Pr... ...ies

"The edge-of-your-seat plot, sinister backstory, and smart, brave, and irreverent main character made this whodunit unputdownable."
—*Justine*

"A compulsive read. Scarborough has created a thrilling book brimming with life, murder, and adventure."
—Carrie Jones, *New York Times* bestselling author of *Flying*

"An intense, engrossing debut. Readers will root for Erin to find answers, laugh at her friends' antics as they play detective, and struggle to identify the killer in a plot full of red herrings and multiple suspects."
—*Booklist*

"A tense, storming heartbeat of a thriller. Scarborough's tightly woven story merges forensic intrigue with friendship, romance, and family, nailing the dynamic stylings of *Veronica Mars* and the playful spirit of *Bones*."
—Cori McCarthy, author of *Breaking Sky*

"The fast-paced plot and Veronica Mars–esque protagonist make this book a good fit for avid mystery readers."
—*School Library Journal*

"A relatable cast and well-thought-out plot make this mystery a Sherlockian puzzle sure to impress the most hardened crime-procedural fanatic."
—Mary Elizabeth Summer, author of *Trust Me, I'm Lying*

"There are enough red herrings everyone entertained all the way

BOOKS BY SHERYL SCARBOROUGH

To Catch a Killer
To Right the Wrongs

TO RIGHT THE WRONGS

SHERYL SCARBOROUGH

TOR TEEN

A TOM DOHERTY ASSOCIATES BOOK
New York

TO RIGHT THE WRONGS

Copyright © 2018 by Sheryl Scarborough

A Tor Teen Book
Published by Tom Doherty Associates
120 Broadway
New York, NY 10271

www.tor-forge.com

Tor® is a registered trademark of Macmillan Publishing Group, LLC.

The Library of Congress has cataloged the hardcover edition as follows:

Names: Scarborough, Sheryl, author.
Title: To right the wrongs / Sheryl Scarborough.
Description: First Edition. | New York : Tom Doherty Associates, 2018. | "A Tom Doherty Associates book."
Identifiers: LCCN 2017039436 (print) | LCCN 2017054152 (ebook) | ISBN 9781466885493 (ebook) | ISBN 9780765381934 (hardcover : alk. paper)
Subjects: | CYAC: Mystery and detective stories. | Forensic sciences—Fiction. | Criminal investigation—Fiction. | False imprisonment—Fiction. | Kidnapping—Fiction.
Classification: LCC PZ7.1.S33 (ebook) | LCC PZ7.1.S33 Tom 2018 (print) | DDC [Fic]—dc23
LC record available at https://lccn.loc.gov/2017039436

ISBN 978-0-7653-8194-1 (trade paperback)

Our books may be purchased in bulk for promotional, educational, or business use. Please contact your local bookseller or the Macmillan Corporate and Premium Sales Department at 1-800-221-7945, extension 5442, or by email at MacmillanSpecialMarkets@macmillan.com.

First Edition: February 2018
First Trade Paperback Edition: March 2019

Printed in the United States of America

D   0   9   8   7   6   5   4   3   2

To Mason

Because family is who you say it is. Period.

TO RIGHT THE WRONGS

► 1 ◄

Normal is an illusion. What is normal for
the spider is chaos for the fly.
—MORTICIA ADDAMS

Care to guess where you wind up after you and your friends
help police catch a killer? It isn't Disneyland.

To my great relief, it isn't the *Today* show, either. They called
to extend an invitation, but my guardian, protector, and de
facto mom Rachel was solidly against it. She didn't want to
have to relive the worst day of her life on TV any more than
I did. Thankfully, our fame was distilled down to two and a
half minutes on the local news, and a front-page article in the
paper.

The important thing is we caught the man who killed my
mother and my biology teacher. I stood up to him after a lifetime of looking over my shoulder and being afraid. And, I *re-
membered* something, too. A small sliver from that horrible
night fourteen years ago.

Now, supposedly, I can go on with my life and just be normal.

How exactly does that happen?

Do I flip a switch, turn a dial?

Today begins the *normal* last three weeks of my sophomore
year of high school. I'm pacing between my bedroom and the

tree-shaded balcony that overlooks the street, watching for Journey's battle-scarred van to rumble into view.

The warm, lazy air makes me glad we're finally in summer countdown. Soon, I'll be able to spend my mornings lounging in bed with the French doors wide open and a stack of books I've been dying to read.

I check my phone again.

He's not that late. Maybe only a minute or two. I'm just anxious.

A few weeks ago, I thought I knew everything there was to know about him and he didn't even know I existed. Now, I'm officially his girlfriend. He said it right out loud in the TV interview. After those words came out of his mouth I couldn't answer any more questions. But it was worth it.

I'm wearing a new green tank top, which brings out the color of my eyes, and a pair of white shorts. The outfit may not look like that much of an effort, but before I started hanging out with Journey my morning routine was to pick the least rumpled navy blue T-shirt out of the laundry hamper—my T-shirts were all navy blue because that paired best with jeans, and navy blue and denim blend really well into the background.

It wasn't that I didn't have a sense of style before Journey. It's that my *normal* back then meant not standing out. When a tragic event steals your childhood, and puts your name in the headlines for weeks and months, you become *that girl* forever. Now I'm hoping that I can quietly morph into just a girl.

The worn-out shocks on Journey's van squeal as he pulls into the driveway. His brakes harmonize in protest.

I grab my purse and backpack. The small, round wooden heels of my sandals tap out my excited departure on the stairs. I blast through the kitchen, past Uncle Victor, who is camped out at the table with a cup of coffee and some paperwork.

"Bye. See you later." I barrel toward the back door.

I glance back in time to see him grin and hoist his cup.

The van has added a new, asthmatic wheeze to its soundtrack and the passenger door complains loudly as Journey opens it for me from inside. His hand remains there to help pull me up into the belly of this ancient beast. I slide into the seat and lean across the wide-open space. He meets me halfway and plants a quick peck on my lips.

Humph.

Our last actual date was prom, two weeks ago. Since then we have been pushed together and separated. We have been interviewed, interrogated, analyzed, and seen by specialists in PTSD. We've also been fussed over by family and friends and hounded by reporters. All of this activity has meant virtually no PDA. So now that we're finally allowed to go back to school and we're alone, I was hoping for a little more than just a peck.

"Sorry," he says.

"For the kiss?"

"What? No. Because we're late." The transmission crunches into reverse and he pilots the van out of the driveway.

I should just be happy that he's giving me a ride to school. I'm not exactly on his way. It takes him at least an extra twenty minutes to pick me up. Rachel has offered to buy me another mode of transportation to replace my scooter that got munched, and I'll take her up on that eventually . . . but for now I'm enjoying riding to school with the guy who has reclaimed his status as hottest senior on campus.

We ride quietly for a few minutes, each in the silence of our own thoughts, because that's just how we are with each other. We don't have to fill every moment with chatter.

"Three weeks and I'm free." Journey does a quick fist pump.

"How's it feel?"

"It'd feel better if I knew for sure I got into OSU."

"Don't worry. You'll get in." I don't know why I'm saying that. His grades are good, but his application was late.

As he pulls into the parking lot my gaze drifts to the spot where Principal Roberts used to stand and survey everyone's arrival.

It's weird. Same spot, new principal.

This one's tall, probably over six feet, with a back as straight as an ironing board and feet planted in a wide stance. The way her arms are crossed over her chest is more defiant than defensive. Her dark hair is wrenched back so straight that it looks painted on, the tight twist at the nape of her neck an afterthought. A dark band of sharply designed wraparound sunglasses cover her eyes. Her regal, *what's-that-smell* expression is the same look she gave the TV reporter when she was asked if she was proud to have a group of student crime fighters in her midst.

Miss Blankenship, our new principal, made her feelings very clear. She is impressed by high test scores. That's it.

"Can you snag a ride home with Spam or Lysa today?" Journey asks. "I have to leave early to drop my suit off at the cleaners for graduation."

"Yeah. No problem."

Am I imagining it or are her eyes following us as we drive by? I must be imagining it, since I can't actually see her eyes through her sunglasses. Anyway, I get it. Journey's van is a huge eyesore that groans and squeals. I guess anyone seeing it for the first time would be inclined to stare. I rub the well-worn door panel lovingly. We almost died in this wreck.

"Don't forget, you promised to teach me how to drive a stick this summer," I say.

Journey pulls into a parking space, pops his seatbelt, and wraps a long arm around my neck. He strokes my jaw with his thumb and gives me a sultry look through thick eyelashes. "Which stick are we talking about?"

I playfully bat his hand away.

But he leans in for the longer kiss that I was waiting for. At the first sign that he's pulling back, I gently grab his lip with my teeth to draw out the kiss. Then he does it back to me and we both try to keep from giggling. The warning bell rings as we're finishing up. We pull apart breathlessly and I catch something moving out of the corner of my eye. Holy cra— The new principal is standing right in front of the van, staring at us through the window.

I jump away from Journey as if we were doing something wrong. "What the heck?"

Journey bounds out of his door with the enthusiasm of a golden retriever. Hand out, smile on. I proceed more cautiously.

"Hi. Journey Michaels." His charm goes into overdrive. "You're the new principal, aren't you?"

She glares at him, arms crossed over her chest. "Where's your parking pass?"

"Oh." Journey digs out his wallet and pulls the parking pass from inside. He holds it up to show her. "The little thing that attached to the mirror broke off. Should I just put it on the dashboard?"

"You should go to the office and get a new one. Bring it out here and hang it on the mirror. Then hurry to class. If you're late it's on you."

Seriously? Her lips move but nothing else. I expect her voice to sound flat and metallic.

Her gaze swivels to me with such intensity that for a second

I worry that maybe I said that out loud. But I'm pretty sure I didn't.

Journey barely seems to notice her odd mannerisms. He sways slightly. "I'm on it," he promises her. "Don't worry. But I'm a senior. We're basically done with classes, so it's not that big of a deal."

She makes a pinched face. "You won't walk if you have any demerits on the books. If I were you I'd hurry."

I'm standing here witnessing crazy train in action when she again shifts her reptilian gaze in my direction. "Why are you still standing here?"

I open my mouth to explain or introduce myself and decide silence is the better option. I hurry off in the opposite direction from Journey. We glance at each other once and share a small wave.

And I thought our last principal was a psycho.

Actually, our last principal *was* a psycho.

But since there aren't any other unsolved murders lurking in Iron Rain's past, we're probably not in any real danger.

I hurry into the building where my first class is and a group of freshmen girls flock around me like birds on a scrap of bread.

"Erin. Erin. Look what we got. We ordered them from the website where you got yours. They just came yesterday." They're all talking at once and twirling multifilament fingerprint brushes like the one I use. The newspaper article mentioned the contents of my supply kit and where I got everything. Which is so funny because after Lysa and Spam and I admitted our forensic activities, our parents extracted promises from each of us that we won't be doing any more favors for our friends at school. Cheater Checks is DOA.

"That's cool," I say. "What are you going to do with them?"

"Lift fingerprints. What else," the blonde says. "Look. We

already did some." She holds up a white card that's covered with smeary, black smudges. "What do you think? Do those look like a match?"

I blink and back away. "Okay, so first you need to work on your technique. A lot. Those aren't fingerprints. They're black blobs."

She whips the card out of my hand. "Whatever, it was my first try."

She moves off with her friends in tow and I head for my locker. Strolling along the rows, I see splashes of black and neon colors all over the place. Geez, what's going on here? Then I come upon a couple of guys blowing neon green fingerprint powder against the metal door. Some of it sticks, but most of it is going to waste on the floor.

They laugh hysterically.

I pause and consider telling them they're doing it wrong, but when the second warning bell rings I shake it off and head to class. As I pass them I hear one whisper to the other.

"Hey, that's *her*," he says.

Ugh. No matter what, I'm always going to be *her*.

I shudder and hurry to class.

Normal. What does that even mean?

2

We're all pretty bizarre. Some of us are just
better at hiding it, that's all.
—ANDREW, *THE BREAKFAST CLUB*

Being confined to class is slow compared with the frenzy of the last few weeks. Now it's all cramming for finals and thinking about Journey. These days I'm always thinking about him.

Since I knew I wouldn't see him after school, I wrote a little "thinking of you" kind of note. Just a little dreamy thing, with hearts and stuff, like what we used to Snapchat. Not that we don't still Snap. But this was an actual note, which seems more personal. It's something he could keep as opposed to a *see-it-whoosh-it's-gone* Snapchat.

What I didn't realize, before I blathered on for a whole page and then folded it up into a tiny triangle of love, was how hard it would be to squeeze something this thick into a locker through one of the slots.

As I pushed and pried with my glamorous broken and gnawed fingernails—managing to get the note stuck halfway between in and out—I realized, of course, *this* is the reason everyone Snaps.

And yes, I did ask for a bathroom pass so I could pull off my little note adventure. But how else do you surprise someone with a surprise note if they're standing right there?

Anyway, Blankenship picked this moment to troll the halls. She wrote me up for *three* infractions: loitering, tampering with a locker that did not belong to me, *and* littering.

It should be noted that the littering charge occurred when she snuck up behind me and ordered me to drop what was in my hand.

So, instead of getting to go home and change into comfortable clothes and have a snack, I'm heading to room 101, to serve detention.

Except when I turn the corner and approach room 101, I'm stunned.

There's an overflow of at least twenty people milling around outside the room. I wedge past the group and peer in through the open door. The Detention Dungeon is packed to overflowing. Every chair and desktop is supporting a body and there's a line around the room of people sitting on the floor.

I'm shocked to spot my two best friends, Spam and Lysa, in the corner. I make my way over. "You're kidding me."

It's a question, even if it doesn't sound like one.

They roll their eyes.

"I seriously did nothing wrong," Spam insists. "*Noth*-ing."

A smile tugs at my lips. Out of the three of us, Spam has logged more detention hours than Lysa and me and possibly five other students combined.

I pat her shoulder. "It's okay, Spam. It happens to all of us. Like . . . now."

"She doesn't believe me," Spam says to Lysa. "Tell her."

Lysa looks toward the heavens. "She's right. This time she didn't do anything. And I'm here because I defended her."

"What?"

Spam's indignation roars to the surface. "It was right after the first lunch bell. The first one. I wasn't in a hurry, because my next class is right there across from my locker. Anyway, I was leaning against the lockers trying to sync this little electronic thing I made to the app on my phone. And suddenly there she was. She literally swooped out of nowhere, like Batman." Spam flaps her arms in frustration.

"So it was the phone?" Official school policy dictates no phones in sight, except during lunch. We try to be covert about it, but anywhere you look you see visible cell phones on campus. And Spam has been nailed for this more times than I can count.

"No," she squeals. "I tucked that thing up into my sleeve so fast she never saw it." Spam demonstrates her move with sleight of hand worthy of a magician. "What she took was a little electronic device I was working on for my father. She thought I was going to use it to graffiti the lockers. She cited me for loitering *and* attempted vandalism."

"Wait. What?" I thought my infractions were crazy.

"She was seriously just making stuff up," Spam says. "I put this tiny electronic beacon in the case of a fat highlighter pen because I figured my little brothers wouldn't notice if I stuck a highlighter in one of their backpacks. My dad can keep tabs on them through a tracking app when they go out, like to the mall or something."

"But she just thought it was a highlighter pen?" I say.

"Yes. She's a nutjob," Lysa says, agreeing with Spam. "You should hear her list of infractions: littering, loitering, hanging out, hurrying, the dreaded PDA, too loud, too *sneaky*, racing, lagging. Everyone's in here for some crazy, weird stuff. Hey, why are you here?"

I shake my head. "Basic crazy, weird stuff."

Brianna squeezes past me and gives us a disgusted look. "You guys are the geniuses; can't you do something about her?"

Brianna was our first Cheater Checks client but she wasn't the only one. A lot of people in this school suspected their boyfriends or girlfriends weren't being truthful. She must've had a thing for bad boyfriends, though, because she hit us up more than once.

"*Her* meaning the principal?" I ask.

"Yes. Blankface," Brianna replies.

"Want us to build a time machine and send her back to the future?" I ask.

"I'd be happy if you just tied a bell around her neck like a cat so we'd hear her coming," Brianna says.

"We'll see what we can do." Brianna moves off across the room. "She was our best customer," I say with a sigh.

"Hashtag-frowny-face. I hate that we promised not to do Cheater Checks anymore," Lysa says. "Not only was it a great side hustle, it was our thing. It made us special."

"Tell me about it," I grumble. "Have you seen the lockers in C-building? They're covered in neon fingerprint powder. Neon. I didn't switch to that until my prints were perfect with plain black. Victor says that's how you learn."

"You guys . . ." Spam's eyes grow wide and she gets *that look* on her face.

"What?" I ask.

"I can do that," Spam says in an almost trancelike state.

"Do what?"

"What Brianna just said." Suddenly energized, Spam's thumbs work overtime as she punches stuff into her phone. Her head swivels toward the door.

"Shhhush," she hisses loudly. "She's coming."

A wave of action ripples through the room as everyone sits down and opens a book. A few seconds later, Principal Blankenship enters. A notebook is cradled in her arm with a fat purple highlighter clipped to the cover. She quietly stalks the room, taking in the prescribed quiet studying in progress. Finding nothing, she stalks out.

A few moments later a harried Coach Wilkins arrives. "Whoa." He's visibly shocked to see so many people in this room. He holds up a piece of paper. "Okay, sports fans, I'm sending around a detention sign-up sheet. You want credit for today, make sure your name is on it. Stay like this for the next forty minutes and we'll be all good."

▸ 3 ◂

If you witness a crime, it's important to record your memories
as soon as possible; otherwise there's a risk that what
you remember will become warped by hearing
other versions of the incident.

—VICTOR FLEMMING

So, after an hour of our lives that we'll never get back, we drag
ourselves out of the Detention Dungeon and wander toward
the parking lot with the rest of the incorrigibles. The group is
so huge it feels like half the school. Lysa and Spam are bicker-
ing over which one of them should give me a ride home. Personally, I don't care. I wouldn't even mind walking today. This
new principal thing has me feeling very weird and unsettled.
Just when things were supposed to finally fit into place. Now
we have *her* to deal with.

I can tell she's definitely not keen on us.

We stop on the front walkway next to the flagpole. If I'm
going to ride with Spam, she parks in the lot to the right. Lysa,
who is rummaging in her bag for her sunglasses, parks in the
one to the left.

"Spam, how did you do that? How did you know Blankenship was coming?"

"It was amazing, wasn't it?" She peers at her phone as if it's
magic. "It totally worked."

"She was expecting us to be goofing off," Lysa says. "Did you see her face? She was disappointed that she couldn't add to our misery by handing out *more* D-slips. No doubt she has severe rules about misbehaving *in* detention."

"But seriously, how did you know?" I ask.

Spam looks up from her phone. "That purple highlighter clipped to her notebook was mine and it has a tracking beacon hidden in it. There's an app on my phone programmed to track the beacon. When I turned it on I could tell she was coming toward us."

"Is the beacon expensive?" Lysa asks. "Can you track her wherever she goes?"

"The electronics are cheap, just a few dollars. As for tracking, I think you need to be fairly close. But I could probably work on the range. Why?"

Lysa finds her sunglasses. We wait while she puts them on and checks her look in the mirror on the back of her cell phone case. "Ahh, that's better. We hate giving up Cheater Checks because it made us special. But we *promised* . . ."

I instantly get where Lysa's going. "So, what if we sell apps instead? Knowing when someone is lurking around might be valuable."

"It's genius," Spam says. "Both of you. Why didn't I think of that?"

"The highlighter might be a problem, though. If everyone started carrying one it could be suspicious." Lysa, the practical one.

"Good point. I'll figure out another type of bell for our cat," Spam says.

"Seriously, how weird is she?" I slip my head through the strap of my bag and adjust it so it hangs cross-body style. "A massive number of detention slips, and she's like this super-spy or something."

Lysa removes her sunglasses to polish them on the hem of her skirt. "I think she's just establishing her Alpha power over us. She'll calm down."

"Did you not see the same thing I did?" I say. "Everything about her is deliberately calm . . . calm and grim, like a little boy pulling the wings off flies. She *enjoys* torturing us."

Spam fluffs her hair. "Have you ever noticed how the first thing Lysa says is always something nice, whether it's the truth or not? You have to wait awhile for her actual feelings to rise to the surface."

"That's not true," Lysa argues. "I say what I feel inside. Especially to you guys."

I hide my smile because Spam's right. Lysa does tend to paint things in a sunny light.

"You actually believe that after that impressive show of force, she'll drop back and become a *normal,* everyday principal?"

"Hey." Spam spins in a circle as a guy we've never seen before zips past her on a skateboard. He's so close, his wake ruffles her hair.

Skateboarder guy skids sideways to a stop and flashes a huge smile. "Hey yourself, shortcake." He points to the GoPro attached to his helmet. "Smile." Then he frames the shot with his fingers.

On command, Spam offers up more than just a smile, moving quickly through a series of silly fashion model poses while the skateboarder slowly pans all three of us. Spam ends with a kiss blown off her palm. "What's your name?" she says.

"The Lone Ranger." He flip-kicks, swiveling his board, and rides off.

It's not until this moment that we notice the car speeding toward us.

The car surges straight for the skateboarder, but he manages to pivot and deflect danger by pushing off the front fender with his fingertips. As he swerves around the moving vehicle, the driver overcorrects and aims for us.

We scream, grab for each other, and tumble backward.

There's a series of terrifying scrapes and bangs as the car jumps the curb and slams into the flagpole with a teeth-jarring, metallic thwang.

For a second everything is silent.

Then people scream and run in all directions.

The flagpole teeters briefly before it snaps and plunges forward, landing on the roof of the car with a giant crash. The force of the falling flagpole explodes the car windows, and glass flies in all directions. More students scream and run.

Coach Wilkins and a security officer appear at the vehicle and try to wrench the door open. But it's bent in such a way that it won't budge.

A trail of smoke drifts up from the crumpled hood in a question-mark shape.

My movements are slo-mo. I'm barely aware of distant sirens and warnings to run because the car is going to blow. I sit up alongside Lysa and Spam. We contemplate the black skid mark that runs across the cement only a few inches from our toes.

A familiar chill compels me to turn my eyes into a recorder and take in the whole scene. My suspicious mind goes to a dark place. Was that really an accident?

"Holy crap." Spam scoots back.

Blankenship stands off to the side, arms crossed over her chest. She's not looking where I would expect her to be looking, at the rescue operation for the driver of the car. No, she's staring at us, and the scowl on her face suggests that she thinks we had something to do with all of this.

A shiver traces through me.

Lysa is babbling. "I skinned my knee. But it's fine. It doesn't even really hurt. Everything is fine, though. Are you fine? Because I'm fine."

"Erin. Erin. Oh my god!" someone yells.

Spam and I help each other up, then reach down to help Lysa up too.

Everything is shrouded in a strange fog and nothing makes sense right away.

Especially because the voice yelling my name belongs to Journey and he's racing toward me across the open area between the Administration building and what used to be the flagpole. Victor is a few feet behind him, but veers off to help the driver out of the car. The chief of police is here too, walking fast and talking on his cell phone. But Journey's not supposed to be here at all.

The sirens are suddenly loud and upon us.

I go through a minimal check for injuries.

"Yep. Skinned knee. That's all for me. What about you?" Lysa asks.

Spam sticks her finger into a new hole in her jeans. "Tore my jeans a little. But they actually look better like this."

Journey arrives at my side. He grabs me and pulls me into a protective hug. Then he holds me out at arm's length and brushes the hair off my face. "What happened? Are you okay?"

I stretch out my neck. "I'm fine, I think. But why are you here? I thought you had to leave early to take your suit to the cleaners?"

Journey shifts from one foot to the other. "I did. Or I was supposed to but then Victor called me to come to his office. We were just finishing up when we heard the crash. When I saw you on the ground I was so scared."

I shake my head to clear the cobwebs. "Wait a minute. What office? And why did Victor want to talk to you?"

Journey slips his arm around my shoulders and starts to lead me toward the building. "Come inside and I'll tell you."

Spam and Lysa are still adjusting their clothes and their bags. Lysa obsessively cleans off her sunglasses with the hem of her dress again.

"Lysa. Spam. You guys come too," Journey says. "We need to make sure you're okay."

Spam and Lysa hold on to each other.

"We are a little shook up," Lysa says.

Spam shakes her head. "I don't even know what happened."

The Fire Department arrives and hauls out a giant tool to pry open the car door. They're helping the driver out and to her feet as we pass. We pause to watch the end of the rescue. There's some blood on her face from all the broken glass, but otherwise, she looks okay.

"She just looks like somebody's mom," Spam whispers.

She does look harmless. Maybe it was just an accident— wrong time, wrong place.

"It was that skateboarder's fault," the woman says. "He cut in front of me and caused me to lose control of the car."

"What skateboarder, ma'am?" a fireman asks her.

"The skateboarder!" The woman points at us. "You girls saw him. He was wearing a blue jacket."

Lysa, Spam, and I exchange pensive glances.

Spam shields her mouth with her hand. "She's lying," she hisses. "He was wearing a plaid Pendleton."

Not that it means anything, but I notice that Journey's jacket happens to be blue. "Maybe she's just confused," I say.

"He never left the walkway," Lysa whispers. "She was aiming for him."

"Or us," Spam adds.

"But why lie?" Lysa murmurs.

"Come on," Journey says, and we follow him. I'm anxious to see this mysterious office, but at the same time I'm wondering if there's a mystery here with the woman and the skateboarder, or if it's all what Rachel likes to call my overactive imagination.

► 4 ◄

A coincidence is not an acceptable explanation. The smart, guilty
criminal anticipates being linked to the crime scene, so
they will come prepared with a plausible story
to explain the connection.
—VICTOR FLEMMING

Journey leads us around the back of the administration building to a set of ancient cement steps that descend into a dark
basement area under the main building. Steps I never noticed
before.

"Where are we going?" I ask.

"I told you," he says. "Victor's office."

"Since when?" I ask.

"Since today, I guess," Journey says. "I don't know. You'll
have to ask him."

The stairs empty into a long, dark hallway with two doors
to the right. Journey opens the first one and leads us into a
huge, rectangular science classroom that is nearly twice the size
of Miss P's classroom. I know it's a science classroom because
alongside each four-person lab table is a sink.

Even though this is still in the basement, a strip of ground-
level windows along each end of the room allows a warm slant
of light to wash over the desks, chasing the dark and giving
the room a cathedral feel.

But I'm still not getting it.

"Why would Victor use this as an office?" I ask.

"No. This is the new science classroom and lab," Journey says. "Victor's office is over here."

He leads us through a door to a large, unfinished space, roughly the same size as the classroom. There's a folding table and a couple of chairs. In the middle of the table is Victor's distinctive pile of papers.

"*This* must be Victor's office because that looks exactly like our kitchen table at home."

Journey sets up a few more folding chairs.

Lysa and Spam and I each take a chair, but our eyes are bouncing all over the place. The main attraction is a large whiteboard on a stand. Journey moves it to the side and pulls up a chair for himself.

"Victor and the chief just gave me the whole rundown and they're going to tell you guys, too. But here's the deal. This part is going to be a crime lab. The new Iron Rain *crime lab*." He pauses, eyebrows peaked, waiting for us to squee or something. But we all kind of sit there. I don't know about Lysa and Spam, but I'm a little too stunned to react.

"Seriously? Here? Right here? On our actual campus?" It's all I can manage to croak out.

"Yes. Right here on our actual campus." Journey grins.

"But how?" Lysa asks, and she sounds just as astonished as I am.

"Miss P, man." Journey makes a wide gesture. "This is what she was working on when she was killed. The new science classroom was never a problem, which is why that part's almost done. It was the crime lab that Principal Roberts objected to."

Principal Roberts was paranoid that somehow his DNA

would wind up in the system and ultimately implicate him as the man who murdered my mother. "The fact that Iron Rain was without a crime lab for all these years worked in his favor."

"It did," Journey says. "It's only because Victor agreed to stay on to teach at the school *and* run a part-time crime lab that this project is still going forward."

I let my gaze roam around the room as I contemplate my dream come true. "I knew Victor wanted to set up a crime lab. I didn't know it would be here at the school. This is amazing."

Spam gets up and wanders the space, trailing her fingers along the cement block. "I'm not even into all that alphabet science stuff and I'm plenty wowed by this idea."

Lysa touches up her lip gloss. "My father says our city has needed this for a long time. You'd think that's the last thing a defense attorney would want, but he says when the only evidence you've got is eyewitness testimony, that can tank your case in a hurry."

I wander over to the whiteboard. There are some photos randomly taped in different sections and some notes scribbled in various spots.

"What's this?" I ask.

"Oh. Victor started a murder board for my father's case," Journey says.

"Oh my god. Seriously?" I lightly clap my hands. One of the best things that came out of Journey and me teaming up to catch Miss P's killer is that Victor agreed to take another look at the conviction that put Journey's father, Jameson Michaels, behind bars. "Show me. Show me. I want to know how this works."

"Basically, the purpose of the murder board is to reconstruct all the details of the case against my father so we can examine every piece." Journey points to the different sections on the board. "My father's in prison because someone trespassed on our property and wound up dead." Journey's expression hardens. "We think it was more like an accident or a setup rather than murder, but unfortunately a jury saw it differently."

I look at the board, there are a few photos under the witness column. "There were witnesses?"

Journey tilts his head to the side. "No one saw the actual shooting. These witnesses were brought in to give their impressions of the broken-down wreck of the cannery and what they thought were my parents' states of mind."

I squint and point to a photo that looks familiar. "Is that Coach Wilkins?"

Journey chuckles. "Yeah. He was a college student then."

"But he testified against your dad?"

Journey shrugs. "I haven't read the transcripts yet, but you know I told you how my parents bought the old cannery because it was a cool building with a lot of history. They wanted to turn it into a hotel. According to my mother, almost as soon as they arrived, strange things started happening. Someone was messing with them and the property. They called the police but they could never find any evidence of anything. When it came to my dad's trial, Coach Wilkins and a bunch of other people testified that the cannery was haunted and all the weird stuff my dad described was because my parents were New Yorkers who didn't fit in around here."

"Wow. Someone can get convicted of murder just because they don't fit in?"

"It happens all the time. Ask Lysa," Journey says. "I'm sure she'd tell you."

I point to another photo of a woman. "So who's that?"

Journey shrugs again. "I don't know. Like I said, I haven't read all the transcripts yet."

"She looks kind of familiar, though." I gesture to the board.

"So, *this* is why Victor called you down here?"

Journey shifts his feet. "Well, yeah. Sort of."

I take out my phone and aim it at the murder board, but before I can snap the photo Journey puts out his hand and pushes my phone down.

I start to turn toward him, confused, but the door flies open and Victor and Police Chief Culson enter.

Victor gives us a quick scan. "Everybody okay?"

The three of us nod.

"I skinned my knee, but it's really fine," Lysa says.

"Apparently, it was just a crazy accident." Victor comes around the table to an empty chair and settles in. "But I'm really glad you're still here because I wanted to show you what's going on, and I have an offer for you."

The chief steps up. "One second, Vic." He points to me and reads off his phone. "I gave Rachel a heads up about the accident, and let her know that you were completely safe. She thought you should have been home over an hour ago."

Dang. I forgot to let Rachel know about detention.

"Long story. I'll explain when I see her."

I try not to outwardly cringe. But why is the chief all up in my business with Rachel? He's not a bad guy exactly. But there's a sudden *everyone-loves-the-chief* fest going on and it's starting to bug me. Not that long ago, Police Chief Charles Culson was my prime suspect in Miss Peters's murder over exactly this issue: a crime lab for Iron Rain. I was betting he didn't want our city to have one because it would take some of his power away. Also, he and Victor seemed to have an uncomfortable history.

Turned out I was wrong.

Now they're best buds, working on a crime lab together, and there's a definite bro-mance blooming right before my eyes.

The chief looms over us with a notepad in his hand. "Can one of you provide me the name of that skateboarder?"

Lysa, Spam, and I shrug and shake our heads.

"He didn't look familiar," I say.

"Never seen him before," Spam adds.

"But he is a student here," the chief says. "Right?"

"Not necessarily," Lysa says. "Why?"

"Because that boy is responsible for an accident that could have injured many people and actually did cause a great deal of property damage. That's why."

"Wait wait wait," I say. "We were right there. He didn't cause the accident." I glance at Lysa and Spam. "He never left the sidewalk."

Spam nods. "Erin's right." She replays the accident with her hands. "The skateboarder—who was super cute, by the way, which is how I know we don't know him—was way up here, on the sidewalk with us. That woman came from way over here."

The chief tilts his head to the side and gives us a sweet smile. And by sweet, I mean phony. He's not buying our version of the story. "Look, girls, I know you think you know what you saw. But I spoke to that woman and she was very clear about the instigation of the skateboarder and when we find him, he'll probably be charged."

"With what?" My words tumble out. Nothing makes me angrier than an adult blaming someone my age. Because they always do it. Somehow, in their minds, everything's our fault.

"Erin," soothes Victor. "Relax. Chuck's simply doing what police do. Trying to get to the truth. The boy was involved in an accident. At the very least we need to find him and make sure he's okay."

Hmph. Bro-mance.

I look from Journey to Victor. Do they not remember how this went down when the police were "just trying to do their job and get to the truth" the night they wanted to charge Journey with Miss P's murder? And the only reason he was a suspect was because I said I saw him there.

But Journey and Victor just look balefully back at me. A glance at Spam and Lysa tells me I'm not alone with my feelings, though.

"Did you take any photos of that boy or the area that we could use to identify him or the other people at the scene? If you did I'd like to collect your phones for evidence." The chief smiles. "But don't worry. You'll get them back in three or four weeks."

Without even looking at each other, we all shake our heads.

"Nope," Lysa says.

"Not me," agrees Spam.

"Yeah. It all happened too fast for photos," I say.

Spam's head suddenly snaps up. She turns to stare at the door.

I follow her gaze and within seconds there's a *click, click* of high heels and Miss Blankenship enters. She cradles the ever-present notebook against her chest like a shield. A hard hat wobbles slightly on her head. She's followed by a burly guy dressed in work clothes and a thick plaid Pendleton jacket. He's carrying a clipboard.

I glance at Spam. She flashes me her phone. It features a pulsing red dot.

Victor gets out of his chair and ambles over to greet her. "Taryn. Come in. We're just going over the new plans."

Blankenship pauses to swivel her head in my direction and a flow of ice trickles down my spine. Under her shriveling gaze I scoot my chair a little behind Journey.

Without a shred of emotion, she blinks a few times, then wets her lips. "Great. This is your contractor, Clay Kirkland."

Victor glances at the chief. "I thought we hired a guy named Dawson?"

The chief checks his notepad. "That's right. Bob Dawson."

Blankenship inches forward, gesturing toward Clay in much the way Vanna White would indicate a new vowel. "Exactly. And Mr. Kirkland is your *new* Dawson."

"But why?" Victor and the chief exchange frowns.

"I'm happy to report that he came in with a lower bid." There is nothing about her expression that suggests she's happy about anything. In fact, the level of excitement she shows, she could be making funeral arrangements.

"Was Dawson's bid a problem?" Victor asks the Chief.

He shakes his head. "I didn't think so."

"I'm afraid . . ." Blankface drags out the word as she plucks a piece of lint from her sweater. "Dawson had some . . . shall we say . . . *gritty* things in his profile."

"Gritty?" Victor says.

The chief nods knowingly. "Ah. I think she's saying he failed the security background check. We have to be careful of stuff like that around children and schools."

Blankface looks relieved. "Exactly," she says. "But Mr. Kirkland is just fine."

Victor's head twitches slightly and I wonder if he believes her. "Okay."

At this, Blankenship turns and starts to click her way out.

"But," Victor adds. "We need to be on the same page here."

Blankface stops and swivels again. "What page is that?"

Victor gestures to the classroom. "The classroom is *your* domain. You can make any decisions you want about that area. But the lab is mine. It needs to stay autonomous. It's here to support the police department and the city of Iron Rain. Which means, with all due respect, if there's a problem that involves the lab, you come to Chief Culson or myself. We call all the shots on this area. Nonnegotiable."

We're frozen in place watching Victor and Blankface square off. She's just as tough as he is. She doesn't blink, sigh, or so much as roll her eyes. There's not a single facial tic.

"Let's get something straight, shall we?" she says. "As principal—"

Victor interrupts. "Acting principal."

She nods, her lower lip becoming rigid. "As acting principal, I call all the shots at my school. It's the very definition of my job."

Victor's jaw tightens. "As long as you respect the definition of mine, we'll be fine."

"Fine," Principal Blankenship says. Her jaw is drawn even tighter than Victor's. She turns and stalks toward the door. Victor follows her out.

As soon as the door closes, Clay shivers comically. "Is there a draft or is it just me?"

Victor returns almost immediately and we stifle our giggles. He pauses, shakes it off, and then strides up to Clay.

"If she becomes a problem," Victor says, "she'll be my problem, not yours." He glances at the rest of us, pinning a pointed gaze on me. "For the record, this is not me saying the new principal is a problem."

"Don't you mean acting principal?" I say.

Victor gives me a warning look, but ignores my smart comeback. Instead, he offers to shake Clay's hand. "Welcome to the team. We can set up an appointment to go over the specs when you have time."

Clay accepts Victor's handshake. "Sounds good. I'll get out of your hair for now." Victor walks him to the door and the contractor slips out.

As Victor returns to his chair, he makes a wide gesture. "Surprised?"

"I guess." I glance around the room still not exactly sure what's going on here.

"Well, if you aren't now, you will be," Victor says.

5

There's nothing to say mistakes can't happen in a crime lab. They can and do. But before there were crime labs and DNA tests, literally hundreds of people were wrongly sent to jail and there was no way to prove their innocence.

—VICTOR FLEMMING

Victor gestures for us to get up. "Time for a tour. Come on. Up, up." He leads us into the classroom area. "This will be your new, state-of-the-art classroom with me as your teacher."

I wander over and inspect the lab tables. Lysa heads for the storage cabinets and Spam tests the water in the sinks. "It's gorgeous," I say.

"You can thank your bio teacher. She did all the heavy lifting. This part is basically done, we just need to finish out the storage room and paint."

He leads us back into the unfinished room and his table piled with papers. "But here's the exciting part." Victor begins moving papers around on the table. "Chuck and I spent all morning hammering out the details."

I curtail a snort. More bro-mance.

Victor gestures to the large set of drawings covering the table. "These are plans for a fully functional crime scene lab and evidence storage facility. They are for the most part on point. With a few modifications, we can have this all up and running in a few weeks."

He moves that page to the side and produces two more. "The school paid for the classroom, and the PD is forking over the cash for the lab." He adds a third page. "I can scrounge the NIJ and probably get most of the necessary equipment donated."

My eyebrows creep higher.

Victor glances up. "The National Institute of Justice. They're extremely generous with grants and donations to small communities for exactly things like this and I don't mind working with last year's model."

"This is an amazing opportunity." I'm very nearly breathless imagining all the things I can do in here.

"Hold your horses. I'm not even to the part about you yet." The way Victor reads my mind is uncanny. He continues to flop pages this way and that, apparently digging for one more page. He finds it and slaps it on top of the stack, pinning me with a steely gaze.

"Now, here's where you girls come in." He adds a wink. "It's going to be kind of last minute, since summer is basically upon us. But if we can pull off a six-week, forensics-style summer camp and get a minimum of twenty kids to sign up, we will qualify for a government grant that will cover the cost of all of our educational materials for an entire year *and* pay for two full-time camp counselors."

He gestures, arms out wide, big Victor grin plastered across his face. "What do you say, Erin? Do you and one of your friends want a job for about six weeks this summer?"

"As camp counselors?"

Victor holds up a finger. "Not *just* camp counselors . . . *CSI camp counselors.*"

A grin tugs at the corners of my mouth. It does sound fun.

"Admit it. You love the idea," Victor teases. "This is like me saying, *Come here, little fox, I have a job for you in the hen house.*"

I break into a full smile.

He looks to Lysa and Spam. "How about it, girls? Is one of you up for a summer job? You could both do it and job-share if you wanted."

Spam raises her hand. "Lysa should take it. I work at my dad's computer store in the summer."

He swivels his gaze to Lysa. "What do you say?"

She's all smiles. "I'd be honored. I needed a summer job, too. No job, no car."

Spam and I smirk and side-eye. *Honored.* Lysa is so PC— parentally correct.

Victor shuffles all the papers back into a stack and rolls the plans up into a tube. "Okay, Chuck, it's settled. Let's do this." He glances at Journey. "You can start right away helping me get the lab built out and acquire all the equipment."

"Stoked," Journey says. "But I'll have to give notice at my job first."

Suddenly, the sour cloud that had been hanging over me all day is back.

"Wait, what's Journey doing?" I know I sound like a petulant child, but I can't help it. Ever since we solved the murders— actually, to be 100 percent accurate, *I* solved the murders—okay, Spam and I, but by the time I dragged her into it I already knew Principal Roberts had Journey and Victor. Anyway, ever since *all that,* Journey and Victor have practically been joined at the hip.

No one answers me.

"What's Journey going to be doing . . . at the camp?"

Journey's gaze shifts from me to Victor and back to me. There's a distinct "deer in headlights" look. He says nothing, which actually says a whole lot of something.

Victor stands and slides a fatherly arm around Journey's

shoulders. "Your boyfriend won't be working at the camp, per se. Instead, he has accepted the offer to be my intern *and* right-hand butt monkey."

Journey laughs.

I frown.

"Wait. *He* gets to be your intern?" I can't help it. The words just blurt out. Shock and disappointment have flattened me. Heat creeps up the back of my neck. My face flames in blotchy patches. I leap to my feet, itching to bolt. It's humiliating to suddenly have to struggle to control my emotions. I was always the girl who could bury her pain and trauma behind a cool, no-caring exterior, but these last few months . . .

I don't know what's happening to me, but I don't like it. The only thing that holds me back is Victor. His praise and respect is all-important to me and I know that charging out of here like a baby won't get me that. But I'm panicking. Right this second, I sense a confrontation and I don't know how to handle that.

"Journey's a college boy now. Or, he's going to be. And he's majoring in criminal science," Victor says, slapping Journey on the back.

"Wait, what?" My mouth literally drops open. Devastation is all over my face. "You got accepted?"

He waves his phone. "Oh yeah. Sorry. With the accident and everything, I forgot to tell you. OSU." He raises his arms in a mini-cheer. "My mom texted me an hour ago. Cool, huh?" Judging by the way he shoves his hands in his pockets and shrugs, he knows how badly all this is landing on me.

I nod stiffly. It's as if my jaw has been wired shut. "That's great. Really great. I'm happy for you." And I am. It's just weird to find out about my boyfriend's important news in such an offhand way. Spam is closest to me so I grab her sleeve and pull her to her feet.

"Well, everything is super great." My voice is freakishly shrill and I try to lower it. "But we need to go. Right, Spam?"

She nods. "Yeah. My . . . uh, dad is probably wondering where I am."

"I have to go too," Lysa says, grabbing my other arm and following us as we edge toward the door. I feel like the walls are closing in on me. I need out of here before I completely come apart.

I head for the stairs.

"Wait," Journey calls after me. I stop and look back. "I have to be at work in twenty minutes, but I can still drop you off."

I wave my hand over my head. "No need. I'll ride with Spam, but you have a good night." My voice is set to cherry-candy sweet.

Victor, abnormally clueless, waves happily. "See you at dinner."

If Journey wanted to say anything back, I drowned him out with the machine-gun-style sound of my rapid steps up the stairs.

Screw him . . . screw all of them.

► 6 ◄

Step one, collect all the evidence and let it
give you the road map to step two.
—VICTOR FLEMMING

We climb the dark basement steps in a crush and spill out into the daylight. The fabric of Spam's sweater is still balled in my grip and Lysa is clinging to my arm as if we're about to board a roller coaster.

"Ugggh." I groan.

Lysa swivels around to face me even though that means she's now walking backward. We stroll slowly, in this position, toward the parking lot. Lysa's finger is in my face. "Okay. This isn't Journey's fault," she says.

My shoulders sag. "I know. I'm not mad at him. And I get why Victor would hire him as his intern. I truly do. It makes sense, right?"

"It's the same reason he's hiring us to work at the camp," Lysa says. "He trusts us."

I nod. But making sense has nothing to do with how completely stabbed in the back I feel. After my biology teacher was murdered and I found her body, Rachel asked her FBI criminalist brother, Victor, to come home and make sure I was safe. She had no idea he was my idol.

"It's just I got to watch him work. We worked together. We bonded. It was amazing. I know I can't be his intern . . . I'm still in high school. But why Journey? I just feel swept aside."

"But hey, CSI *camp*. Focus on that." Spam pries my fingers off her sleeve. "You guys will probably be doing *crime scene s'mores* and *roasted weenie body parts* or something super cool like that." She turns her attention to her phone.

"She's right," Lysa agrees. "CSI camp sounds like a lot more fun than being Victor's intern."

"Don't forget butt monkey." Spam grins, wrinkling her nose.

We come around the side of the Administration building and pause at the sight of the wrecked car crushed by the flag-pole. A reminder of how close we came to disaster.

"At least no one was hurt," Lysa says.

A young police officer stands out near the parking lot, keeping an eye on things. He notices us and smiles.

We smile back.

Our shoes crunch over the broken glass. Spam stops at the spot where we were nearly killed less than an hour ago. She stoops to pick something up off the ground.

"What's that?" I ask.

"A token," she says. "From Family Fun Arcade."

"You and your gamer crew," I say.

"Yeah, but this isn't mine. It is from my favorite game, though." She tucks the token into her pocket and steps in front of me, lowering her voice. "Do you have your kit?"

I pat my messenger bag. "Always. Why?"

"The skateboarder pushed off the front of that lady's car."

"Yeah . . ." I'm not sure where she's going with this.

"Look." She nods at the shiny hood of the car. "His finger-prints are like right there."

Lysa and I exchange confused looks. "And . . . ?" I say.

She rolls her eyes, a little exasperated. "And you can just grab one. Whoosh. Like that. Lysa and I will distract the cop."

"Okay. I can . . . but why do I want to?"

"Because . . ." Spam turns her phone to show us the latest news alert. It's barely been an hour and already: SEARCH ON FOR SKATEBOARDER AS SCHOOL TALLIES PROPERTY DAMAGE.

I gasp. "You want me to lift his prints so we can turn him in?"

This is very un-Spam-like.

"No," she says. "So we can find him."

I give her a hard look.

"He needs our help." I look at her phone again, then at her. There's got to be more to this for Spam.

"What?" She balks. "Okay, he's supercute, he got me to model for him, and he called me shortcake." She flashes a devilish smile. "I kinda liked that."

There it is. I hesitate, not sure about this.

"According to the chief he could be in a lot of trouble," Lysa says.

Okay. I go into my bag for my fingerprint kit, which, for a girl like me, just looks like extra makeup. "I can grab the print easy-peasy, but without access to Detective Sydney's AFIS computer there's not much I can find out about it."

"Remember what you always say," Lysa says. "Step one, collect the evidence and let it give you the road map to step two."

"This isn't Cheater Checks, right?" I say, thinking out loud. I promised Rachel.

Spam nods. "It's definitely not."

"But . . . are we tampering with evidence?" Lysa asks. "We can't do that, either."

Spam rolls her eyes. "Hold on. I'll find out." She strides over to the officer and strikes up a friendly conversation. She asks him when the crime scene guys are coming.

He shakes his head. "This isn't that kind of a crime scene."

Spam looks knowingly over her shoulder.

"But so why are you here?" she asks.

"Oh, I'm just waiting for the tow truck," the cop replies.

I raise my eyebrows at Lysa. "Sounds like we're good to go."

She wanders over to help Spam with distraction.

I quickly bring out the brush, powder, and a square, two-inch hinged fingerprint lifter card that Victor gave me to practice with. The car looks freshly washed and shiny so the skateboarder's prints are all very clear. I determine his thumbprint to be the best one.

I kind of huddle to one side and pretend like I'm checking my makeup. I even use my compact mirror to monitor Spam and Lysa and the cop behind me.

I slip my left hand into a glove so I don't contaminate the print with my own. Then I load a supply of red fluorescent fingerprint powder onto the brush and sprinkle it over the area. I dab lightly to allow the super-fine grains of powder to drift into the ridges of the print, defining it.

With great detail and flamboyant hand gestures Spam is describing her favorite video game to the cop. Turns out he plays it too.

Thanks to the hinged lifter I can almost pull this off one-handed. The lifter contains two parts, connected in the middle. One side is a smooth, shiny card where the actual fingerprint will be preserved. The other side is sticky lift tape. I spread the hinged part open and carefully peel off the protective film, revealing the sticky side.

I say carefully because I've learned that if it actually sticks to the glove it will not come off.

Holding the sticky part by the edges, I firmly apply it over the print and smooth it down with my gloved hand. Then I peel the whole thing off in one smooth move.

Once the print is removed from the hood of the car I close the sticky side against the shiny side and the print is sealed inside forever.

I'm just sliding all my tools back into my bag when Journey ambles up.

"Erin, what's going on?" he asks.

"Nothing. Just a little makeup fix." I swirl my finger around my face. "I was—you know—breaking out."

Dang. I just lied to Journey and I'm not even sure why.

He blinks, nods, and frowns all at the same time, which means *Okay, girl stuff.* "So, you aren't mad at me over this Victor thing, are you?"

Sigh. Yeah, the Victor thing.

I shake my head. "I'm happy for you." I reach out and grab the hem of his jacket and pull him toward me because I really am happy for him. "I'll admit that I maybe got a little disappointed there for a minute. Because you know how I feel about Victor."

He nods. "I do know. But he just came at me out of the blue and offered me this job. I didn't know what to say."

"I know. You're fine. It'll work out," I say.

"So, I really do have to get to work." He gives me a peck on the cheek. "And I don't have time to take you home now. I hope that's okay." I nod and give him a hug and he strides off across the parking lot just as the tow truck arrives.

The cop guides the tow truck driver into backing up to the wrecked car. Lysa, Spam, and I watch as the tow truck driver hooks up his rig to the damaged car. Within minutes he's sliding his hands all over the area where the fingerprints were, so now I don't feel bad about lifting one.

Lysa and Spam resume debating who should drive me home, and Victor strides toward us.

"Why don't you just ride with me?" he says.

We all shrug. Perfect. It's settled.

Victor waits while I quick hug first Lysa and then Spam. But as I follow him to his car the unsettled feelings close in around me, like storm clouds. The ride home won't take long, but it will be just the two of us.

I don't even understand why I'm having these feelings all of a sudden, which means I'm nowhere near ready to talk about them.

▸ 7 ◂

Trusting an eyewitness can be tricky. Extreme stress, the presence
of weapons, or even a bland suspect can affect what
and how much one remembers.

—VICTOR FLEMMING

Victor's phone rings as he unlocks the car.

I get in.

He checks his phone. But doesn't answer it. Just checks it.

He silences the ring, then stashes his briefcase in the backseat area before getting in and buckling up. The phone rings
twice more. And he silences it each time, without looking at
the screen.

I pretend to read, thinking that will cut down on the
chitchat and I won't have to worry about revealing my hurt
feelings.

"Good book?" He shoots me a typical Victor smile. I nod
and offer him one back. It's not my usual easy-breezy smile,
but it's the best I can do under the circumstances.

His phone rings a fourth time as he's starting the car.

"Gah!" Frustrated, Victor yanks the phone out of his pocket,
reaches around the back of his seat, and slams it in the general
direction of his briefcase. He puts the car in gear and begins to
exit the parking lot. He's clearly agitated about something.

I watch him out of the corner of my eye.

He stretches out his shoulders. Rolls his head around on his neck. Taps his palm on the steering wheel. He even obsessively rubs one eyebrow.

I don't know exactly what's going on, but this is not the laid-back version of Victor that I'm used to. Silence in the car builds quickly until it threatens to blow out the windows.

I close my book. "Is everything okay?"

Victor puts both hands on the wheel and gives me a forced smile. "Sure. Why?"

"You look upset. You're making sighing sounds . . . and stretching your neck."

He lifts his chin. "What about you?"

"What do you mean?" I thought I was hiding my feelings well.

"Usually you're a little chatter bug. You stormed off earlier and now you've only said two things to me."

"You seemed busy." There's a lack of conviction in my voice.

He shakes his head. "Not buying it."

"Yeah. Well, I'm not buying that you're all hunky-dory either." I shove my book into my bag. "You tell me what's got you all tweaked out and I'll tell you mine."

Victor chuckles, but his direct gaze on me doesn't waver. He unexpectedly flips on the turn signal. "Using my own tactics against me, are you?"

"Maybe."

"Fine," he agrees. "But I think this'll go down better over a couple of shakes. What do you say?"

"Chocolate and you've got a deal." I feel the warmth returning to my limbs. This is Victor at his best. He lets nothing stand in the way of uncovering a problem.

Not even milkshakes before dinner.

Victor pulls into a drive-thru and orders the shakes, then pulls up to the window to wait for them.

"Do you want to go first?" he asks.

"No." I'm not even sure I want to go second. But I'm definitely not going first.

Victor nods. "Fair enough. Remember when I told you I thought I might be getting fired?"

"Because someone sabotaged your lab."

"Right. But I couldn't prove that," he adds. "So, yeah. That situation's back."

"But you quit, so what difference does it make?"

"An innocent man died as a result of that mistake. Also, I didn't quit . . . I resigned so I could move home and switch careers."

"Right."

"Bottom line, quitting—or resigning—didn't make that problem go away." He presses his face into his hands and rubs as if he's trying to remove the thoughts that are bothering him.

"It's going to be okay, though. Right?" I ask.

"Honestly?" Victor says. "I don't know. All I can do is tell the truth and see how it all shakes out."

The drive-thru window slides open and the employee hands out the shakes. Victor rolls down his window and takes them. He hands one off to me and preps his own straw. Once the drinks are good to go he pulls out onto the street and heads for home, which is only a block away.

He takes a sip of his shake, then nods in my direction. "Okay. Your turn."

I inhale a lung-full of courage. He followed through so now I have to. "Why did you choose Journey as your intern?" I try to keep the hurt out of my voice, but it cracks anyway.

"And butt monkey," Victor adds. "Don't forget butt monkey, because that is a key part of his job."

I want a serious answer, not a joke. I glare and exhale, stopping just short of an actual snort. "You know what I mean."

Victor sobers a little. "Explain to me why you're upset and maybe I'll know better how to answer you?"

I sit back in the seat with my shake in one hand and arms crossed protectively over my middle. Is he that clueless?

"Look, Journey's starting college. He'll be studying criminal science. We have his father's case to work on . . ." Victor explains.

There it is. My temper flares, dissolving Victor's face into a white blur. "You said it wasn't kosher for someone to work on a case they were connected to by blood." Accusation drips from every word and I regret it the minute it happens. But there's no holding it back. The floodgates to Erin's psyche are now open.

Victor nods. "I did say that, specifically in relation to your mother's murder case and *you* handling the actual evidence. And it's still true. I stand by that statement. But Journey's father is alive, possibly erroneously imprisoned. The work he will be doing is primarily research, not forensic investigation. He will pick up every lead from his father's case and follow it all the way through to its conclusion. His role will be fact-checking, research, and documentation. It will work very much like the Innocence Project run by some law schools, but because he's working with me, his focus will be on the evidence and the forensic angle of the investigation, not the legal one."

Victor pulls into our driveway and parks up near the garage.

"I'm happy for Journey. I really am." I gather my bag and

start to get out of the car. "He doesn't even remember his father, so I know how important this is to him." I just don't know what to do with *my* feelings. But I can't bring myself to say that out loud.

"I get it," he says. "You're happy for Journey but that doesn't change your feelings of disappointment."

"You said you liked working with me. That we clicked. I thought *we* were a team."

Victor reaches his hand across the console to me. "We were. We are. We're all of that. Erin, *you* are the whole reason I left my job in Virginia and moved back home. We're not just a team . . . we're a family. But there's a place in this for Journey, too." He stops and cocks his head to one side, thinking. "Wait a minute. You two didn't break up, did you?"

Hot, angry tears peck at the back of my eyes. I press the heels of my hands into my forehead and refuse to let the tears leak out. I wave him off and swallow back the fist of emotion in my throat. I get what he's saying and I want to be okay with this. But I can't help feeling shoved to the side.

"We're fine." I get out of the car. One of us has to break the tension. I dab away the tears and adjust my attitude. I don't need Rachel asking a bunch of questions right now, especially when I'm not even sure exactly how I feel.

Victor follows, grabbing his briefcase and phone. We tromp up the back stairs. Victor opens the door and allows me to go first.

Rachel is stirring something on the stove. She smiles, happy to see us, then immediately frowns.

"Milkshakes? Before dinner?"

Victor speaks as if the kitchen were filled with people. "Everyone's always saying we need to bring back the good old days. Well, sis. Don't you remember when *we* used to go for milkshakes after a rough day?"

Victor's charm strikes again. Rachel visibly melts. "Aw," she says. "Where's mine?"

"Oh no, Rachel, did you have a bad day too?" I open my arms for a hug.

"Not milkshake bad," she says. "But I'll take that hug anyway."

I bend my knees to make it easier, since I'm nearly as tall as Victor. Over Rachel's shoulder I watch him turn off his cell phone and slam it into his briefcase, which he then kicks into the corner. He slumps into his spot at the table.

"Oh." Rachel walks to the credenza in the dining room and retrieves a FedEx envelope. "I almost forgot, this came for you today, brother dear." She lays the envelope on the table before moving off to her bedroom.

Victor scans the label; his eyes darken and turn wary. Rachel might just as well have laid a snake in front of him. He rolls his lower lip between his teeth, chewing thoughtfully. Finally, he glances up at me, making eye contact.

The effect is unnerving.

I don't know what's in that envelope. After his admission about the problems at his old job I would normally think it had to do with that. But his odd reaction to me gives me pause. Then something else pops into my head. It happened in such a strange moment that it was easy to sort of forget another recent incident with Victor and a FedEx envelope.

Emotions were running super high the day Victor showed up in my hospital room to tell me we had done it. Principal Roberts had been arrested and he confessed to murdering both my mother and Miss P.

Victor made a lot of promises that day.

He decided to come home and become part of the family with Rachel and me. He promised to take over teaching Miss P's biology class with a forensic focus. He also promised to help find my father. To that end, he'd handed me a buccal swab for my mouth and instructed me on how to move it around and scrub vigorously to get the best DNA cells. When I was done, I handed the swab back to him. He dropped it into a tube, sealed it, and then dropped that into a FedEx envelope. He'd said he was sending it to his former lab at the FBI.

And here's the thing. Not five minutes later, I looked out the door of my hospital room and watched Victor, at the nurse's station with his back to me, swab his own mouth and drop that tube into the same FedEx envelope with mine.

I didn't know what it meant then . . . and I still don't exactly. But his actions strongly suggested that Victor thought he could be my real dad.

At the time, I was all fluttery about that notion. *Biggest fan discovers legend is her father.* Seriously, this is the stuff those "girl finds her destiny" stories have.

But today feels different. And it's not because my feelings for Victor have changed. They haven't. He's still a legend.

I'm just not sure how I feel. I mean, it's not like I don't want Victor to be my dad . . . and it's not like I do want him to be, either. Having my actual dad in the picture threatens to change everything.

What happens to Rachel then? She's my legal guardian and my mother in every way. But she never actually adopted me.

I want to know, I guess . . . I just don't want anything to change.

Principal Roberts confessed to killing my mom and Victor confirmed that man wasn't my father. That settled the most important fact for me.

Not sure what the next step is in my need-to-know-who-Erin-is epic.

Victor and I are locked in a stare-down across the table. My thoughts are racing, so his probably are too.

Suddenly, Spam bursts in the back door and breaks the spell.

Victor and I blink at each other, then turn to look at her.

She waves her finger between the two of us. "Are you guys doing that who-blinks-first thing?"

"What? No," I say. "Why?"

"Because that's what it looked like when I peeked through the window."

"You peeked through our window?" I say.

"Well, yeah," she says. "I always look before I just barge in."

"And there's a reason for not knocking?" Victor asks.

Spam waves her hand. "We almost never do that."

I try to focus on Spam but my mind is on Victor and the FedEx envelope. As if he can read my thoughts, he taps it on the table. Then, with steps that seem heavier than normal, he walks the stiff cardboard envelope back into the dining room, where he sets it in a prominent place on the credenza.

"You're not going to open it?" I ask.

"What?" Victor looks startled.

"Never mind." I drop the subject. But I can't help wondering what does *that* mean?

Rachel comes back to the kitchen. "Hey, Spam. I thought I heard you come in."

"Hey, Mama-Rach," she says. "Smells amazing."

"Chicken Dijon," Rachel says. "Want to join us?"

"Oh, I wish I could. My dad is making dinner for us. But I wondered if I could borrow Erin for a few minutes?"

Rachel checks her watch. "Fine. Just be back in thirty minutes for dinner. Okay?"

"Will do." I get up and follow Spam to the door. I pause and look back at Victor. He smiles a normal Victor smile.

"Have fun," he says.

► 8 ◄

Facebook has a larger database and a better facial
recognition algorithm than the FBI. True story.

—SPAM RAMOS

Spam practically drags me down the stairs by my sleeve.

"What's up?"

"We have to show you something."

"We?"

"Lysa's in the car."

"You can't show me here?"

"No."

"Not even in my room?

"No."

"My attic?"

We round the corner. Lysa is parked behind Victor's car. As
we approach she shifts her car into gear.

"Is this a getaway or something?" I'm joking, but Spam and
Lysa don't even crack a hint of a smile.

"Back or front?" Spam never asks. She always takes the front
and will knock you out of the way to get there. When I hesitate, she whips open the door and slips into the back.

"Who are you and what have you done with my friends?" I
joke.

"Just get in," Lysa says.

I climb into the passenger seat. "I have to be home in thirty minutes."

"Me too," Lysa says. "We thought you'd handle this better in person."

"Handle what?" All this intrigue is lighting me up. And, I'll admit, scaring me, too.

Lysa drives around the block and parks. She turns in her seat toward us. "Me first. So, you know our Cheater Check email account still exists, right?" She pulls out her phone and reviews. "So far, I've received three videos, five stills, and six witness statements about the accident. And that's just since we left school."

"What are they saying?"

"They're all defending the skateboarder, of course. Everyone says the accident wasn't his fault. But no one wants to talk to the new principal or the police about it. They want *us* to do it."

Spam flashes a wide-eyed grin. "Because we're amazing."

"What do you guys think we should do?" I ask.

"I think we should gather everything, get all the statements and evidence, and then hand it over to Victor," Lysa says. "He'll know how to present it to the chief."

Victor . . . dang. I drift a little as the image of the FedEx envelope looms.

"Earth to Erin?" Lysa says. She and Spam are both staring at me.

"Sorry. Yeah. Victor would probably be cool with that. Are you taking me home now?"

"There's more." Spam leans over the front seat with her laptop open. She clicks some keys. "I was just messing around and thought I'd run the photos through a couple of databases to see if I could ID the skateboarder. . . ."

"Wait." I look from Spam to Lysa and back to Spam. "You're plotting his defense. And you're stalking him."

"He was so cuuute," Spam says.

"How could you tell? Everything happened so fast I barely saw him."

Spam gives me a serious head-tilt. "Oh, trust me, he's cute. And yeah, a facial recognition search might sound a little stalker-y—"

I twitch. "Facial recognition . . . like the NSA does?" I drop my voice to a hush. "Spam, that's not stalker-y, that's invasion of privacy."

"Not really." She scoffs. "FYI, Facebook has better facial recognition algorithms and a larger database than the FBI."

"I don't believe that."

"True story," Spam insists.

Lysa waves her hand. "Just show her."

"Does this mean you know who he is?" I ask.

"No," Spam says. "But the woman driving the car was in the background of the photo. And I matched to her."

"So? Everybody knows who she is," I say.

"Right," Spam says. "But not everybody knows her picture is on Victor's murder board." Spam clicks some keys and brings up a photo of the woman behind the wheel of the car, compared to a photo of the woman on the whiteboard. There is a green border around each photo and the word   T H.

"She's a suspect," Lysa says. "Or a witness. I wasn't sure."

"Wait. You took a photo of the murder board?"

"Of course," Spam says. "So did Lysa. You didn't?"

"Hmmm. I was going to . . ."

"Her name's Arletta Stone," Lysa says. "She's head of the Iron Rain Historical Society. She tried to block the sale of the cannery to Journey's parents. She also testified that the cannery is haunted." Lysa starts the car. "I'll research more about her tonight."

Lysa puts the car in gear and heads back to my house.

A familiar chill envelops me. "Wait, does it mean anything that someone related to Jameson's case crashed her car at our school, nearly killing us?" I ask.

"You know what you always say about evidence—if it's there it means something." Spam shrugs. "Anyway, it creeped us out."

"What if she saw us and thought the skateboarder was Journey? She could've been aiming for him," Lysa says. "The newspaper article had all of our photos and mentioned how, with Victor back in town, certain cases might be reexamined. If there are any guilty people out there, hovering below the radar, that statement has got to make them nervous."

"Interesting theory," I say. "But running over kids with a car in front of a bunch of witnesses at their school doesn't sound like the best plan of a criminal mastermind."

"Sometimes criminal masterminds just freak out and panic." Spam shuts her laptop. "Case in point, Principal Roberts."

True.

▸ 9 ◂

When you find evidence, you don't always know what it means.
But if you found it, you can bet it means something.

—ERIN BLAKE

The girls drop me off at the end of my driveway.

Victor is out shooting hoops, and judging by the huge damp patches on his shirt he's pushed himself to a punishing workout. He pauses as I walk up.

"Where'd you go?" he asks.

"Nowhere. We just drove around. You know, girl talk."

He nods. "Are they excited about CSI camp?"

I nod. "Oh yeah. Very excited."

"Good," he says. "This camp stuff will be the perfect outlet for your forensic curiosity, which should keep you from messing with any real cases that might come up."

I blink. Did he really just say that?

Victor bounces the ball to me. "A little one-on-one?"

I bounce it back to him. "Nah. I'm kind of tired." I wander into the house, dazed about everything: the creepy new principal, the classroom, the lab, the accident, the skateboarder, Arletta Stone, Journey as Victor's intern . . . and the big one: Victor doesn't trust me.

"Perfect timing." Rachel greets me with a friendly hip bump

and hands me a stack of dinner plates. All I want to do is retreat to my bedroom sanctuary, but first I'll have to make it through dinner.

I drift around the kitchen gathering utensils and setting the table. The structure of the routine grounds me and allows me to swallow back the bad feelings, at least temporarily.

It helps that Victor followed me in and went straight upstairs to wash up.

What does he mean, messing with *real* cases? Is the strange and violent appearance of Arletta Stone the beginning of a real case? What about gathering witness statements and photos about the skateboarder? Would that be helping or messing something up? I used to think I understood the parameters. Now I'm not so sure.

I silently assist Rachel in ferrying the food to the table. I can feel her gaze on me. She wears her worry like a gorilla suit. I offer her a thin smile, knowing it's not enough.

Oblivious, Victor drops into his seat at precisely the right moment and in mid-conversation.

"I have some great guidelines on how we'll structure the CSI camp. I'm thinking each week will have a theme that supports one of our core forensic techniques. We'll offer two hands-on science experiments and pair that with some flashy crime scene setups. The rest of the time we'll focus on learning important skills like observation and deductive reasoning."

The more he talks, the more his enthusiasm builds.

"Sounds fun." The words are there, but admittedly my enthusiasm is weak.

Rachel is quietly listening and watching both of us. Finally, she puts down her fork and rests her elbows on the table. "I'm not sure that luring kids into a camp by promising *flashy crime scene analysis* is a good idea, Vic."

He looks confused. "What?"

"You're not a parent," Rachel says. "You've never spent much time around kids. There are things that might seem simple and straightforward to you, but could actually trigger an emotional trauma."

Victor tilts his head, arching one eyebrow. "I'm not planning anything 'triggering.'" He uses air quotes around that word.

Rachel shifts her gaze to me, briefly, then looks back at Victor. "What I'm saying is . . . you don't know a lot about kids and how they behave, so you might not understand what this kind of stuff can generate." She trails off by glancing back at me.

"Sis, you need to be specific. I lecture on this stuff. I've testified in front of juries. I know about boundaries and how to use them. They write books on this stuff for sixth-graders."

He doesn't get it, but I do. "She's talking about *me*."

Victor looks from me to Rachel and back again. Rachel pinches her lips together. An awkward silence attacks the room.

"*Are* you talking about Erin?" Victor asks. "Are you worried about her working at the camp?"

Rachel inhales noisily and wets her lips. "'Worried' might be too strong a word. I'd like to see Erin diversify. Get into art or dance or something other than *crime*."

"Rachel, please don't say I can't do the camp." My emotions squeeze the life out of me from the inside. I might be upset with Victor right at this moment, but I don't want to be blocked from working with him. "It's an amazing opportunity." I'm trying so hard to appear normal that I can hardly breathe. My voice is a desperate gasp.

Rachel balls up her napkin and sets it beside her plate. I recognize this motion. What's coming next is Rachel's "end of discussion" bottom line.

Victor spots it too. He waves his hands to calm us both down. "Look, sis. Obviously, you have data and experience that I don't have."

She acknowledges his comment with a slight nod.

"But I also have data and experience that you don't have."

Rachel opens her mouth to speak, but Victor silences her with a raised finger.

"Here's my suggestion," he says. "Let's not decide anything today. I'm sure that what I have planned will ease your concerns—we are including kids as young as sixth grade, so everything will be very tame. But let me get the program together and present it to you before you decide. Okay?"

Rachel thinks for a minute. "Okay," she says, flashing me a happier face. "I'm willing to table this for now."

I breathe a sigh. I'm sure if I get my emotions under control I'll be able to handle Victor's attitude and my limitations. But once Rachel says no, it's impossible to get her back to yes.

"I could use some help getting the classroom set up. You don't have any objections to Erin and her friends helping with that after school, do you?"

"No. That's fine." Rachel stands and starts to bus her plate from the table.

"Leave it, Rachel," I say. "I've got it."

"Oh. Thank you." She looks a little surprised and a lot grateful. "Okay then, I'm going to head over to Charles's for a bit. We're going to watch a movie."

There have been a lot of surprises over the last few weeks, not the least of which is that I found out that Rachel had been secretly dating Chief Culson for over a year. Things are out in the open now, but when I first heard it I was in shock.

"Have fun," Victor says.

After Rachel leaves I start to clear the table. Victor listens until he hears her get to the bottom of the stairs, then he picks the conversation right up from where we left off, completely ignoring Rachel's concern.

"You probably know this, but there's already a summer camp program at the school that's run by Coach Wilkins."

I nod as I remove Victor's plate from the table.

"We'll be an offshoot of that," he explains. "A much cooler and more fun offshoot." He grins. His attitude is infectious.

"Definitely cooler and more fun," I agree.

"We'll operate the same five days, Monday through Friday, and during the same hours. The kids will bring a sack lunch; we'll provide a snack. I'll handle the heavy lifting, which will be a great way to ease me into the teaching environment. And you and the girls can teach them all your tricks."

By tricks I assume he means all those things I did to uncover what Principal Roberts had done and what Victor now considers "messing with a real case." "Do you mean teach them how to lift prints and chromatography?"

Victor's gaze travels around the room as he thinks about my question. "Chromatography, definitely . . . because that has a strong science base. Not sure about the fingerprints. I still have to get some approvals from the new principal." At the mention of Miss Blankenship, we both make a spontaneous "there is no emoji for her" face. "You saw her opinion about this stuff on the TV interview. So, I'll have to consider how much she will let us do."

I shiver just thinking about Blankface. She is the coldest person I have ever met. If someone told me she was a robot, I would totally believe it. I plan on keeping my distance from her.

"Sounds good," I say, loading dishes into the dishwasher.

I want to ask him about the FedEx envelope, too. Get all my angst and trauma over in one swoop. But I don't know how to broach the subject. He has no reason to think that I suspect anything. And there's also a good chance that envelope deals with his work problem.

In the end, I focus on taking care of the dishes and trying not to worry about Victor or the FedEx envelope. When I'm done, I head upstairs to my bedroom.

I flip on the bedroom light and survey my overflowing laundry basket in the middle of the room. It might be all in one place, but it's not going to wash itself.

Ugh. Maybe later.

Instead I retreat to my attic with my book.

I step into my giant walk-in closet and pull the cord dangling from the ceiling. A set of narrow stairs accordion down and I climb up through the dark hole. At the top of the stairs I flip on the light, washing the area in a gentle glow.

When I first discovered this space, I kept it a secret from everyone, including Rachel. I used it to hide my secret Cheater Checks lab—and my mother's murder box. It turned out I wasn't the only one hiding things. Rachel had stashed my mother's belongings up here—her furniture, photographs, and letters. Everything. Once I saw it and lived with it, there was no way Rachel could take it away.

Victor helped me convince her that keeping this space sacred for me, and me alone, would help me process all that I had lost. The murder box of evidence went back to the police department, of course. And there's not really a lab up here anymore. But there is a sofa and coffee table and lamps. And there's even a desk and cabinet on one side. It's a cool place to hang out and it's the one place I never let get messy like my bedroom.

I lay back on the sofa and try to feel her presence. "Hey, Mom," I whisper. My new ritual doesn't include anything gruesome like hugging a box of murder evidence or lying on top of an outline of her body. I just spend time thinking about her and trying to remember things.

I lie down, close my eyes, and think of the very earliest thing I can remember. I continue to hope that one day I'll grasp an actual memory of her. A memory of my mother's touch or of an expression or gesture. I'd even love to be able to lock in on the way she smelled. But I was very young when she was murdered, so there's not much there to work with.

For years, I was irrationally terrified by the tiny shadow of a cross. But I didn't understand why until the night Principal Roberts admitted what he had done. Finding my mother's things hidden in our attic and having access to what was contained in her murder box filled in some of the blanks for me. The photo on the front of the old newspaper filled in even more.

It was taken the night Rachel discovered us—me, curled alongside my mother's cold, lifeless body. The photo showed the front of our house, surrounded by flashing lights, officers, and crime scene tape. In the foreground, a stunned, tearstained, and disheveled Rachel sits on the bumper of an ambulance, gripping baby me, wrapped in her jacket.

Her finger is pressed against my chin to avert my face from the activity in the house. But my eyes are trained on the action as a body is wheeled out, shrouded in dark plastic.

I'd like to think I understood that was the last time I would ever see my mother. But I'm unable to grasp the memory to confirm that. Periodically, I try to tap into it using various relaxation, breathing, and visualization techniques, because if I don't, I risk forgetting about it altogether. And that's something I'm not willing to do.

Just as I'm starting to relax into my memory I hear a squeak from the closet stairs. I sit up as Journey's head pops up through the hole in the ceiling.

► 10 ◄

Feelings of dread, flashbacks, nightmares, and even a loss of
personal identity, also known as a fugue state, can be
expected after an intense, emotional,
or life-threatening event.

—WIKIPEDIA

Journey has a way about him that's so easy, it's as if I've known
him my whole life. And yet this boyfriend/girlfriend thing is
still new and exciting, which explains why my heart goes all
drum solo the moment he enters the room.

"Hey, you." I smile extra warmly. "How'd you know I was
up here?"

"I could see the light around the edge of the window when
I pulled in the driveway," he says. "Plus, Victor said you were
upstairs." He drops a stack of bound notebooks, each about two
inches thick, onto the sofa between us before bending over to
give me a kiss.

I cringe a little remembering the overflowing laundry basket he had to maneuver around to get here. But then I rise to
meet him halfway and slide my hand around the back of his
neck. We share a nice, simple, *glad-to-see-you* kiss. Though he
lingers just a bit. After a few seconds, he pulls away and plops
down on the sofa.

"What are these?" I point to the notebooks.

"Transcripts from my father's trial."

"Oh my god!" My hands flutter. "I have something to tell you. But you have to promise not to get mad."

I nervously topple the stack of notebooks into my lap and randomly flip the pages. I'm not actually looking at them, just giving my fingers something to do while I try to figure out how to tell him about the link to his father's case. After Victor's comment, I don't want Spam to sound stalker-y. Also, I'm leery of admitting that both Spam and Lysa took photos of the murder board.

Frowning, he scoots a little farther away from me on the sofa. "Let me go first."

"No," I interrupt. "Mine's important."

"So's mine." He gently takes the notebooks out of my lap and moves them to the coffee table . . . out of my reach.

This resembles being scolded, but maybe I'm being oversensitive after Victor's comment. I sit back, pinch my lips together, and fold my hands in my lap.

"First," he says, nodding to the stack of notebooks, "Victor expects *me* to read those."

"Of course." I curl one leg under me. "You'll read all of them. I just thought I'd read some too, so I can help. And then we can talk about the case and come up with theories and stuff. Seriously, Iron Rain has had its share of murders. Right? I'm surprised that I didn't know anything about this case before I met you, but I started reading about it."

"How much do you know?" Journey asks.

"Hardly anything."

"Let's hear it."

He's so serious and finger-pointy that it's kind of freaking me out. "Okay. Well, I know that the victim was a kid."

"He wasn't a little kid," Journey says quickly. "He was sixteen, same as you."

"Right. And that's still really sad."

"Agreed," Journey says. "But the fact he was a kid went hard against my father."

Something's wrong with this conversation. There's something Journey wants to say, but isn't. "I'm not getting a good vibe here. You do want my help with this, right?"

"Don't get mad." He draws in a ragged breath. "I know you and your friends mean well. Your intentions are all good. But here's the thing. In your situation, nothing was going to bring your mother back."

I gasp. It's true, but he says it so bluntly it's like being punched in the face.

"My father's alive. And if we do everything right there is a slim chance we could bring him home." Journey's gaze is intensely piercing. "I can't risk screwing that up by not following the rules."

I nod and try to swallow, but a chunk of humiliation blocks my throat. My lip trembles. "You're saying if I get involved I'll screw it up?"

"Erin, you stole your mother's murder box," he says.

"Yes. Yes, I did." I get up from the sofa and start to pace. "And it was a good thing I did, too. Because that was the only way we knew that the person who murdered Miss P was the same person who murdered my mother."

"But it so easily could have gone the other way," Journey argues. "If Principal Roberts hadn't tried to kill us, any evidence contained in that box would have been inadmissible in court simply because you took it. He could have gone free."

"Okay." It feels like total crap to have my mistakes thrown back in my face, but I hear what he's saying. The horrible thing is there's no way I can tell him about Spam's discovery now. He'll never understand or believe it was accidental. "I promise

I won't mess with your father's case. I just want to be supportive and share in this huge moment."

Journey pats the sofa next to him. I move back and sit down.
He puts his arm around me and pulls me close. "I know. And
your support means everything to me," he says. "We wouldn't
even be getting this opportunity if it hadn't been for you. But
from what I've read so far, this case is going to get messy."

I wince. "What happened? Did your father and this kid get
into a fight, or what?"

Journey makes a dejected cluck. "Worse. My father set up a
motion-activated trap . . . with a gun."

"So, he meant to kill an animal?" I'm tentative because let's
face it, killing a defenseless animal isn't great either.

"At the trial, he claimed he wasn't trying to kill anything—
that he armed the trap with a paintball gun, not a real one. And
he did it to prove that someone was harassing our family."

"Oh wow," I say. "That's intense."

"Exactly. And it's why I can't let anything mess this up."

I take a deep breath. "Okay." I pick up my own book. "We
can just hang out here and read together." I sit back and put
my feet up on the coffee table.

"You're not mad?" he asks.

"I get where you're coming from." I'm not mad. I want to
help Journey, not make things worse.

Journey lies down on the sofa with his head in my lap and
opens one of the notebooks. I let my fingers play through his
hair in between turning pages.

Every now and then, he takes my hand and kisses my palm
gently. When he does I pause to study his face, and wonder if
he really thinks I'm that much of a screwup.

It's not long before we hear the squeaky stairs and Victor
sticks his head up into the attic. "Hey, kids. Rachel just sent

me a text reminding me that school isn't out yet, which means Erin has a curfew. So, you know . . ."

"Oh yeah." Journey checks his phone. "Sorry. I didn't realize it was so late."

"Me either."

We close up the attic and I walk Journey down to his car. Our goodbye is brief and quiet. Soft kiss. He's probably as deeply alone in his own thoughts as I am in mine.

When I get back to my room I send a joint message to both Spam and Lysa: E SE ON T ENTION THE WO   N IN THE R TO O RNE I E   IN TER

It's the best I can muster under the circumstances.

Maybe I'll feel different after a night's sleep.

▸ 11 ◂

Shotguns are weapons of impulse. They're heavy, loud, imprecise,
short-ranged, and hard to conceal. Which is why they're
generally not the choice of most criminals.

—VICTOR FLEMMING

The lunch table at the side of the cafeteria has apparently become ours, since we're the only ones who ever sit here and
every time we show up, it's empty. I arrive first and while I'm
waiting I take out my notebook and start a list of the growing
number of mysteries swirling around.

There's the crazy driver, who's linked to Journey's dad's
case. *Strange.*
There's Spam's elusive soul mate, the skateboarder.
Mysterious.
There's the creepy new principal. *Ugh, so creepy.*
There's Jameson's case—which I promised to stay out
of. *Compelling.*
There's Victor's problem at work—which he says he's
dealing with. *Scary.*
And the FedEx envelope—which Victor is clearly *not*
dealing with. *Crazy making.*

I look over the list. More than enough to keep a mystery addict engaged. But the things calling to me the hardest are the ones I really should stay away from.

I'm hoping Lysa and Spam will arrive before Journey so I can head them off about discussing his father's case. But when I see all three of them coming toward me at the same time I resort to a quick text to Spam and Lysa: SRS   I IT   O T WO   N RI ER IN RONT O O RNE

Lysa checks her phone as she's walking. She makes eye contact and nods. Spam checks her wrist. I'm hoping for the best.

I slide over to make room for Journey next to me. Spam and Lysa take places opposite us. Today it appears we've each bought a different food item from the cafeteria. Mine was supposed to be a chicken sandwich, but when I unwrap the package the breading on the outside is so thick it looks like a clump of kitty litter.

"Gross." I wrap it back up.

Journey peeks in. "Is that the chicken san? I wanted it but they were gone by the time I got there."

I shove it in his direction. "I'm not sure it's really chicken, but it's all yours."

He waves his own wrapped food item. "Anyone want a bean and cheese burrito?"

"Oh. Me." Spam reaches grabby hands across the table. "I'm starving and seriously need carbs." She passes her lunch to me, which is two apples and a banana. "Here, eat mine."

I shrug. "Hmmm. Perfect."

Lysa looks at her salad. "I'm still happy with you."

Spam nudges Lysa. "How many do you have now?"

My insides jump and I die a little. I haven't had a chance to talk to them yet. I sneak a worried glance at Journey; fortunately he's absorbed in devouring his sandwich.

Lysa pulls out her phone and scrolls through. "Six videos. Fifteen witness statements and seven stills." She looks up. "They all say the same thing: The driver was not watching where she was going."

Journey perks up. "What are you talking about?"

Lysa sets her phone aside. "We're gathering witness statements from the accident."

"Did someone ask you to do this?" Journey asks.

I shoot him a quick look. It's day one and he already sounds like Victor.

Spam scrunches her mouth to the side and gives me a pointed look before answering him. "No . . . why?"

Journey backtracks a little. "I thought you guys promised no more stuff." He makes a waffling hand gesture.

"We promised no more Cheater Checks," Lysa says, stashing her phone. "But this is different."

"Is it?" Journey asks.

"Uh, yeah." Lysa, Spam, and I all say it at the same time.

"Don't you remember when *you* were on the receiving end of this kind of tyranny and blaming by the police?" I realize that "tyranny" is maybe taking it a little far. But Journey knows my commitment to the truth. Especially for people our age.

He brings his hands up. "Fine. I'll stay out of it. Which means you need to leave me out of it. Because I'm pretty sure Victor expects me to report stuff like this to him."

I gasp. "Did he say that?"

Journey shakes his head. "No. But intern is like boots on the ground, have your back—"

"Butt monkey." Spam coughs into her fist as she says it.

Journey levels a serious look at Spam. "Dude. Did you just *insult-cough* me?"

Spam shrugs.

Lysa and I stifle giggles.

Journey gets up. "I have to go. Duty calls." He wads up his sandwich wrapping.

Now it's my turn to say it. "Don't be mad."

He plants a kiss on the top of my head. "Not mad, late for a game. See you later." As he passes a trash can he slam-dunks his lunch trash with full basketball style. He glances back to see if I was watching and blows me an air-kiss as a reward.

I blow an air-kiss back and my eyes stay on him until he disappears out the door.

I turn back to Lysa and Spam and find them smushed together, frozen in a goofy pose: Spam's pulling down the skin around her eyes and Lysa's sticking out her tongue.

"Stop."

"We can't help it," Lysa says. "You guys are just so darn cute it makes our faces freeze like that."

Spam leans forward. "So, Journey's narcing us out to Victor now?"

I hedge. I don't want to point-blank say Journey forbids us to work on his father's case. But I have to tell them something. "He's just really sensitive about Jameson's case. You know how that is."

They frown, not buying it.

"I started reading about it online, and wow," Lysa says.

"FYI, me too," admits Spam. "I wouldn't want to talk about it either."

"No. Wait." I panic. "That's not why he doesn't want to talk about it. I mean, it is and it isn't. Basically, you both should stop reading about it."

"Right, because you're not?" Spam gives me her famous one-raised-eyebrow look.

"I'm not . . ."

Spam tilts her head at me. Then she and Lysa share a chuckle. "It's just us," Spam says. "So, you know, keep it real."

"I'm real. Really real," I say. "It's just Journey asked me—us—not to get involved."

Lysa smooths her napkin on the table and shares a sideways glance with Spam. Their indignation rises. "Why does he care what we do?"

"It's not that. It's that—well, this isn't about us."

Now they're both laughing.

"Stop it, you guys." I harden my look. "Lysa, *you* try to get us to follow all of our parents' rules every single time. But *this* time you're blasting me for not reading up on a case we were told to stay out of."

Lysa hangs her head a little, but a sneaky grin tugs at her lips. "C'mon. You know the urge is burning inside you. You want to try to figure it out too."

"Fine. I do. But Journey's worried we might do something to damage his father's chances for a new trial. He says he'll tell me things as he reads them in the transcripts, and I'm content with that."

Spam points. "Which means you are curious."

"Transcripts are public record. Anyone can read them," Lysa says.

"Calm down, both of you. I'm trying to be supportive of my man and not cause any trouble."

"It's a really sad case. The victim was a runaway," Spam says.

Unbelievable. She just goes on talking about it as if she hasn't heard a word I've said.

"Yeah. Apparently, he had a pretty tough life," Lysa says.

They're not listening to me.

"But they managed to trace him back to his family," Spam says. "So that was good."

"How'd they do that? How'd they trace him back?" I'm pow-erless to resist. It's always the details of a case that suck me in.

"I'm not sure," Spam says. "I haven't read that far yet."

"They called the shooting accidental." Lysa slips into her judgmental mom voice. "But what adult doesn't know that rig-ging a shotgun up to a motion sensor is asking for something bad to happen?"

"Journey says it was a *paintball gun*." I don't want to be de-fensive, but a definite tone is creeping into this discussion. "And, by the way, you sounded just like your father when you said that."

Lysa wrinkles her nose and gives me a sour look.

"Why did he use a gun at all?" Spam asks. "That's pretty crazy, if you think about it."

"Journey says his family was being harassed and the police wouldn't believe them. His father thought paint splashed on a person would be proof. Evidence they could see. Instead, every-one just wanted to believe the cannery was haunted."

"Right. But he could have set up a camera to get proof just as easily as he set up a gun," Spam says. "Maybe easier."

"What if he didn't own a camera?" I say.

"Erin, your number one rule is always follow the evidence," Lysa says.

"And I stand by that," I say.

"Then tell me this, why did Journey want Miss P to test his father's DNA when the main evidence in this case was a gun? And not a paintball gun, either. Police never found one of those at his house," Lysa says.

She throws me with the DNA question. "Maybe they found DNA on the gun."

"Not possible," Spam says. "There was no crime lab back then, so even if there was DNA, there was no one to find it."

I sink down, forced to admit that Jameson's case doesn't sound very winnable.

"Look, my father says it's really hard to overturn a murder conviction," Lysa says. "And he was Mr. Michaels's attorney."

"We can't turn our backs on this. What if Journey's father is innocent? Don't we have to try?" My voice slips into pleading mode. "Doesn't everybody—us included—have to do everything we possibly can to right a horrible wrong?"

Lysa and Spam exchange a look.

"You're the one who promised we wouldn't get involved," Spam says.

"But I get it now. I can't be fully supportive of Journey and his father's case because I don't have enough information about what happened. And not having enough information creates too many questions, which makes Mr. Michaels look guilty."

Like Victor says: Information is power.

"We need to re-create the Jameson murder board," I say. "*We* need to do what we do. Ask the questions no one else is asking. Not to meddle, but because we might land on something they missed. It's happened before."

"It totally has," Lysa agrees.

"I just don't want to do it in the attic because . . ."

"You don't want Journey to see it," Lysa says.

"Or Victor."

"My basement then," Spam says. "I can get rid of the littles by letting them watch TV in my room. But we have to keep working on the skateboarder case, too. It's important." She pauses. "And not just because he's cute . . . even though he totally is."

"I agree," Lysa says.

"Okay. Spam's basement, skateboarder, and murder board." I raise my hand for a high five. "Chinese for dinner?"

▸ 12 ◂

Rigging a shotgun up to a motion sensor is asking
for something bad to happen.
—LYSA MARTIN

"Everything's set up," Spam says. "There are two laptops and
four iPads, all charged. Whiteboard, markers, printer."

Lysa is laying out the food on the table. "Egg rolls and dim
sum. Yum."

"I also have these to show you." Spam dips into her pocket
and spills out a handful of plastic discs slightly larger than a
quarter. The design on the disc is a primitive black volcano
with a red sky pierced by a plume of gray smoke.

"Volcanoes?" I ask.

"School pride, baby," Spam says. "It's technically our mascot, right?"

True. Our football team is known as the Crater South
Volcanoes.

"And you did this because . . . ?" I ask.

She digs into her other pocket and pulls out two friendship-
type bracelets with volcano discs attached to woven string.

"These are prototypes for you guys to test."

As Spam helps Lysa into hers I notice that Spam's already
wearing one.

"They do something?" I ask.

"Ahhh," Spam says. "You want magic?" She keys some numbers into her phone. "Once I program them, they'll light up white when any of the three of us are near each other."

As she talks, she programs each of our discs on her phone.

First mine and Spam's light up white . . . then Lysa's. They look so cool. The white light makes the gray plume of smoke glow.

"Wow," I say. "That's so cute."

"The secret part?" Spam says. "The little hole on the volcano lights up red and vibrates if Blankenship is near."

Lysa claps her hands excitedly. "It's a bell for the cat. Have you told Brianna yet? She'll buy one for sure."

We put our fists together so Spam can snap a close-up photo of the three glowing volcano bracelets. "Yes on Brianna. I also Snapped my partial list and already have twenty orders. This pic will easily get us twenty more."

"How much did they cost to make and what are you selling them for?" I ask.

"They don't cost much," Spam says. "My dad buys the electronics in bulk, and I printed the volcano discs on my 3D printer. I wrote the app to program them. Anyway, I priced them at twenty dollars."

"There's barely three weeks of school left. Will anyone buy this for just three weeks of tracking Blankenship?" I ask.

Spam grins. "Dude. Have you met me? I have maximized the power of my device. Each disc can be made to track up to eight people. It comes programed to track Blankenship. But someone's nosy mom could be added. Have a bratty little brother? You can track him, too. All you need is the beacon part they wear or carry, a volcano bracelet, and a smartphone. This is basically a bell for any number of cats you want, up to eight."

"Spam, it's genius. What do you need us to do? What are we going to call it?" I ask.

"I'll need you guys to help me build, assemble, and code them. Plus, spread the word."

"Bella," Lysa says. "I think we should call it *the Bella*."

"The Bella side hustle. It's perfect," I say. "Next order of business."

I ladle some Chinese food onto my plate and choose a fork from the bag. Lysa and Spam do the same, though Lysa also unwraps a pair of chopsticks.

Spam takes a bite of egg roll, then dusts her hands off. "Skateboarder. We've received six videos, twenty statements, and nine stills."

"Have you looked at them yet?"

"No, but we should," Spam says. She brings out an iPad and begins streaming the videos.

The first three videos are similar. Blurry and quick, only about twenty-three seconds. They show the skateboarder in motion, dodging the car, at the last minute. The other videos are shot from angles farther away but they prove what we said. The skateboarder was up on the sidewalk with us the whole time, not crossing the driveway like Arletta Stone claimed. Unfortunately, none of the videos has a clear shot of the skateboarder's face.

"I can't tell who he is from these," I say. "Anybody?"

"I don't know him." Spam goes to the whiteboard and begins a list labeled ES RI TION.

Lysa shrugs while demonstrating perfect chopstick form at grasping a dumpling, dipping it in sauce, and popping it into her mouth.

"Your skill with those is why I hate you," I say.

Lysa smirks. "It's not the only reason, either." She giggles.

"I put him at about five-nine. Shoulder-length, curly brown hair. Caucasian. The video is too quick to see his eyes. What else?" Spam asks.

"He's wearing a plaid Pendleton *and* plaid cargo shorts." Lysa points at the screen. "Which may be leaning a little hard on the plaid pedal."

"Shut up. I think it's just the right amount of awesome," Spam says.

Of course Spam would love an unconventional dresser.

"What about age?" I ask. "Anyone have a guess?"

"I'd say he's in our range—fifteen to seventeen," Lysa says.

"I agree," Spam says.

"Some of the witness statements are hilarious." Lysa reads. "But I love this one: About an hour after school, this radi-cool dude came through pro on a Klein special–Dream deck. He passed the cute crime girls, who he definitely caught on video because his GoPro was lit. All of a sudden, a crazy woman in a dark green Subaru Outback charged across two lanes, veered into the drop-off area, and slammed into the flagpole. She nearly wiped out the boarder and the crime girls, which would have been a straight-up trag. The gnarly part came when the flagpole smashed onto the car." Lysa looks up and grins. "Hey, we're cute."

"And us getting killed would have been a straight-up trag," Spam says. "Not a tragedy, but a trag."

"Klein special–Dream deck. That must be the skateboard," I say. "Write that on the board. Could anyone ID his shoes?" I'm obsessed with shoe prints after that's what helped crack the case of who killed my mom and Miss P.

"No. The videos didn't really show his shoes. Let's check the stills." Spam taps a few things on the iPad and swipes through the photos. "Hm. That's weird."

"What?" I ask.

Spam turns the iPad to show us. "Here's a pic of him coming in, probably. It's a nice action photo." She squints at the screen. "I don't see a time stamp, but look who's standing right there."

"Coach Wilkins?" I squint at the photo.

"Yep," Lysa confirms.

"You guys know the rules. No skateboarding on campus. That guy is zooming right behind him and the coach isn't paying any attention," Spam says.

"Weird. He's staring at the street like he's waiting for someone," I say. "Put the coach's name on the board."

"Okay. Anything else on the skateboarder?" Spam says. "Any ID?"

I shake my head. "Your skateboarder is a true man of mystery. Not much else we can do for now."

"Let's do the murder board now," Lysa says. "I need to go soon. I have a couple of finals I'm a little worried about. I need some study time. Here's the photo I took." Lysa lays her phone on the table in front of us.

Spam excitedly swivels the whiteboard to the blank other side. She bounces on her toes. "I'm crazy excited to do this." She touches the supplies. "I have markers, magnets, superthin red tape to make the connecting lines. This is going to be awesome."

I study the photo on Lysa's phone. "Journey told me about all this stuff, like the dates across the top are the number of times his parents called the police. And the photo of his parents, that was taken when they first moved here. Don't they look happy?"

Spam draws a couple of stick figures on the board with hearts around their heads, then sketches ten lines across the top. "We can put in the dates later."

"Below that are three columns of photos. Looks like: suspects, witnesses, and testimonies. In that order. Evidence is the last column on the far right. Just make little boxes for right now. We can fill it in with photos later."

"Okay." Spam re-creates the murder board with various boxes and lines.

"It's weird." I scrutinize the photo. "The driver at the accident and Coach Wilkins both appear on the skateboarder incident *and* Victor's murder board."

I look up to see if they think this is weird or not.

"Could just be a coincidence," Lysa says.

"Yeah, Victor says crime scene investigators never accept a coincidence as an explanation because a smart murderer anticipates being linked to the scene of a crime so they will find a way to explain away that connection," I say. "And Journey says this is exactly the kind of thing that Victor's looking for. Someone who seemed innocent at the time but who also had a grudge against his family."

"That won't be easy to find after all this time," Lysa says.

"We didn't think it would be easy to find the person who killed my mother either," I say. "And look how that turned out."

"Exactly," Spam says. "Fourteen years later that creeper was still hanging around, practically watching your every move."

"We need to come up with the profile of someone who would have benefited from Jameson going to prison." Lysa doodles cat faces on the edge of her notebook.

"Journey says everyone thought his mother would sell the cannery once his father was sentenced, but she couldn't bear to let it go," I say.

"So, we start by looking at people who wanted the cannery," Lysa says. "Like we know Arletta Stone wanted it. Anyone else we can think of?"

While Lysa and Spam try to one-up each other with various facts they've picked up about Jameson Michaels's case and the urban legends surrounding the cannery, I drift off into some learning of my own.

I start by scanning the articles that came up after I searched his name. But right off I'm forced to admit the facts of this case don't exactly line up in his favor. Why would someone with a toddler rig up a gun to a motion sensor? Any gun, even a paintball gun. Also, why would someone store their dangerous shotgun under the seat of their truck? Even if they believed the gun wasn't loaded, why would they keep it *there*? Isn't that asking for trouble? Aren't guns supposed to be locked up?

The deeper I read only makes it worse. Mr. Michaels claimed he never bought shells for the shotgun and yet the police found at least half a dozen spent shells just lying around on the property.

I go over to the whiteboard and sketch in my notes. Under evidence I write: shotgun, spent shotgun shells. No paintball gun. And finally, someone's lying!

I exchange disheartened looks with the girls. We're used to making progress that feels hopeful. This is anything but hopeful.

"We've done as much as we can do tonight," Spam says.

"Will the whiteboard be safe here?" I ask.

Spam opens a door to a storage closet tucked under the stairs. "Yep. I can roll it right in here," she says. "No one ever goes in here but me."

‣ 13 ‣

There is legal innocence and factual innocence. Legal innocence
means a person could actually still be guilty, but found
not guilty due to a technicality.
—PRINCIPAL BLANKENSHIP

As Spam and Lysa cross the cafeteria toward me I get a text
from Journey saying he has to run an errand for Victor at lunch.

"It's just us today," I say as they take their seats across from
me. "Journey's running an errand for Victor."

"Working through lunch," Spam says. "This must be the
butt monkey part of his job."

"We shouldn't make fun of him," I say. "It's a big deal to be
Victor's intern."

"And snitch," Spam adds.

"Come on, I wouldn't let Journey talk about you guys like
that."

"How are things going with you and Journey?" Lysa asks.
"Will this new connection with Victor change anything?"

I sigh. "Well, it's only been a couple of days." The truth is I
do feel like things are changing. Journey's graduating, going
to college. He has this new job with Victor. Victor could be my
dad. But I'm not ready to talk about any of this yet. Not even
with Spam and Lysa. "I think everything's okay."

Lysa takes the top off her salad and pours on some dressing.

Spam has two cookies and a hard-boiled egg. I brought leftover meatloaf.

"The skateboarder case is getting weird," Lysa says. "He still hasn't come forward and now someone has put up a one-thousand-dollar reward for anyone who can identify him."

"Who would do that?" I ask.

"The driver?" Spam says.

Lysa shakes her head. "It's some organization. But the mystery is why isn't he coming forward?"

"Maybe he doesn't know they're looking for him." I say.

"He'd have to be living under a rock," Lysa says.

"Does anyone have any photos of him yet?" I ask.

"Not yet." Spam grins. "I think we have them all."

There's a buzz against my wrist. The spot inside the volcano on my Bella glows red. I slide my hand off the table.

Spam ditches her phone into her sleeve and we all sit up a little straighter.

A few seconds later, Blankface strolls up. She pauses, eyeing each of us in turn with a sinister, stoic glee.

"Hello, Ms. Blankenship," Spam says, offering her most adorable, friendly puppy smile.

Blankface responds by swiveling her customary alien blankface in Spam's direction. "It's Miss." She's cradling her ever-present notebook, which still has the same fat purple highlighter clipped to the top of the binder. She slips it off and lays it on the table in front of Spam.

"Unless I'm mistaken," she says, "this belongs to you."

We sit in stunned silence, collectively holding our breath and waiting for Blankface to drop the hammer on Spam. I'm convinced she's figured out what Spam is up to and now we're all going to be pressed to explain our way out of it.

But Spam is way ahead of us and much smoother than I

thought possible. She picks up the highlighter and hugs it to her chest. "Thank you. It was my favorite."

"Hmpf. Well, it's dry." Even Blankenship's comments are devoid of emotion.

"Miss Blankenship, I have something for you, too." Spam pulls out a laminated bookmark with a volcano logo at the top and *Go 'Canoes* down the center. "It's a bookmark. I made it on my 3D printer."

Blankenship takes the bookmark and inspects it like it's a bug under a microscope. "Go canoes?" she says. "Like little boats?"

"It's go *kay-noes*, like Volcanoes," Spam says. "The school mascot."

Blankenship continues to inspect the offering, first one side and then the other. She tests its flexibility by bending it a little. She even runs it under her nose, giving it a sniff. Finally, she tucks it in between the pages of her ever-present notebook.

"Thank you," she says. "Now, please give me the name of that skateboarder involved in the accident on Monday. Because I'm new I didn't recognize him. But I'm sure you did. Right?"

She's being somewhat casual and offhand, but there's a definite whiff of danger. Sort of like when a cobra raises its head to eye level.

Spam and I shake our heads.

"He's not a student here," Lysa says, trying to be helpful.

Blankenship's gaze snaps onto her. "You know that because . . . ?"

"Ohh. You're right. I guess I don't actually know that," Lysa says. "Because . . ." She fails at having a reason and tries to blow it off. "Yeah, I don't know why I even said that."

Blankenship leans in over our table. "I don't know why you said it either."

Lysa clamps her mouth shut and sinks a little lower in her chair.

Blankenship pauses and looks each one of us straight in the eyes. "But if you suddenly decide that he does go here and you know his name, you'll come tell me. Right?"

She turns her gaze on each of us and waits until we nod.

"I was reading something today that you might find interesting." Her tone is suspiciously conversational. "Did you know there are such things as legal innocence and factual innocence? Legal innocence means a person could actually be guilty, but found not guilty due to a technicality."

I don't know where she's going with this and apparently neither do Lysa or Spam. We shake our heads.

"I didn't know that either, and I found it interesting," she says. After a moment of silence, she turns and stalks off.

Once she's gone we all breathe again.

"Oh my gosh." Lysa shudders. "Usually, I'm the one who can stretch the truth, but that woman totally unnerves me. And, Spam, you can't lie for anything. But you handled her like a boss."

"Because I wasn't lying," Spam says. "I really did make these bookmarks on my printer and Volcanos really are our school mascot."

"That's your secret? You can lie if you're not lying?" I ask.

"Something like that," Spam says.

I check out my wrist. The red dot is still there. I glance at Spam.

"No worries," she says. "I just have to reprogram it to track the bookmark."

"But what if she ditches the bookmark?" I ask.

Spam opens a pocket on her backpack. "Then I have the school pride pin . . . the Volcano carabiner key ring . . . a bendy straw, she might not go for that, but I have one . . . oh, and I have a hair clip, too. Though I think her hair is actually painted on her head."

"Wow," Lysa and I say at the same time.

The lunch bell rings, and we dutifully gather up our stuff, dump our trash, and head off to our next class.

▸ 14 ◂

Crime hasn't changed that much over the years. But the
popularity of crime shows on TV has changed both
the attitudes of the public and the way
we handle investigations.
—VICTOR FLEMMING

After school, we're at a table out in front, not far from the flagpole area. The wrecked car and broken flagpole are gone, but
several strips of crime scene tape are still visible flapping in the
breeze.

Victor asked if we would hang out here for an hour or so to
distribute flyers, answer questions, and gather names of students who might be interested in the CSI summer camp. The
response is crazy enthusiastic. We're instantly engulfed in a
chattering crowd of kids and parents wanting details all at
once.

The parents want to know how much and how long. Our
friends are asking if we'll be teaching our signature Cheater
Check *tricks*.

Lysa tries being cagey, since Cheater Checks is retired. But
Spam, sassy as ever, promises Cheater Checks and *more*.

The word's out about the Bella, too. If anyone asks, Spam
slaps a small card into the palm of their hand containing a QR
code. If they scan the code with a smartphone it takes them to

a YouTube video she made demonstrating how the Bella works, how much it costs, and how to order it.

I'm just about out of flyers and my voice is shot when Spam grabs my arm. "Where'd he go?" she asks.

I glance around. "Who?"

"Him." Her eyes are wide and insistent. Her pinch on my arm is urgent.

When I don't clue in right away she hisses in my ear. "The skateboarder. He was just here."

"Really?" I stand up and look around. Gratefully, the crush of people is thinning. But I don't see anyone scooting away on a skateboard.

"Kind of risky of him to show up on a skateboard two days later," I say.

"He wasn't on a skateboard." She steps up onto a chair and then up onto the table to continue scanning the area.

Lysa joins us, talking low into her hand. "Are you sure it was him?"

"Oh yeah, it was him. Tall, curly hair. He's wearing glasses today, but still tons of plaid. An awesome amount of plaid, in fact." She steps down off the table. "He looked straight into my eyes and said, 'Hey, Shortcake' . . . His eyes are blue, by the way." She holds up a small flash drive. "And then he pressed this into my hand. I'm guessing it's his view of the accident from his GoPro."

"Well, he's gone now," I say. "Everyone else is drifting to the parking lot."

Spam circles a finger over her head for us to follow. "Computer lab, stat." Lysa and I grab our stuff and fall in behind her.

At the computer lab Spam picks the most discreet computer possible, at the end of a row, in the corner. Lysa and I squeeze in behind her. She plugs in the flash drive and clicks to view its contents. It's an .mov file.

A video.

She presses play. It opens with a view of the three of us standing out by the flagpole.

Lysa squints at the screen. "Uck, that color makes me look washed out. I need to purge it from my closet."

"It does not," I insist.

The camera passes us, darts around a little. Then comes back to rest on us while Spam does her modeling routine.

"Wow. This guy unleashed your inner Kendall Jenner." I give Spam a friendly shoulder-nudge.

"Shut it," she says. "I was going for his attention, not yours."

The view switches suddenly to the incoming car. The woman is visible through the windshield and she's steering the car with her forearms while doing something on her phone.

"Bam!" Spam says.

"She was texting," Lysa gasps.

A moment later, the video follows the car as it rams into the flagpole. There's a shaky ending. After a few seconds, some makeshift credits roll:

Starring:
Sorry, Can't Tell You That
If you'd like to help:
Tell them to focus on her cell phone usage instead of me.

The video cuts abruptly to black.

Spam removes the flash drive and clears the computer. We sit there stunned for a second.

"Okay, you're right," I say. "That was him."

"I told you," Spam says.

"But we still don't know who he is," I say.

"He said *I can't tell you that*," Lysa says. "Why can't he tell us?"

"Maybe he has a girlfriend," I say.

"She probably goes to our school." Spam looks miserable at the thought.

"That's not it," Lysa says, shaking her head.

"Why?" I ask.

"Two reasons," Lysa says. "One, if he had a girlfriend who went here she, or someone in her family, would recognize him, and two, he would've given *her* the video."

Spam raises her arms in a victory cheer. "Awesome. He doesn't have a girlfriend."

"It still doesn't make any sense," Lysa says. "He and his parents could take this video to the police. Then he'd be cleared. Giving us the footage only complicates things."

"Maybe there's a reason he doesn't want to deal with the cops," I say.

"No one wants to deal with them. That's why everyone is sending their videos, photos, and statements to us," Lysa says.

"Maybe he just wants to get to know me?" Spam says, smiling.

"Introducing himself would be easier," Lysa says. "Why all the secrecy?"

"He's a man of mystery. I like my theory the best," she says. "So, I'm staying with that."

We pack up and head over to the new science lab to tell Victor his CSI camp is going to be a huge hit.

As we step inside, he's giving a tour to Coach Wilkins.

"This is a huge space," Coach Wilkins says. "I don't know if you know this or not, but when the school was first built these two rooms down here were the boys' and girls' gyms."

"Huh," Victor says. "I didn't know that."

"Yep. Boys' and girls' sports were separate back in those days. Then they built us the big gymnasium, which is beautiful. I'll admit, I was kind of hoping my department could get this space back to use for my summer camp. But it's cool, you beat me to it."

Coach Wilkins chuckles, but it's a little hollow and I'm not sure that he really thinks it's cool that Victor got his space.

"It wasn't me," Victor says. "It was the bio teacher."

"Miss Peters." The coach nods.

"Anyway, this space isn't all just for the camp. Only this part is classroom," Victor says. "Over there will be crime lab."

"Like a CSI crime lab?" the coach asks.

"Exactly," Victor says.

"Will this be a real one or a play school one?" Coach wonders.

"Oh, it's a real one," Victor says. "Not like we have an abundance of crime in Iron Rain, but now at least when we do have one, there will be a lab to handle the evidence."

The coach looks amazed. "They mentioned this in the newspaper. But why put a CSI lab at a high school? That doesn't sound very safe."

"Oh, it's completely safe," Victor says. "The lab will be off-limits to the students, but still available as a teaching tool. Plus, the school and the police department split the cost of hiring me to teach science and run the lab so it's win/win."

"Fascinating," Coach says. "I'll have to stop by and check it out. Every now and then I catch one of those forensic shows on TV and I'm always amazed by the stuff they find."

"You'll be able to stop in and see it firsthand, right here." Victor slaps the center wall between the two rooms. "We're cutting into this wall and installing a waist-high window all the way across for classroom viewing. There will be mic and sound, too."

"Wow. Full display." Coach Wilkins indicates the extra-wide opening between the two rooms. "You're going to need a door on here or something, especially with a wad of campers running around. I usually have about fifty kids sign up for my camp and keeping tabs on all of them is a chore, let me tell you."

"Don't worry," Victor says. "We're installing a floor-to-ceiling, custom, tempered steel mesh material to seal off this opening. There will be a door, made from the same material, so we can go back and forth."

Clay Kirkland, the contractor, is on the floor making notes on his clipboard. "I'm taking the measurements for that steel now," he says. "We'll have it up in plenty of time for the camp."

"Great," Victor says. "The last thing we need is a bunch of teenagers traipsing through here."

Victor glances up in my direction and I get the point . . . vividly.

The sting of Victor's comment shrinks my insides. I cross my arms over my stomach and wander away from the group just to be able to breathe a little. There are a couple of police officers taking measurements in an alcove at the end of lab area.

Victor follows me, leading the coach into the alcove. "This will be the evidence room. We're enclosing this area here with the same steel mesh material. And I've ordered a bank of high-impact steel evidence lockers. Our evidence will be kept under double security. A breach will be impossible."

I notice the same strip of narrow windows along the ceiling of the alcove. "There's easy access to those windows from the outside. How are you going to secure them?"

"All the windows will be replaced with bulletproof glass," he says. "It's a requirement for crime labs, you don't want people breaking in and stealing or destroying evidence."

"Roger that." I pinch my lips together. It's not just my imagination. He is aiming these comments at me.

▸ 15 ◂

Did you know there is virtually not a single thing you
can do in this world without leaving behind
a trace that you've been there?
—PRINCIPAL BLANKENSHIP

"You'll want to check out the six o'clock news tonight," Spam
says as she drops into the seat across from me and begins un-
wrapping a sandwich.

Lysa is only a few steps behind her. "Why? Are you going to
be on it?"

"No. But the skateboarder's video is. I sent it to the tip line,"
she says.

"What?" Lysa says. "We said we didn't have any videos.
What if they ask us about it?"

"They won't. I sent it anonymously from the computer lab."
Spam plays with her napkin. "The important thing is *he* will
know and I'm hoping he'll find a way to come back to thank
me for clearing his name."

"What about the other videos and statements I've been com-
piling?" Lysa asks.

"I haven't decided yet," Spam says. "I don't think they'll do
the police much good. None of the photos were clear enough
to identify him."

"His video was pretty definitive evidence that the driver

was distracted by her cell phone," I say. "They probably don't even need the other statements." I peel my orange—a food decision I made because I was feeling Miss P–ish today.

▼   ▼   ▼

There's a vibration against my wrist and a flash of red. The three of us turn toward the door, expecting Blankface to walk through at any second.

"What are we looking at, ladies?"

Instead, it's as if she just popped up out of the floor on the other side of our table.

"Whoa." I'm surprised but try to conceal it. "I was just looking for the time," I say.

"The door," Spam says.

"I don't know." Lysa's comment comes a moment behind mine and Spam's.

Blankenship shakes her head at Lysa. "Young lady, if your grades weren't so good I would have real concern about this befuddlement issue you seem to struggle with."

Lysa opens her mouth to say something, then thinks better of it.

"Anyway," Blankenship says. "I need to see all of you in my office."

"When?" I ask.

"Now's fine." She abruptly turns and *click click*s toward the door.

We gather up our lunch stuff. "This can't be good," I say.

Lysa shakes her head. "Not good at all."

▼   ▼   ▼

We file into Blankenship's office. The only change from Principal Roberts's office is that all the sports décor and photos are gone. Now, it's just a big, bare office with old wooden furniture. She has a laptop open on her desk, but other than that, there isn't a single personal item on display. Not a photo, personal coffee cup. Nothing.

She motions for us to sit. As we take seats in a line in front of her, she studies each of us in her odd, almost clinical way.

There's a strong "bug under a microscope" vibe.

"Was I unclear when I asked you to provide me with the identity of the skateboarder who caused that accident?" She's not smiling, but her voice is syrup sweet. I'm pretty sure she has something on us. I'm just not sure what.

I pause to process what she might or might not know about our activities. It's my strategy to try to let the story unspool before commenting. I would rather not get caught in a straight-up lie.

Lysa slides down a little lower in her seat and nervously chews on a ragged nail. Wise, considering how easily Blankface unravels her.

"I wish we knew who he was," Spam says, sitting forward in her seat. "But we don't."

"And yet . . ." The principal spins a paper from her side of the desk to in front of us. "I'm guessing it was one of you who sent a video of the accident to a TV news reporter."

Spam's eyes widen and she sucks in a breath.

Lysa stares at her shoes.

I'm scrambling for any diversion to take some of the heat off them. Like wouldn't it be amazing if my hair could magically catch fire and then, when this was over, be normal again?

When none of us speaks, she continues. "The email was sent through an anonymous link. But you girls know the drill probably better than most. Did you know there is almost nothing you can do without leaving behind a trace?"

I wish she would just say it and get it over with. This toying with us is excruciating.

As if she can read my mind, she sits up and reads off the piece of paper in her hand. "This is from an email I received about thirty minutes ago stating that a reporter, who incidentally recently interviewed the three of you, received a video of the accident a short while ago. The ISP it came from is here, at the school."

The three of us swallow hard.

"My guess is it was sent from the computer lab, wouldn't you agree, Samantha?"

"That's logical." Spam nods and clears her throat. "But FYI, lots of people have access to that lab."

Blankenship calmly laces her fingers in front of her on the desk and it has the effect of a spider spinning a web completely around its prey. "They do. And it's not like we could dust every keyboard on campus for fingerprints. And, even if we could, that wouldn't tell us what we need to know. Would it, Erin?"

I shrivel as she directs her gaze at me. I shake my head.

"Are you familiar with forensic linguistics? It's the study of how certain authors use words that stand out. Like here: FYI, on the first line." She taps her finger on the page. "FYI isn't really a high-school acronym. Not like LOL or TBH or FWIW. Or even YOLO. But one of you likes to say FYI a lot. When something stands out as different it can be tracked."

My cheeks burn with shame and a bit of shock. She has nailed us completely.

"Are you wondering how I know about forensic linguistics?" she asks.

Lysa and Spam sit completely still. But I can't help it. I nod.

"It's those murder podcasts." She leans in again, as if we're best girlfriends or something. "I'm completely addicted to them and they have the best ideas for catching someone in a lie. Anyway, as I was saying, one of you is very fond of—"

Spam holds up her hand. "I sent the video."

"Ahhh. Finally." Blankenship actually smiles, which is maybe more unnerving than her scowl. "Thank you for that, Samantha." She picks up a pencil. "So now, tell me his name. You might even be entitled to a reward, though I'm not sure that's really fair, since you were also protecting him."

Spam gestures, palms up. "I told you. We. Don't. Know."

"Then how—" Blankenship asks.

There's a light tap on the door and Detective Sydney enters. She shakes her head as she recognizes us sitting in the principal's office. "How am I not surprised?"

My sinking feeling plunges to new depths. Not only will Victor know what I've been up to, but Rachel will get a full report as well.

She speaks to Blankenship. "We paid a visit to the driver and showed her the video." Detective Sydney scowls at us. "You understand that *you* were in that video and you're minors and the TV station cannot run images of minors like that without permission."

Now I sink lower in my seat. What's wrong with us? We should have thought of that.

"This is how easily this stuff gets out of hand. The driver has changed her story. Now she says she was turning into the school driveway when a girl in the drive-up area used a mirror to temporarily blind her while her two friends laughed and she helplessly veered off course and plowed into the flagpole. She's claiming the cause of the accident is that she was pranked by teenagers. And even though she appears to be texting and driving, this video could back up her claim of pranking, laughing teenagers."

"That's a lie," Spam blurts out. "We were laughing at the skateboarder, not her."

"You girls need to understand that this isn't a game." Miss Blankenship turns her laptop around, revealing that the chief has been on video conference this whole time.

"Oh boy." Lysa hides her eyes behind her hand.

"We're sorry, Chief." I glance at Lysa and Spam.

"I'm deeply disappointed in all of you, but especially you, Erin. I thought we had an understanding."

"We did . . . we still do." I'm stammering.

"Now I'm not so sure. And, after this stunt, I'm also not sure that it's appropriate for you three to be camp counselors. This isn't an example of the kind of role-modeling we expect," he says.

All three of us sit up.

"No. Wait. Seriously, we are good role models. This is a fluke," I say. "We honestly, really don't know the skateboard guy. Not at all."

"But how—" Detective Sydney comes around to face us.

"He just showed up yesterday, in the middle of a crowd, and gave me a flash drive with his video on it," Spam says. "And then he disappeared again."

Detective Sydney rests her hip on the corner of the desk. "But you have been gathering statements from other witnesses. Correct?"

I sink a little further into my seat. This isn't getting better.

"People just sent them to us," Spam says. "What were we supposed to do?"

"Turn them over to us!" Sydney and the chief say at the same time.

"All three of you made an agreement with your parents: no more investigations," Sydney says.

We nod.

"This right here is investigating. And it threatens this whole case," Detective Sydney says. "You are unskilled at interrogation, which means you could unintentionally manipulate your classmates' memories of the accident." Syd holds out her hand. "Which one of you has the videos and statements? Hand them over."

Lysa holds up her phone. "I do. But you need to talk to my father before you take this."

Detective Sydney gestures strongly to the mirror back of Lysa's case. "Well, that explains the driver's allegation of a mirror."

Blankenship picks up her phone and presses a button. "Send him in."

The door opens again and Mr. Martin, Lysa's father, strides in.

Lysa looks ready to crawl under her chair. "Daddy?"

He scowls. "Alysa Marie. What have I told you about being called to school on your behalf?"

"Make sure it's for an award," she whispers.

"And am I here to witness you receiving an award?"

She shakes her head.

Detective Sydney nods at Lysa. "She admitted there's evidence on her phone."

He holds out his hand in front of Lysa. She lays her phone across his palm.

He turns to Detective Sydney. "My client is voluntarily handing over her personal property, without admission of guilt, to further the efforts of the department in this case. The password is foreverVans21." He looks at Lysa for verification. "Correct?"

She nods.

The principal takes an envelope out of her drawer and holds it open. Mr. Martin drops her phone into it.

Lysa sighs.

He hands the envelope to Detective Sydney. Turning to Lysa, he says, "I'll see you at home."

Blankenship scribbles out passes. "You three can go back to class now."

"Wait," Detective Sydney says. "I just want to make something perfectly and completely clear. You three are minors. Students. You are not detectives. You do not investigate cases . . . for any reason. Is that clear?"

Lysa, Spam, and I nod.

"Now, is there anything else that you know about that skateboarder that you have not shared with us?" she asks.

"No." I share a look with both Lysa and Spam.

"I don't want the three of you to even think about that boy again," Detective Sydney says. "Now. Go to class."

We grab our passes and flee Blankface's office.

"So much for anonymous tips," Spam grumbles as we hurry down the hall.

"And FYI, no more FYI," I say.

"Roger that," Spam agrees. Then she slaps a nondescript phone into Lysa's hand. "Here, you can use my backup phone until you get yours back. I can program your calls and messages to forward to it."

"Thanks," Lysa says. "Now if only you could program the lecture I'm going to get from my mother to go somewhere else too."

"How much trouble are you in?" I ask.

"Well, generally lying to *them* is a much bigger deal. In situations like this they usually take the position that I have to suffer my own consequences as they are, but they won't add to them," she says.

"So, if we get kicked off the camp counselor job?" I say.

"I'll be asking someone if they want fries with that," Lysa says. "And I'll just have to live with it."

"Oh my god!" I pat my bag. "You guys, I completely forgot. I still have the skateboarder's fingerprint. What should I do with it?"

"Destroy it," Spam says. "They'll use it to track him down like an escaped convict."

"Admitting I lifted the print is going to look pretty bad in light of the lecture we just got from Detective Sydney," I say. "But they're making such a big deal out of this, what if it's really important for them to find him? Shouldn't we help them?"

"It's up to the police to do their own investigative work," Lysa says. "It's their job, not ours. My dad says that a lot. They had an opportunity to take that print before they towed the car."

"But what should I do with it now?"

I look from Lysa to Spam. Blank looks from both.

The bell rings, signaling the transition to our last class of the day. We split off and head in different directions.

▼ ▼ ▼

As I walk out to the front of the school from last period I can't miss Journey's van pulled up at the drive-up area, engine running.

The door squeals open as I hurry toward it. He reaches out a hand to help me up.

"Hi." I pause to give him a peck on the cheek. "Nice surprise after the day I had."

He puts the van in gear and starts to drive out of the lot.

"Are we going somewhere?" I'm hoping for someplace quiet, where we can be alone and just hang out—my nerves are pretty jangled after the meeting with Blankface.

"I can't," Journey says. "I have to go in early to work but I wanted to give you a ride home and tell you some exciting news."

"What?"

"Victor met with my mom and my dad's attorney today."

"That's great. Is your mom on board with reopening the investigation?"

"Not yet." Journey slightly rolls his eyes. "I mean, maybe. She's worried that reexamining any of the evidence will seal his fate forever. She wants to believe there's a better chance to get my father off on a legal procedural error, you know, like if Lysa's dad did something wrong while defending him. But everyone—including Victor—says there's no guarantee of that because the facts are so weird."

"I know Lysa's dad. If you think *she's* an obsessive rule-follower, you should see him."

"That's pretty much what Victor said too."

"Is she going to let Victor try?" If Journey's mom was really opposed to going forward with the investigation, Victor might stop—unless some actual new evidence appeared.

"She didn't say yes—but she didn't say no, either," Journey explains. "She wants my dad to give his opinion. So we're going to the prison to talk to him tomorrow."

My mouth drops open, but for a long moment no sound comes out.

"You're going to meet your father?"

"Yes. Can you believe it? My family is getting this chance because of you. I can't wait to tell my dad the whole story of how this came to be and that my amazing girlfriend is the one who's responsible for it."

"I'm honored. Really. And I'll be thinking about you the whole time."

Journey drives toward my house. "So how was your day?"

"Mmmm." Not sure I want to get into the whole ugly mess about Blankenship, the chief, and Detective Sydney over the skateboarder issue. I suspect Journey's reaction would be that he tried to warn us. "My day was . . . just a day. But it's so much better now. I'm really happy for you and excited."

"Thank you. How about if I plan a special date for us tomorrow night?" Journey says.

"An actual . . . real, like going out kind of date?"

"Yes. An actual real going out kind of date." He chuckles at my inarticulate response. "I'll come up with something special. Just the two of us . . . we can celebrate."

I can't explain the ambush of a sudden nervous flutter. I'm completely comfortable around Journey, and him asking me on a date is a good thing. But my uncontrollable flares of emotion seem to be telling another story altogether. And I don't understand it.

▶ 16 ◀

My father says it's up to the police to do their own
investigative work. It's their job. Not ours.
—LYSA MARTIN

Because Journey is meeting his father today, I catch a ride to
school with Spam. She just texted to say she's on her way. So I
grab my stuff and head down to wait.

At the bottom of the stairs, I pause by the credenza where
Victor has been piling up his mail and paperwork. The FedEx
envelope is still propped up against the wall where he placed
it. I tip it forward with one finger to see if it has been opened—
it's still completely sealed. Go figure.

Spam beeps that she's in the driveway. I race out to the car
and hop in.

Spam backs out and steers us toward school. "How did last
night go?" she asks.

I shrug. "It wasn't as bad as I thought it would be. Rachel
and Victor grilled me a little bit. All they really wanted to know
was how are we connected to the skateboarder, and I told
them the truth. They didn't seem to care that we were gathering statements, but they both clearly draw the line at lying to
the authorities . . . Detective Sydney, the chief, *or* Blankface.
Obviously, I didn't tell them about the fingerprint."

"What about the camp counselor job?" she asks.

"I was afraid to ask. Victor did say it would behoove us to make peace with Blankenship, though. She calls the shots at the school."

"Oh my god! How creepy is she?" Spam says. "She enjoyed busting us way too much."

"No kidding," I say. "Did you hear from Lysa?"

"No, did you?"

I shake my head. "Knowing how strict her parents are, she'll probably get the worst of this."

"Did anyone say why they're all up on the skateboarder?" Spam asks.

I shake my head. "It seems weird, unless they're just suspicious because he's not coming forward."

"But if he didn't do anything they should back off," she says.

"Maybe there have been crimes committed by a rogue guy on a skateboard," I say. "Maybe you dodged a bullet with this one, Spam."

"No way," Spam says. "I looked into those eyes, twice. He's got the heart of a puppy dog."

I can't remember the last boy who captured this much of Spam's attention. It's probably the mystery angle that has her hooked. "You only say that because he called you short-cake."

She grins.

▼ ▼ ▼

All day I think about how it's going with Journey and his father. I've imagined meeting my father many times. I've dreamed of what the first thing I would say to him would be and what I would look at first. I've even dared to ponder the horror and desperation of finding out my father was in prison.

But I've never envisioned going to a prison to meet my father for the very first time. Poor Journey.

As the day drifts into the evening and I hear nothing from Journey I stay completely off all my devices, leaving a wide-open channel for him to call or text or something.

His thundering silence causes me to worry even more. And when he completely misses our date, I'm silently pacing my attic and freaking out.

Miss P always encouraged me to be myself, so before I go to sleep, I lay back on the pillow, open Snapchat, and hold my phone up over my head. I take a picture of my bright hair spilling over the soft blue pillowcase, then I send it to Journey with a message: H IR ISSES O .

I'm hoping he'll remember these words from the early days of our relationship when my dorky moves were more obvious. When he doesn't answer, I turn out the light and drift off to sleep.

By morning, Journey still hasn't answered my calls or texts and my worry is out of control. What if Jameson won't let them revisit the case? . . . What if he got mad and lost it, admitting he really killed that kid after all? And he was glad he did?

My mind races with possibilities, and they're all bad.

"Earth to Erin?" Rachel brings her coffee to the table and takes a seat across from me. I guess she was talking and I wasn't responding. Now she's sighing and giving me pinched looks. "Are you sure you're alright?"

"I'm fine, honest. I'm just worried about Journey."

She drains her cup and walks it over to the sink, then comes back to give me a hug. "You're too young to take all of this onto your shoulders. Let the adults worry about this stuff. It will all work out. I promise. I'm just going in to take care of some paperwork. I'll be home to make dinner."

"Okay, Rachel. See you later."

I'm still sitting at the kitchen table when Victor comes down.

"I can give you a ride to school," he offers.

I blink. Has he not noticed I'm wearing pajamas?

"Victor, it's Saturday."

He pauses to think. "I guess you're right. I'm so busy I've lost complete track of the days. Anyway, I am going in to meet with the contractor. I also have the camp themes written out. If you want to come in with me and hang out for a bit, you and your friends can work on the schedule."

I take a very long pause.

"I thought we had to earn back the trust to be your counselors," I say.

Victor leans back against the counter. "Yeah, Chuck mentioned that he felt the lying required a pretty stiff punishment." Victor crosses his arms over his chest. "And listen, I don't necessarily disagree with him. Let's say you can come back on probationary status. But one more step out of line and you're done."

"Sold." I leap up and head to my room. "Ten minutes."

▼ ▼ ▼

Within ten minutes, I'm dressed and we're in the car and headed to school. I've texted both Lysa and Spam to see if they want to meet me there and work on the camp schedule. Spam texted back that she'll be on her way soon. I haven't heard from Lysa.

"Shouldn't we be shopping for some transportation to replace your scooter?" Victor asks once we're in the car.

I shrug. "It's not that big of a deal. I always seem to have a ride when I need one."

"But Journey will be heading off to college soon, so you can't really rely on him for too much longer."

"Have you heard from him . . . or his mom?" I'm hopeful for news that he's okay.

"No," Victor says. "Have you?"

I shake my head.

Victor gives me a sympathetic look. "This is a little like you wanting to know the identity of your father. Even though knowing won't change much about your life, you feel like a part of you is missing because there's this big thing about you that you don't know. I'm guessing Journey has some similar feelings."

I nod. "Yeah. I can understand that."

"Just be patient with him," Victor says. "He'll come around."

"I will."

I don't know what Journey is feeling, but I do know that everyone is different when it comes to understanding and accepting who you're connected to. It's even possible that my situation of not knowing who my father is could be the easiest of all.

▸ 17 ◂

You can't appeal a case just because you think the jury
got it wrong. You have to find a mistake
that was made, and then prove it.

—MR. MARTIN

We arrive at the classroom/lab. Victor unlocks the door and
holds it open for me. I marvel at the changes he's made in just a
week. The center wall now has a giant window cut into it. A
heavy metal frame has been installed in the doorway between
the rooms. And the alcove on the classroom side is now an en-
closed storage room, thanks to the addition of a wall and a door.

Victor heads into the lab area. Instead of following him, I
take a seat at the teacher's desk at the front of the classroom.
From here I have an almost unobstructed view of the murder
board. When Victor isn't looking I shoot a couple of photos
with my phone. Not investigating . . . just researching.

"Knock, knock?" Coach Wilkins sticks his head in the door.
"Oh, hi, Erin."

"Hi, Coach."

"I thought I saw Victor's car in the parking lot?" he says.

"He's in there." I point toward the lab area.

Coach Wilkins heads over there. He and Victor greet each
other cordially.

I'm not really listening to their conversation, but every now and then a few words drift my way. It sounds like the coach is worried that more students will want to sign up for Victor's camp than his.

After a few minutes, Victor walks the coach back through the classroom. They're still talking. "I don't think that what we have planned will mesh very well with a sports camp," Victor explains. "What we're doing is more science experiments, classroom stuff. But let's put a pin in it and revisit after sign-ups, okay?"

Coach nods. "Sounds great, Vic. I like that idea."

The door opens again and a woman peeks in. Coach Wilkins is not happy to see her. "Letty, what are you doing here?"

"I've been waiting out front for you for ten minutes," she says. "Finally I checked with the office and they said you might be down here."

It's her voice, more than anything else, that causes me to raise my head and study her. Holy crap!

She steps inside and pauses to take in the room. "Wow. This is really nice."

My eyes are bugging out of my head because Letty is Arletta Stone, the driver of the car that almost hit us and the skateboarder. I wonder if Victor knows that. He glances over at me and I quickly look down to keep from revealing my flush of interest.

The coach gestures. "Victor, this is my cousin, Arletta Stone. Letty, this is Victor Flemming. He's our new science teacher but he used to work for the FBI."

Letty offers Victor her hand. "I know. I've read your books. Big fan."

Victor shakes hands with Letty. "Thank you."

She peers around him. "Is that the spiffy new crime lab over there? The one they wrote about in the newspaper? I can't wait to get a look at it. I watch the shows, I read the books. I'm a huge fan." She edges toward the lab area. "Are you really re-opening a bunch of cold cases?"

The coach steps sideways, blocking her. "Not now, Letty. They're busy. I'll give you a tour another time."

"Yes. You'll have to come back for a tour," Victor says. "Once it's all put together."

"I'd love to," Letty says.

The coach and Victor shake hands. "Anyway, thanks for everything, Vic," the coach says. "I have to take her to get her car, but it's going to be exciting having you around here."

"Thank you," Victor says. "I'm excited to be here."

The coach and his cousin leave.

Victor kind of shakes off the encounter and then pulls up a chair to join me at the desk. "I have your mission, should you choose to accept it," he says.

"Why wouldn't I choose to accept it?" I'm confused. "Isn't that why I came in with you today?"

Victor laughs. "Sorry, that's a line from *Mission Impossible*."

"What?"

"Never mind," Victor says. "Old TV show, which means I'm showing what an old guy I am. Anyway, first day of camp is only three weeks away. I have a budget for about forty hours of prep time. Here are the themes I'm looking at."

He hands me a piece of paper.

"Week one: crime scene. Week two: hair, fingerprint, impressions . . . Well, you can read the list. If you and the girls would come up with two fun, science-oriented activities per day, along these themes, that would be great."

"By activities do you mean science experiments?" I ask.

He bobs his head right and left, thinking. "They don't have to all be experiments. A game would work too."

"So, even like a crossword puzzle or word search on the theme?"

He grins. "Yes. Anything that you think would be fun and educational."

The door bursts open again.

This time it's the contractor, Clay, lugging a toolbox and a coil of extension cords slung over his shoulder like mountain climbing ropes. "Are you having a meeting?" he asks. "Because I'm going to be installing brackets and that's going to get loud."

"We're almost done here." Victor looks at me. "You know what to do, right?"

I nod. "Spam and I can get a table over by the gym and work there."

"I'd like to have your concepts by Friday so I can approve them," Victor says.

"Will do." I give him a little salute and head for the door.

"Erin," he says. "I'm glad we're working on this together."

I smile. "I am too."

Just as I'm leaving, the contractor is back with more stuff. I hold the door open for him and he gives me a grateful smile.

"Thank you," he says.

I get to the top of the stairs and send Spam a text on where to meet me and start walking toward the gym. There's a buzz on my wrist. I look up and Blankenship is coming straight toward me. She unnerves me, and for no reason at all I panic and turn right. This sets me on a path to the Administration building, which is probably exactly where she's going.

Before I get to the A-building, I turn again, trying to figure out how to not look like a super dork walking in circles. A whistle blows behind me. I turn as Blankenship makes a beeline in my direction. There's a second buzz against my wrist.

Got it. She's right in front of me.

"What's the problem? Are we not awake yet, Blake?" she asks.

I sag. But then I force myself to put on a friendly face. I palm-tap my forehead. "Just got confused about where I was going."

Blankenship looks me up and down. "Good," she says, in a tone that clearly doesn't mean good at all. "Because for a minute there I thought you might be trying to avoid running into me."

She so bluntly nailed the situation that I'm dumbfounded. Speechless. I fumble and stammer. "I better go," I mumble and hurry off.

She makes a rather loud harrumph to my back.

I shiver. That woman gives me the heebie-jeebies.

I select a table in the shade by the gym. Within a few minutes, Lysa arrives and drops into the seat across from me.

"So, it turns out I can read text messages on the phone Spam gave me, I just can't reply to them."

As she sits down she adopts the saddest face I've ever seen, which I'm sure is about what her parents have put her through over the last two days. But she surprises me when she asks about Journey.

"Have you heard from him?" she says.

"No, why?" I'm flooded with fear.

"Apparently, it was awful," she says. "My father said Jameson freaked out when he realized his son was in the room and he wouldn't talk to them or even look at them."

"Oh no." I feel terrible.

"Yeah. Apparently, he ran to the door and pounded on it to be taken back to his cell," Lysa says.

"Journey was so excited to meet him."

Lysa puts out a hand. "It may still happen. They're going back today."

"They are?" That's surprising.

"My father said he has a new strategy. So, fingers crossed."

"No wonder I haven't heard from him."

"Haven't heard from who?" Spam asks, arriving with a tray of coffees and a bag of donuts.

"You are my hero," I say, reaching out with grabby hands.

She hands me a coffee and a donut wrapped in a napkin.

"She hasn't heard from Journey and things didn't go well at the prison," Lysa says.

"Do things ever go well at a prison?" Spam wonders.

"The only good news is that my father's preparations for their second meeting distracted him from severe lecture mode over the skateboarder fiasco."

"So, what did they say?" I ask.

Lysa gives a bland smile. "I get to suffer the consequences."

"What does that mean?" Spam asks.

"They're not going to do anything to get my phone back. I get it back when Detective Sydney gives it back." Lysa sighs. "It definitely could have been worse."

"Don't worry, Syd's pretty cool. She'll just do her job and probably won't snoop on your other stuff."

Lysa shrugs. "It's okay. I deserve it. I'm just glad we didn't totally blow the camp counselor job."

"Yeah. Me too," I say.

Spam hands Lysa her coffee and donut, then punches in some keys on her phone. "Maybe this will cheer you both up. We currently have orders for eighty Bellas, at twenty dollars apiece, less costs." She punches in some more numbers. "We stand to make a profit of about $1,200."

"Wow," I say. "You've done all the work on this, Spam. I think you should keep the money."

Spam shakes her head. "Nah. We're a team, and besides, I need you guys to help me assemble and program these bad boys."

"I'll help," I say.

"Me too," adds Lysa.

"So, you know I've given my father more than a few gray hairs, right?" Spam says.

We laugh, remembering some of Spam's more terrifying antics.

"Like the time you caused the main cell tower in town to shut down?" Lysa says.

"Or when you accidentally played that X-rated meme about the coach and the librarian in front of the whole school?" I say.

Spam scowls at the enthusiasm we put into remembering her mistakes. "I get the point. Nip it," she says.

"Sorry," I say. "Just teasing."

She softens. "Anyway, I showed my father the Bella last night. He was really impressed. He thinks this is my ticket into college. There's a whole bunch of stuff about STEM for girls and the big push to get girls interested in math and science." Spam comically smooths her eyebrows and hikes up her bra. "Can you picture *me* as a role model?"

Lysa gives me a soft look. "Our girl's growing up."

Spam lightly smacks her on the shoulder.

"That's awesome, Spam," I say. "I want you to show us how to code those things too."

"That's right," Lysa says. "We're girls. We need to know."

"Totally," Spam promises.

"By the way, I shouldn't say this, but we have our first connection on the murder board," I say.

"You should say it. You should shout it from the rooftops,"

Spam says, squirming excitedly. "This means I get to use my super-awesome skinny red tape."

"I know. I'm excited about that too. So, the crazy woman driver . . . is connected to Coach Wilkins. She's his *cousin*. He was just downstairs talking to Victor and she showed up. She was very snoopy about the crime lab."

"Hmm," Lysa says. "We still need to research her."

I give her a look. "Because research isn't investigation, right?"

"I think research is just reading," Lysa says.

"Yeah, me too," I agree. "As long as we keep it at just reading. Because here's the deal: Victor says we're on probation as counselors, one more screwup and we're out."

Lysa and Spam exchange grim looks. Lysa moans, putting her head in her hands. "I've never been on probation in my life."

Spam smirks. "Oh, give it a rest, Debbie Do-Right. You've just never been caught. That's the real story."

"We can put our energy into this camp thing and not screw up any investigations," I say. "I know we can."

▸ 18 ◂

It's always the minute details of a case that suck me in.
—ERIN BLAKE

I hand the girls copies of the weekly themes that Victor gave me.

"Victor wants us to start working up activities for the camp—two per day—based on his list of themes for each week."

Weekly Themes for Camp

Week #1   Analyzing the crime scene
Week #2   Hair, fingerprints, and impressions
Week #3   Blood analysis
Week #4   Ballistics testing
Week #5   DNA and electrophoresis
Week #6   The criminal process

"He loved the idea of word search and crossword puzzles," I say. "What else can we do?"

"We could do a crime scene treasure hunt," Spam says.

"How about crime scene charades?" Lysa offers.

"Both ideas are so fun. Let's each take two topics and work up our ideas," I say. "We want to do a supergood job so Victor will be so impressed he'll forget all about the probation."

"I want crime scene and the criminal process," Lysa says. "All I have to do is listen to my dad for three meals in a row and I'll have all the ideas I need."

"I'll take blood and hair, fingerprints, and impressions," Spam says. "I love all that gross stuff that just flicks off while we're walking around being human."

Lysa looks amused. "Your blood just flicks off while you're walking around?"

Spam makes a face. "Don't challenge me. I can get gross and you know it."

Lysa retreats. "Why do I let her do this to me?"

"That means I'm doing ballistics and DNA. Sounds good. Let's show Victor what a smart thing he did by hiring us."

There's a red flash of light from our Bella bracelets. All three of us turn to notebooks and start making notes.

After a couple of seconds, Blankenship strolls up to our table with her notebook shield cradled in front of her. She scans the table and stares at each one of us individually. Then she checks her watch. "Seeing one of you here on a Saturday is one thing," she says. "But seeing all three of you here raises my suspicions. What are you girls up to?"

Lysa and I can barely look at her, but for some reason Spam just talks to her like they're old friends. She waves her hand over Victor's list. "Science experiments for the CSI camp."

Blankenship grunts. "What about finals?"

"We're studying for those, too," Lysa says.

She puts a hand on her hip. "And yet there's not a single book on this table."

"Notes?" Lysa says, at a complete loss.

"It's your funeral," she says.

As she turns and walks away, Spam makes a nasty face to her back.

Blankenship isn't stupid . . . or maybe she's an alien and has eyes in the back of her twist of hair. Either way, she glances back and nearly catches Spam in full prune-face.

Spam makes a quick correction.

Lysa elbows her in the ribs. "She almost caught you."

"Yeah," Spam grins. "But she didn't. The Bella works. We'll always know when she's about to pop up. "

▼ ▼ ▼

We spent the day working on lists for CSI camp and monitoring how our social media is blowing up over the Bella. I'm glad I got stuck with ballistics because before this I didn't know anything about firearms and ammunition. But I'm learning that, as a science, ballistics is as detailed and sophisticated as the study of fingerprints. Maybe even more so. Which makes it totally my kind of thing. I can't believe he's paying us to research this stuff. I'd gladly do it for free.

Victor shows up at our table.

"I'm ready to call it a day, how about you?" he says.

We stretch.

"Yep, I'm ready too," I say.

"I'll meet you at the car," he says.

I pack up my stuff and head to the parking lot. Victor is already there, waiting. I climb into his car. The new leather has a faint smell of citrus. Orange, specifically. A smell that still leaves me so conflicted.

It's great having Uncle Victor in my life. But through all of this I still ache for Miss P. And yet, if she were still here, he wouldn't be. Then again . . . if she were still here maybe Journey and I would be working on things together, not separately.

Although, it's more likely that Journey still wouldn't know I exist.

"What's wrong?" Victor asks as he turns toward home.

"Nothing," I say.

Victor and I used to talk about exciting things, like crime stories in the news and how he would approach solving them. We would theorize about how ordinary, everyday things could be used as evidence. But lately, our typical conversations go like this: Victor asks if we're excited about the camp and I answer yes. Victor asks what's for dinner and I tell him. Victor asks what's wrong and I answer nothing.

I don't want to say that Victor has turned out like all the other adults in my life, but in a way, he kinda has.

"Yeah. That's a full load of nothing," Victor says. "Are you and Journey fighting again?"

"I told you, Journey and I don't fight."

"Fine. I'm just going to stay out of it," Victor says. "Did you make any headway with a list of camp activities?" he asks.

"Yep," I say. "Weeks one, two, and three are solid. And we're working on the others."

"Great." Victor gives me a proud look. "Next week we can set up the classroom. That should be fun."

"Can we put a little shrine to Miss P in the new room?" I ask.

"Shrine?" He glances at me, eyebrows furrowed. "Is that appropriate for a classroom?" Victor pulls in and parks in the driveway. Now I have his complete attention. He turns to look at me.

"Sorry. When I say shrine, I don't mean an actual shrine. I just mean something special to remind us of her. Like a picture or something to keep her memory alive, that kind of thing."

Victor begins to gnaw on his lower lip. This is Rachel's fault. She told Victor he needs to be careful about what he says to me because I process trauma by holding everything inside. And blah blah blah.

He unbuckles his seatbelt and turns toward me. "What's going on, Erin? Is this camp stuff bringing up some feelings you'd rather not deal with?" he asks.

"No. God. How about 'tribute'?" I force my hands into my lap so I don't appear too wigged out. "Is that a better word than 'shrine'? Because it's seriously not that big of a deal." It didn't start out to be a big deal. But now there's that sharp pain again. She's supposed to still be here and she isn't. And I'm not okay with that.

"Erin. Talk to me." His voice takes on a sharp edge. "What's going on? What are you feeling?"

"I'm fine." I rush quickly through the explanation. "Coming up with the camp activities got me thinking about Miss P and how *a tribute* to her would be fun. It will all look very normal. Not like a shrine at all. The class and the lab are beautiful and it was all her idea. It really sucks that she isn't here. I just want to feel like she's still here . . . in spirit."

Victor nods. "I get it. It's going to take some time for all of you to process this loss. Doing something is better than stuffing it down. Promise me you won't stuff it down."

"I promise." Now it's my turn to be worried. "So, what's happening with your job thing?"

Victor exhales and stares out the front window. "I'm working on it."

"But is it going to be okay?"

He glances back at me. "I'm supposed to be the one worrying about you, not the other way around. I'll be fine. Okay?"

"Alright," I say.

"Now let's go see what Rachel is cooking for dinner. I missed lunch today."

As we enter the kitchen I'm expecting to find Rachel either

working on dinner or sitting at the table, reading. But it doesn't look like she's even home yet.

I send her a text: I THO GHT O WERE   ING INNER

She texts back: SORR   GOT ISTR   TE   I   E NT TO SEN
TE T E R IER I   ING   INNER   T H R ES S HO SE
O   N   I TOR SHO   O E O ER HERE

Victor grabs a soda out of the fridge and flops into his regular chair at the table.

"She's making dinner at the chief's and wants to know if we want to go over there."

Victor pops open the soda. "What are our choices?"

I open the door to the fridge and scan the layout. "Leftover Salisbury steak . . . TV dinners . . . pizza . . . or eggs à la Victor." I throw the last one in there to get a smile out of him. "Or, we go to the chief's for dinner."

"What's she making?" Victor says.

People suffering from PTSD require a program of structure
and predictability and lots of time to restore their
sense of security and stability.
—ONLINE HELP GUIDE

Rachel's making my favorite roast chicken casserole for dinner.

I'm not wild about having dinner with the chief, but I can't resist chicken casserole and it beats leftovers or pizza. I'm going as is, but Victor wants to change clothes. I wait at the bottom of the stairs while he goes up to his room.

My gaze drifts over to the credenza and the pile of Victor's mail that continues to accumulate. Underneath it all is the FedEx envelope. My heart pounds as I grasp the corner and pull it out from under the stack of mail. I turn it over.

It's still sealed.

I press it between my palms as if I could squeeze the words out through the cardboard. When I hear Victor start down the stairs I stash the envelope back underneath the mail pile.

The chief's house is only about a fifteen-minute drive from our house. Victor and I ride in silence. I don't know what he's thinking, but I'm becoming a little obsessed with that envelope. Why hasn't he opened it?

Why wouldn't someone open an envelope?

There are only two reasons I can think of.

One: They know what's inside and don't need to look.

Or two: They don't know what's inside and they're afraid to look.

I glance at Victor. He is not someone who scares easily. He's relaxed and driving casually. He detects my stare and gives me a smile but doesn't feel the need to talk.

I admire that. He's not one of those people who needs to fill every silence.

Sometimes it's nice to be *with* someone but *alone* with your thoughts.

Rachel answers the door when we ring the bell and shows us into the house. The chief's house is newer and more formal than ours, but it's still comfortable. He's sitting in the living room in a recliner, reading the paper. Rachel has changed out of her work clothes and it looks like she's wearing one of the chief's white dress shirts over a pair of slender black pants. The sleeves are rolled up and her hair is pulled up with some clips. There's an adorable smudge of flour on her cheek. And I swear there's another kind of glow about her.

My Rachel. The rock of my life, who was always there for everything. That Rachel always had an anxious edge about her. I'll admit this Rachel is new. I've never seen her this content, and it's really sweet.

I bury the pang of guilt that rises in my chest as a reminder that if she hadn't rescued me, she probably would have been this Rachel all along. But then I think, well, at least she and the chief get to be open about their relationship now. Finding out about her secret boyfriend was definitely the best thing to come out of suspecting him of being a murderer.

"Your timing is perfect," Rachel says. "I just put dinner on the table."

Rachel leads us to a dining room off the kitchen. The room

features a long, formal table and matching hutch. There are paintings on the wall of sailing ships being tossed by giant waves. In contrast to the violent ocean scenery, the table is set with a pale pink tablecloth and matching napkins. A short vase of pure white roses sits in the center of the table.

This is an awfully formal setting for chicken casserole.

The chief takes a seat at the head of the table. Rachel sits to his right and Victor to his left. I choose the seat next to Victor.

The casserole and a large, fresh salad are laid out in front of us. My stomach rumbles, reminding me that I skipped lunch too. Victor dives right in, ladling scoops of casserole onto his plate. My hand hovers over the salad server when . . .

"I'm not sure I can wait for dessert," the chief says, taking Rachel's hand in his and patting it with his other hand. His expression is giddy and his gaze lingers on her.

She shakes her head, stifling a giggle. "Not now, Charles. They're hungry."

"They can eat while we talk." He's obviously bursting with some news.

"Really, I think we should—" Rachel chokes up, the words sticking in her throat.

Victor and I side-eye each other. He clearly doesn't have any more of a clue than I do.

"I think we're missing something here," Victor whispers.

"I don't care," I say. "There's no way I'm skipping dinner for dessert. Rachel's roasted chicken thingy is amazing and I'm starving."

Rachel pinches her lips together and her eyes well up. She fans her face with her hand.

The chief takes Rachel's hand again.

At the last second I see it. Something that wasn't there this morning.

"I just asked this gorgeous woman to marry me!" he blurts out.

Rachel pulls her hand away from his and self-consciously displays a sparkling diamond ring on the ring finger of her left hand.

"I said yes," she says, somewhat shyly.

"We're getting married," they both say at the same time.

I'm stunned. My jaw drops open. Maybe I should have been cued to this, but I wasn't. This is the very last thing I ever thought would happen. And it's not that Rachel doesn't deserve it.

I glance at Victor. He's stunned too. But he recovers more quickly. He leaps to his feet and offers his hand to the chief.

"Wow. A wedding," Victor says. "That's terrific. Congratulations. Sis, you'll make a beautiful bride."

"Thank you. Thank you," Rachel says. "It was a complete surprise."

Her gaze is moving past Victor and toward me and I know this means I need to say something. Something nice. And I need to say it now.

But there's one overwhelming, pounding, singular thought, and the minute Rachel looks at me it blurts out of my mouth.

"What about me?"

Everything stops. Silence crashes in around us.

No one speaks.

The earth stops spinning.

I blink and try to focus on my eyelashes because I'm afraid to look anywhere else. My lower eyelids are full of water.

"Oh, Erin . . ." Rachel's voice is low and sorrowful. She glances back at the chief. "I wanted to tell you first. Alone. Just the two of us. Because that is how we do things. I'm sorry. This just—I don't know—got away from me. I—it was a complete surprise. But you know—"

I can't take it. I can't go through another "you're the moon and the stars" pep talk. Not here, in front of Victor and the chief. I know she loves me. I do. I know I'm cared for. My life is good. I get *all* of that.

I even get why she didn't tell me one-on-one, just the two of us, like everything between us has always been for my whole life.

It's because it's not just the two of us anymore.

► 20 ◄

No matter how disturbing or visceral a crime scene is, in order
to be impartial, the investigator must remain
immune to the emotional impact.
—VICTOR FLEMMING

Rachel rounds the table toward me, arms extended. Warm
huggy, on the move. But I don't want any part of it. I don't
want to be comforted. Not right this minute. I need to sit with
this and get my thoughts straight.

I back toward the door. "I just need a minute. Give me a minute."

All three of them stop and stare at me.

"I'll be right back." I turn and swiftly move toward the door.

I open it and the blast of air feels great. I continue moving
straight to Victor's car.

Three sets of footsteps follow me.

I know this is stupid. It's not like there's anywhere I can go.
I get into Victor's car and close the door and breathe in the rich
leather scent.

Rachel's palms flatten against the glass. "Erin, please. Let's
talk about this."

Victor and the chief hang back at the top of the driveway.
Hands in their pockets. Creases between their eyebrows. Uncomfortable as hell.

I'm trapped. Nowhere to go, nothing to say. I'm just going to have to gut it out.

I try to roll down the window, but there's no power to the car. My only option is to open the door. Sigh.

Before the door span is even six inches, Rachel's hands dart in and grab both sides of my face. "Erin. Look at me," she commands.

I turn my face to hers, shocked by her flood of tears.

"Rachel." My voice is steady and matter-of-fact. "I'm okay. I just wasn't expecting it and so I was a little shocked. But I'm fine. It's all good."

"No. You're not good. You're stuffing, I can tell." She hugs my head to her chest. "I'm so, so, so sorry. I should've been more careful about your reaction. I just—"

"You were excited. I get it."

"I got swept up in the moment. I was being selfish." She pulls me out of the car and wraps her arms around me. "Your feelings are okay. They're normal. Natural. Do not stuff them down, please. Nothing will change right now. I promise. Nothing changes until you're ready."

"It's okay. Really. I'm ready. I want you to be happy." And this is true. I feel like complete crap for ruining this moment for her. She always made everything about me, so I never suspected that she might want something more. Now I feel like a complete jerk.

"I *am* happy. I've always been happy. And you know you're the moon and the—" Ugh. Here it comes. I fumble trying to get my hand out of my sleeve and up to her lips. But she grabs my wrist before I can silence her.

"You are our priority. We know you'll need time to get adjusted to this and we are prepared to give you all the time you need. We'll wait years. It doesn't matter to us at all." She pauses, sniffling and blotting her eyes on the edge of her sweater. "Once there's a plan and a timeframe we're all comfortable with, you will have choices. We're not just going to tell you what you have to do. You'll get to choose."

She looks so miserable. I just want her to stop trying to fix it. This isn't a "fix it" thing.

"What kind of choices?" I ask, also blotting my eyes with my sleeve.

"Like where you want to live. Once it's settled . . . and it doesn't have to be right away . . . we figured that I could move in here with Charles. Now that Victor is home he can take over Mom and Dad's house. You, my darling, can choose. We would give anything if you will come live with us here. But if you chose to stay there with Victor, so you can be near your friends, I won't be hurt. We'll still see each other every day. I'm really sorry I didn't plan a better way to tell you the news. Charles means well and he's so excited about all of it, but especially about getting to know you. Through all of this you will remain our priority."

I nod. "I know. I know." I glance over at Victor and the chief silently watching our every move. I dig the toe of my shoe into a crack in the driveway. "Sorry. I'm okay. Really it was just so sudden I didn't know how to react."

"I understand," she says. "Come back up and let's finish dinner." She gently takes my elbow. But I stand firm.

"I'm not hungry anymore. I think I really just want to go home."

"Are you sure?"

"Yes. I'm fine. But I need to be home."

She nods. "Okay. I'll have Victor take you."

I nod and get back in the car and close the door.

Rachel shrugs helplessly at Victor and the chief. Victor takes this as his cue and strides over and gets in on the driver's side. He leans toward me as he buckles his seatbelt.

"Just so you know, I'm game for whatever you have in mind, there just needs to be the promise of a meal at the end of it. Because I really am starving."

He's starving and there's a gaping, hollow pit inside me.

"Take me somewhere," I say. "Anywhere. Somewhere I've never been." I soothe my head against the cool window and breathe out a path of fog. No matter what I do, my future always seems to look exactly like this.

"Roger that." Victor checks his watch. "It's Saturday . . . camp hasn't started yet. I've got this." He starts the car and turns on the lights, washing Rachel and the chief in the beams. The chief has his arm around her and she's nervously twisting the ring on her finger.

"They look happy, don't they?" I say.

"They really do," agrees Victor.

We're both lying. They look like they're facing a firing squad.

"Did you know about the engagement before tonight?" I ask.

"No," Victor answers. "It was a complete surprise."

► 21 ◄

Survivor guilt is real and nothing to be ashamed of. But one must
remember, surviving isn't a selfish act, it's primal.
—VICTOR FLEMMING

Thirty minutes alone in the car with Victor isn't bad.

Rachel would be wearing out her neck flashing me worried
glances every five seconds. He just drives, quietly tapping out
some tune with his thumbs on the steering wheel.

Before I know it, the wheels leave the pavement and crunch
over a bumpy, gravel parking lot. I sit up and take in our dinner location: a small, dark building with a bright neon sign.
The Tender Tavern looks like a bar.

"They serve food?" I ask.

"Best burgers this side of the Mississippi." Victor parks and
glances over. "They have other stuff, too. But their burgers
are—" He kisses his fingertips like a French chef.

"Okay. I'm down for burgers." I open my door and get out
of the car. The cool night air floats a whiff of river brine in my
direction. It's one of my favorite scents and the thing I love
most about living here. I'm always near water.

We crunch over the gravel toward the weathered wooden
door. Victor holds it open for me. Inside the tavern is as worn

as the outside. But where the outside has been roughed into craggy splintered edges, the inside is smoothed to a fine, faded patina. The formerly light wood of the bar has been rubbed to a dark, glossy mirror, while the formerly dark wooden floor features a light, burnished path down the middle.

A waitress with a bar rag tucked into her waistband approaches us. "You here for dinner?"

Victor nods.

She grabs a couple of menus and leads us toward the part of the dining room with more light and several occupied tables.

"What about one of those tables over in the corner?" Victor asks.

"Sure, darlin'," she says. "Anywhere you like." She threads her way through the maze of furniture and drops the menus on the table. Then she scoops up silverware and napkins from an adjacent table and deposits them, too. "I'll be back to get your order in a minute, hon."

Victor pulls out my chair for me and then sits to my right. He peruses the menu briefly before tapping it on the table. There's a hint of nostalgia in his smile.

"I haven't been here in years," he says. "This used to be our hideaway place when we were in high school because they were a little lax in checking IDs," he says.

"You drank in high school?" I'm not shocked that he did, just shocked that he's admitting it.

He raises his eyebrows. "You don't?" Then he puts up his hands. "Wait. Don't tell me. I don't want to know."

I answer him anyway with a shake of my head. "The taste. Yuck."

"Keep it that way if you can. Too many stupid things get done behind alcohol."

The waitress comes and takes our order: two burgers with

everything, soda for me, and a beer for Victor. She scoops up the menus but before she leaves, Victor stops her and cancels the beer, changing it to two sodas.

"I'm going to wash my hands," he says, getting up from the table.

When he returns, his hair is damp and he's grabbed a basket of peanuts in the shell from the bar. He sets it down and cracks open a nut.

"So, you know how this is going to go down, right?" he asks.

"What? Rachel and the chief?"

He plucks another peanut from the basket. "Yeah. My guess is my sister will move slowly and take a lot of time with this. It's her first wedding, after all. You'll probably be away at college before she ever moves him in."

"That's not what she said, though." I look him in the eye. "She told me she wouldn't do anything until I was ready, but basically it's my choice. I can live with them at the chief's house, or stay in our house . . . with you." Saying that out loud suddenly sounds too personal. "So, you know, I can be close to my friends."

He looks surprised, but not in a bad way.

"She said that?"

"Yes. She said she thought you'd like to live in your parents' house for a while."

"It's true. I love that house." His look drifts and becomes misty. Then he brings it back to me. "Lots of memories there. I bet you can say the same thing, right?"

I nod.

"I'm not as good a cook as Rachel, but I have a few skills. I'd be thrilled if you wanted to stay and bunk in with me."

There's no contest between staying in *my house* versus moving in with the chief. But this is way too fast. I haven't had a chance to process it yet. "Full disclosure, I'm not very good with change."

"Me either," he says. "But suddenly we're both faced with a bunch of it." He pauses and rubs his hands across his face. "Full disclosure . . ." He radiates a sudden worry.

"What's wrong?" I ask.

"Nothing. It's just there's something important that I need to tell you. And this might be as good a time as any." He squirms a little. "It's not bad . . . at least I don't think it's bad. Your mileage could vary. But it is important. Honesty is always important, right? And listen—this is important too—I'm getting ready to tell you something and I need to know that you're not suddenly going to jump up and run out of here. I don't think it would look good for me to be chasing you around a dark parking lot in this neighborhood. If you know what I mean."

He's slipped over into babbling. And I have a pretty good idea why. I flash back to the unopened FedEx envelope. I lean forward, pressing my elbows into the table. "Are you getting ready to tell me you slept with my mother?"

Bam! I said it, just like that. I didn't know I had the guts.

"Whoa. What?" Shocked, he scoots back from the table. He glances around for the waitress and blots his mouth with his napkin. Then he chuckles.

"I knew. Well, I didn't exactly *know*. But I saw you in the hospital put the swab in your mouth and then into the envelope along with mine. So . . . I suspected."

He grins, a combination of embarrassed and proud. "You'd make a great poker player. You've got some seriously stealth moves."

"With everything going on the last couple of weeks it kind of slipped to the bottom of my 'things I'm worried about' list."

"But you saw the FedEx envelope?"

I nod. "You still haven't opened it."

"Well, I thought about opening it and then I thought I should wait and tell you first. I wanted the two of us to be on equal footing. I wanted us both to know that this is something that's possible."

"So, it really is possible"—my voice softens and clouds with emotion—"I could be your daughter?"

He pauses, but his look is like a beam of bright, unfiltered emotion. "In this whole world, there's nothing that would make me happier or make my life more complete." His voice catches at the end too.

"Here you go, two burgers with everything." The waitress barges right over the moment. She sets down plates of food in front of each of us. Then she unloads condiments from the various pockets on her apron.

Victor and I are frozen. Struck. Staring across the table at each other. I'm not even thinking about the words. Tiny pinpoints of light explode. All these years I dreamed about this moment and all I wanted was for him—whoever *him* turned out to be—to be happy about meeting *me*.

Victor definitely looks happy.

"Are you two playing that 'see who blinks first' game?" the waitress asks.

"No!" Victor and I say it at the same time, never breaking eye contact.

"Okay." She sounds skeptical, like she doesn't believe us. "Anything else I can—"

"No. We're good," Victor says, looking away.

"Really good," I add, also looking away.

The waitress moves off.

"Just so you know, I was more worried over how I would feel

if it turned out not to be true." Victor shakes his head, swallowing hard. "I'll confess I didn't want to face that alone."

"You don't have to." I set my hand on the table next to my plate. He puts his forward and pats mine.

"That's right. We're in this together. It's been one hell of a night; I say we cap it off by opening the envelope as soon as we get home."

"Yeah. Let's rip it open," I agree. "We can do it together. Each take an end and tear."

I take a bite of my hamburger. "Mmmmm." He's not wrong. Juicy and perfectly seasoned. I adopt an expression of bliss and point to the burger.

"What'd I tell you?" He kisses his fingers again, à la the chef.

"So, when did you . . ." I twirl my finger as I search for the right words.

"First put two and two together?" he asks. "That night, in the hospital. I was filling out the police report after old Carl tried to kill us. I had to call Rachel to get your birthdate. Everything about the report was focused on your mom and dates for specific things and how old you were then and now. And, I don't know, all of a sudden everything just lined up."

"Does Rachel know?" I have always suspected that Rachel knew the identity of my father but wasn't saying. But if she knew Victor was my real father it might explain why she would consider letting me live with him.

Victor vehemently shakes his head. Then he pauses. "Well, let me put it this way: I never said anything to her. But I don't know about your mother."

"My mother never told you either. Right?"

Victor heaves a big sigh. "No. And I have quite a bit of guilt surrounding that. It's the one thing that makes me think this might not be true. I can't imagine what I might have done that would have made your mother feel like she couldn't tell me about you."

"Maybe she knew . . ." I gasp for a second, summoning courage, then forge ahead. "Maybe she knew you didn't love her." These are difficult words but they need to be said. The one thing I always hoped was that my mother loved my father. That I was born out of an exquisite union. And that it didn't matter to her or to me if he didn't feel the same way.

"Let me just say that I *loved* your mother in every way possible. Growing up, I almost can't remember a time when she wasn't part of our family. She *was* family. Then I was gone to the FBI for a couple of years. When I came back for my own mother's funeral, well, your mother was . . . she had changed. Or I had. Anyway, your mother was unforgettable."

"And yet . . ." I call him out with my look.

"Yeah. I know." The guilt lies thick in his voice. "What can I say? I was young and didn't know what I wanted in life. I thought I wanted out of this town. She wanted out too. She was going to Italy and Paris and I was locked and loaded for Virginia. I had just gotten a promotion and a book contract."

He pauses to concentrate on his burger, so I do the same.

After a few bites, he speaks again. "Just so you know, your mother was way out of my league. She was classy and elegant. She knew which fork to use and how to pull together an outfit that looked like it just came off the runway. I was a science nerd. No one would have ever thought I had an actual chance with her."

Somehow, we manage to finish every scrap of food on our plates. Victor sits back in his chair. "Do you remember the speech I gave you that day in the hospital?"

"About coming home and wanting a family?"

"Yes. I said it then and it's still true to this very minute. You changed me, Erin. I honestly don't care what it says in that envelope. You and me . . . we're family."

Amazing how one night can go from lowest low to highest high in just a couple of hours.

► **22** ◄

The spiral in a snail's shell is the same mathematically as
the spiral in the Milky Way galaxy, and it's also
the same mathematically as the
spirals in our DNA.
—JOSEPH GORDON-LEVITT

Victor opens the sunroof for the drive home, then blasts the
heater.

It's the perfect night. We drive mostly in silence with little
pockets of conversation here and there, until . . .

"So, you must've had some notions about what your father
would be like. Any thoughts you'd like to share?" he asks. "You
know, so I'll know what's expected of me."

He's not wrong. I've had a lifetime of notions and fantasies.
"Mostly what I imagined was the 'big tall guy on white horse
rides in to save the princess' kind of stuff."

"Really?" He sounds incredulous. "That surprises me, because
you are one hundred percent the capable princess who saves
herself *and* the dad. And come to think of it, that *is* exactly
what happened."

We share a laugh. "I really like how you talk to me."

"How is that?" he asks.

"Like I'm a regular person and you're not being overly cau-
tious and worried that I might break. Or overprotective. Or
concerned that I might be too sensitive." I pause to think it

through and wonder if I'm properly expressing myself. "Yeah. You just talk to me straight. And I really like that."

Victor nods. "Straight talk. Check. Anything else?"

"Wait. Now I'm worried," I say.

"About what?"

"Well, you don't think that opening the envelope will—" A sudden flood of emotion closes my throat again. I struggle to croak out the rest of my question. "Change things between us. Do you?"

A car passes going in the opposite direction and the headlights sweep over us. I glance at Victor's face. His lips are pinched together. A quirk I've noticed when he's thinking.

"Good question," he says after a pause. "I believe that opening the envelope *will* change everything . . . but for the better. Right? It could prove we're actually related."

"Or not."

"True. Or not."

"But we've already agreed we're related no matter what the envelope says. So, opening it or not opening it won't change anything," I say. "Or will it?"

He pauses then emits a full-bodied chuckle. "Dear lord, we have Schrödinger's cat."

"I love cats."

Victor is suddenly ramped up and excited. This is exactly how he looked the night he came home with all the supplies to run a DNA test in our kitchen. "How much do you know about quantum mechanics?" he asks.

I give him my very best raised-eyebrows look.

"Yeah. Okay. Follow with me here," he says. "So, scientific theory is based on facts that have been observed. You know that, right?"

"Yeah. Miss P was big on our observations."

"Quantum mechanics describes probabilities, or what *could* happen over time. In fact, there was this one physicist who believed that our observations actually caused the results."

"Wait . . . I'm getting confused," I say.

"Hang with me," Victor says. "Schrödinger's cat is a scientific way to describe probability without screwing it up by observing it. Are you with me?"

"Maybe."

"So, Schrödinger posed a question: If you sealed a live cat in a box with a radioactive particle, what would happen to the cat?"

"It would die. The radioactive thingy would kill it."

"Probably. But maybe not." Victor smiles. "Maybe the cat is really strong and the radioactive thingy is tiny and weak. *Probabilities*. That's the key word."

"So?"

"So, this might freak you out a little, but the theory is that as long as you never look inside the box the cat is *both* alive *and* dead."

I sit up. "Wait. I understand this."

"You do?" Victor chuckles, sounding surprised.

"Yeah. It's like a Choose Your Own Adventure novel."

Victor laughs. "Believe it or not, those were about the only books I actually read as a kid."

"I devoured them too. But you have to admit they're a little like Schrödinger's cat for books."

"They are," Victor says. "Those books are Schrödinger's cat in a nutshell. You're amazing, Erin."

"You're pretty amazing too, Victor. You're going to make a great high school teacher."

By this time, Victor is driving down our street. It looks the same, even though everything changed tonight.

"So, we agree. We're not going to open the envelope?" I ask.

"That's right," Victor says. "Envelope stays sealed . . . unless one of us needs a kidney."

► 23 ◄

Some 5 million children, or roughly 7 percent of all children
living in the U.S., have a parent who is currently
or was previously incarcerated.

—childtrends.org

Victor pulls into our driveway and angles his car around to the
side of Journey's van.

Wait. Journey's van?!

Journey's leaning against the door, peering at his cell phone.
He looks up and flashes that brilliant smile that grabs my heart
and pulls it straight out of my chest.

"Oh my god," I whisper.

I still experience an actual, physical chill when I realize that
Journey Michaels is *my* boyfriend. In a million years, I never
thought anything that cool would happen to me.

But then I remember, he's not just my boyfriend, he's also
Victor's intern. "Is he here to see you . . . or me?"

Victor shrugs. "I didn't make a date with him, so he must
be here to see you."

I squeal and vault out of the car before Victor has even
turned it off. "See ya later." I stop before closing the car door
and glance back inside. "Thanks . . . for everything . . ." I pause.
"I really mean that."

Victor smiles and nods. "We're a team now. Or, more than

a team. Have fun. Be safe. And, oh yeah, if I'm in charge now, what time will you be home?"

I glance over at Journey's brilliant smile. "I won't be late. I promise." I close the door and dance all the way to Journey's van.

Journey slings an arm around my waist and pulls me to him. He presses his lips into my hair and murmurs, "I stood you up for our date last night. Don't hate me."

I throw an arm around his neck and give him a huge hug. "I could never hate you. And it's okay. I was worried but then I heard you had a pretty tough day."

Journey looks past me at Victor getting out of the car. He waves and smiles. Then, lowering his voice to a whisper, he says, "I thought maybe we'd head over to the Point for a while . . . unless you're hungry?"

I pull back and inspect his face. The Point is the town makeout spot. Our relationship is so new we haven't done the Point thing yet. But tonight, I'm feeling bold.

"The Point is perfect."

"It is?" He looks surprised.

"Yes. Let's go." I'm not exactly thinking of making out, although I'm not opposed to that either. What I am thinking is that the Point is perfect for the private, uninterrupted conversation we need to have.

Journey helps me up into the van and then goes around to his side.

Once he's steered us out onto the road he launches into a conversation. "I met my dad today."

"That's so crazy. How was it?"

"Both better and worse than I expected," he says.

"Confusing, I'm sure."

"It was better because now I have a real person to match up with my image of him."

"He's not angry that you came to see him?" I ask.

"Not today. He was smart and calm and really cool. He apologized for freaking out yesterday."

"And it was worse because . . . ?"

"He's still in there. And if we can't change that, he'll stay in there for at least another ten years." Journey goes quiet while he makes the winding drive up to the Point. And I contemplate the notion of another ten years in prison. "Yeah. Ten years," Journey says as if reading my mind.

"What did he say about reopening the case?"

"He's excited and extremely grateful to Victor . . . and to you."

We arrive at the Point, which is a bluff overlooking the spot where the Pacific Ocean and the Columbia River come together. It's dark, but not gloomy. The star-strewn sky glitters like it's dressed for a night on the town.

Journey pauses his story to concentrate on finding a place to park. There's room for about ten cars up here, without being right next to each other. He pulls into a spot, sets the emergency brake, turns off the engine and the lights. He slides his seat back and turns toward me, patting his lap. "I got to tell him about you."

I release my seatbelt and move over to sit on his lap. "What'd he say?"

"He wants to meet you and hopes you'll come next time."

"There'll be a next time?"

"Yes. He said I could start coming regularly." Journey's voice grows thick with emotion. "I'm a man now and he needs to get to know me."

I lay my head on his chest and melt into his warm hug. "I can't wait to meet him."

"You will, I promise." Journey digs in his pocket and pulls out a small, hand-carved wooden disc about the size of the palm of my hand. "He also gave me this."

I take the disc and run my fingers over it. It's an elaborate scene of two dolphins rising out of the water carved inside the circle, making it more of a ring than a disc. "It's beautiful. What is it?"

"Apparently, this was one of my toys when I was a baby," Journey says. "My parents said I used it for teething."

"Awww." I give it a closer inspection. "So cute. There are tiny teeth marks on it."

"Yeah. What's not cute is where it came from."

I give him a questioning look.

"My parents don't *know* where it came from. They suspect it came from Rodney, the boy who—"

"The victim?" I can't disguise my surprise.

Journey is surprised. "How'd you know?"

"I've been reading." Off Journey's frown I quickly add, "Just reading, though. That's all."

He nods. "Anyway, I like using his name. I think it's the right thing to do."

"I agree. He had a name. We should use it."

"Apparently, he was an artist. My parents think he carved it and gave it to me. My mom said it was one of my favorite toys."

"Wow. Do you think he was sending your parents a signal by giving you that toy?"

"Good question," Journey says. "The part I haven't told you—which is the creepy part no one ever told me—is that the harassment my parents were dealing with wasn't as harmless as the newspaper made it sound. They would wake up in the morning and find me out of my crib. They were sure it wasn't possible for me to climb out by myself."

"Are you serious?"

"Yes," Journey says. "Most days I'd be sitting on the floor playing with toys. Then, one day, they found me in the kitchen, playing in a pile of flour."

"Holy crap. How do you play in a pile of flour?" I ask.

"You don't," Journey says. "Apparently, I drooled and it was gross and sticky."

I run my finger across his lower lip. He pretends to bite my finger.

"Anyway, it got real one morning when they woke up and I was gone. Completely gone. They checked every room in the house."

"Oh my god. That's terrifying."

"I know. And then they found me outside, playing in the dirt near my dad's truck."

"Which is where he kept the shotgun, under the seat." I say.

Journey gives me a warning look.

"I'm researching ballistics for camp week and I knew there was gun evidence in your father's case. I was just reading a little."

He hugs me tighter and plants a kiss on my head, which I hope means my snoopiness is okay.

"Yeah. Who checks under the seat of the truck every day to make sure the shotgun is still there? It could have been taken at any time. My dad had no clue. Anyway, they called the police, multiple times, reporting things like trespassing or attempted kidnapping. My dad said the cops never believed them. Their theory was that either I was an escape artist or one of my parents was a sleepwalker."

"They didn't investigate?"

"What was there to find about a kid out of his crib? My father changed the locks. Put a fence around the property. He installed an alarm system. He tried everything. There was other stuff, too. They would come home and the shower would be damp. Small amounts of food went missing."

"They could have checked for fingerprints," I say.

Journey gives me a sideways glance and ruffles my hair. "It's adorable that you think they might have thought like you. But no. They weren't going to do that."

"To be honest, the police didn't do all that much when my mom was murdered either," I say. "So I get what you mean."

"Anyway, after finding me outside the house, my dad just flipped out and quietly rigged the trap with a paintball gun. He believed the paint would be a great way to prove that someone was there. Even if they didn't catch him, there would be an outline of paint on the wall indicating that an actual human had been there and not a ghost."

"What about the DNA test that Miss P was trying to do for you? What would that have proven?"

Journey sighs. "Miss P knew it was a Hail Mary try. There isn't a lot of actual evidence in my father's case. There's the shotgun and the motion-activated harness and some spent shells. My father never disputed that those things belonged to him. And, because there was no crime lab, his DNA isn't on file anywhere. Miss P wanted to try to get a baseline on him. Then we could ask them to test the shotgun."

"But didn't they already test the shotgun?"

"They verified that the gun was his and that it fired the fatal shot but that was all they did," Journey says. "But you know how you load a shotgun, right?"

I nod. "Sorta."

He demonstrates. "You crack open the barrel and push the shells into the barrel with your thumb. Miss P explained that DNA tests are much more sensitive now than they were back then so it's possible that simply scraping a thumb across the metal edge of a shotgun barrel could leave enough epithelial cells behind for a test."

"And, if that DNA belonged to anyone but your father . . ." I chime in, following the logic.

"Exactly," Journey says. "It could prove his story that someone rigged the gun and that would be enough to get him a new trial. That was our goal, to get him a new trial."

"What does Victor say?" I ask.

Journey reclines his seat a little and pulls me closer. "Victor thinks the DNA theory is risky. It's likely if they found any DNA at all that my father's DNA would be there too. And that could be confusing and could make his situation worse. Victor wants to do more than just get a new trial. He wants us to find something they missed or find someone new to blame." Journey cuddles me up in a warm hug.

"If anyone can do it you know it's Victor," I say.

"I know." Journey buries his face in my hair. "So, I'm sorry I didn't answer your texts. The last two days were surreal. But I especially loved the Snap of your hair."

I feel my cheeks getting warm. "It's okay. I just felt bad for you, is all."

"I made it through. So, how was your day?"

I pause to give him a kiss. And then another. And okay, one more.

I sit up a little on his lap and lean back against the door. "My day was pretty surreal, too. Rachel and the chief are getting married . . ."

"What?" Journey studies my face. "You're kidding, right?"

"Not kidding."

"Whoa. A murderer's son dating the police chief's daughter sounds like a movie of the week."

"It's stepdaughter, and your father is innocent. Wrongfully accused."

Journey sighs. "I always believed that. But after meeting him, I believe it even more."

"Then we have to do everything—leave no stone unturned— we have to get this right." In my mind, there are banners and flags waving and music blasting as I say this.

Journey raises his eyebrows. "We?" he says.

Dang! "I mean the collective we. Like you, Victor, Mr. Martin, the chief." I chuckle self-consciously. "You thought I meant we as in you . . . and me . . ."

"I thought you meant we as in you and me and the girls," he says.

"Yeah. No. The girls and I, we're busy setting up the camp." I'm nervous stammering, so it's time to change the subject. "In related news. I might have actually met my father today too."

"What?" Journey squeezes me excitedly. "That's amazing. Who? Tell me."

"Well, it might be Victor," I say.

"Wait. I thought he's your uncle." Journey frowns. "How does that work?"

"You know the deal. Rachel was my mom's best friend and Victor is Rachel's brother, so we're not related . . . or, maybe we are. I'm not sure, there's a chance, possibly. A big one. Victor could be my actual biological dad."

Journey is a little hesitant. "Are you okay with that?"

"Sure. I'm great with that. Aren't you?"

"It doesn't really affect me," Journey says.

"You're his 'intern.'" I put air quotes around the word as I say it.

"Ah yeah, well, Victor's cool. I'm not worried about that. But wow for you. That's a pretty big day. When will you know for sure?"

"Yeah, that question doesn't have an exact answer," I say.

"Because?" Journey asks.

"Because we decided not to find out for sure." Journey reacts with an expression that's half confused, half silly. "It's a long story," I say.

My phone pings and I slide it out of my pocket. It's a text from Spam. Her timing is hilarious. A straight emoji line of kissing lips. I flash my phone toward Journey. "Spam."

He chuckles.

I text back: WHERE RE O

   S N I ST .RO E ST O

WHERE RE O GOING NOW I ask.

        TO   HO SE she replies. O SHO   O E WE   N

I   THE ITT ES O T O THE   SE ENT N   SSE   E SO E

E S

I glance up at Journey. "She wants to know if we want to go to her house."

He gives me a soft look. I know what he's thinking.

"I'll tell her no. We haven't been alone in days." I start to key in a text response, and after a few seconds Journey lays his hand over mine.

"I have a better idea," he says. "How about I drop you off at Spam's and I go home. Today has just kind of been—I don't know. I'm still in shock and overwhelmed and—" He swipes the hair off the side of my face and tucks it behind my ear.

"Would it be okay with you if we call it a night? I really needed to see you, but now I'm kinda wiped out."

I nod. "I completely understand. I'm exactly the opposite. I'm wound up."

When I don't move out of his lap right away we go ahead and make out a little. It's soft and sweet. Tentative. No pressure. Just like things have always been with Journey.

But at least we've made it past The Point. That's a relationship milestone.

◂ 24 ▸

The FBI created AFIS, a fingerprint database. Then they added
CODIS to preserve DNA evidence. And now, their newest toy
is NGI (next generation I.D.), which employs biometric
response and can provide IDs in ten seconds.

—VICTOR FLEMMING

I climb the stairs to Spam's back door. Mr. Ramos waves through
the window. He's wearing a bathrobe and doing dishes.

It works the same at her house as it does at mine.

"Hey, Erin." Mr. Ramos opens the door and launches right
into his favorite joke. "Knock, knock."

"Who's there?" I reply.

"You," he says.

"You who?" I roll my eyes. Mr. Ramos has been telling this
joke for as long as I can remember. It used to make me giggle
out loud and even now, having heard it a zillion times, it still
brings a smile to my face.

"You hooligans are causing trouble again, I see," he ad-libs
and waves his fist.

"What?" I'm used to him saying: *You don't have to yell, I'm
right here.* "Mr. Ramos, you changed the punch line."

"I didn't change it, Benji changed it," he says.

"What does Benji know about hooligans?" I ask.

"Good question. You have to ask him." Mr. Ramos nods
toward the stairs. "They're downstairs."

"Thanks, Mr. Ramos."

His eyes twinkle. "I thought Spam said you were bringing the infamous Journey. I was looking forward to meeting him."

"He had to go home," I say. "But you'll get to meet him soon."

"I'm looking forward to it. Have fun." He waves and heads off down the hall.

Down the stairs and around the corner, I find Spam and Lysa at a long game table littered with the Bella makings.

"Why are you smiling?" Spam asks.

I wave my hand. "Your dad called Journey *infamous*. It was adorable."

Spam rolls her eyes. "He's so annoying. Where is Journey?"

"He was pretty stressed and overwhelmed after his day meeting his dad so he went home." I survey the stuff scattered on the table. "So, what's all this?"

Spam gestures. "These are the pieces for all the Bella orders we've received so far. If we work together, we can have them done in less than an hour." She walks over to the closet. "But, since Journey isn't here, we can also update the murder board." She rolls the whiteboard out into the room. Down in the corner, there's a sketch of cartoon eyes, a mustache, and something that vaguely resembles a penis. "Ugh. Little brothers. Updates?" she asks, erasing the scribble.

"Yes," I say. "Journey showed me a small carved, wooden ring with dolphins and stuff that his parents think the victim secretly made for him."

"Hmm." Spam contemplates the board. "Not sure where that goes."

"Put it under evidence," Lysa says.

Spam writes it on the board. I call up a photo on my phone. "Here it is. I took a photo of it."

They look at it and nod.

"Also, you can put a red tape line from Arletta Stone to Coach Wilkins, since we know they're cousins."

Lysa consults her laptop. "I found out some stuff about her. Arletta Stone and her family are fourth generation in Iron Rain. She runs the historical society, which is a little hole-in-the-wall office in town that hands out sightseeing maps to tourists. The historical society is who put up the one-thousand-dollar reward for the identity of the skateboarder. Apparently, Arletta Stone's real dream is to own a full-blown museum about the fishing and sailing industry in this area, which dates back over a hundred years."

"Let me guess," I say. "She wanted to buy the cannery?"

"Exactly," Lysa says. "Before Journey's parents moved here, the cannery had been vacant and up for sale for years. Arletta was working on gathering investors and then . . ." Lysa claps her hands together.

"Journey's parents," Spam says.

"Exactly. Uppity young family from New York City swooped in and snatched it up." Lysa clicks a few keys on her keyboard and adjusts the screen. "They paid cash. And Arletta, who had already been accumulating items for the museum, lost everything. She filed bankruptcy the same year Jameson went to prison."

"That could be a motive," I say. "But Ms. Stone would also need means and opportunity."

Spam puts a dollar sign with a red circle and slash through it next to Arletta Stone's name. "I've got something too," Spam says.

She turns her laptop around, revealing Coach Wilkins posing next to a large trophy with a rifle in his hand. "That is our very own Coach Wilkins . . . cousin to Arletta Stone . . . accepting a Civilian Marksman trophy for Distinguished Rifleman."

We register looks of surprise.

"A cousin who is a distinguished marksman and who was also on the witness list at Jameson's trial." I walk over to the whiteboard. I tear off a piece of red tape, connecting Coach Wilkins under the suspect column now too.

"One might assume that sending Journey's dad to prison would cause the cannery to come up for sale again," Lysa says.

"But they were wrong," I say.

We stare at the board in quiet contemplation.

"Why does this always happen to us?" Lysa says. "We figure things out, but then we can't tell anyone."

Spam lays her head on the table. "We've got the 'you're on probation' blues."

I shake my head. "It's okay. It's not like one of these people is going to suddenly go crazy. It will take some time for me to feed these thoughts to Journey, but I will. What about the skateboarder?" I ask. "Any more news on him?"

Spam sags. "Sadly no. Not a peep."

She takes her place at the table and slides the little piles of discs, twine, and tiny plastic bags in front of each of us. "Okay. Now we should finish the Bellas." She holds up a silver disc by the edges. "This is a wearable electronic platform. I've already installed the LEDs." She glances up at our blank faces. "LEDs are the lights." She lays the plastic volcano design over the top of the silver disc and snaps the two together. "You snap the cover over the platform and twist it so it locks in place. Then you tie on the single slipknot bracelet."

"That's it?" I ask.

"Then pass them to me. I'll pair and program them with whatever tracking device was ordered," Spam says. "Most people are combining the bracelets with pride pins, though the hair clips are popular too."

"How many do we have to do?" I ask.

Spam checks her phone. "Thirty."

I groan. "Sounds like work."

"What if I told you they're worth six hundred dollars?" Spam asks.

"Dude, what are we waiting for?" I reply.

► 25 ◄

Computers are so sophisticated at recognizing faces that
facial recognition is already replacing fingerprints
as the ID of choice.
—VICTOR FLEMMING

The Iron Rain Memorial Day festival is the official kickoff to
summer. After this there are only two weeks of school left—
one for cramming for finals and one for the finals themselves. Then finally a big celebration for Journey's graduation.

The fairgrounds have been transformed. There are games,
rides, and rows upon rows of booths. You can find food, crafts,
and even a farmers' market. And today, you can sign your kid
up for CSI summer camp, right here in Iron Rain.

The flyers we passed out last week said sign-ups would begin
today, at the festival. Victor and Coach Wilkins are sharing a
booth for camp sign-ups. Cheerleaders and athletes work on
one side of the booth, talking about sports camp; while Journey, Lysa, Spam, and I work the other and talk about CSI camp.

It's weird studying Coach Wilkins today after what we
learned last night. He's beyond competitive, practically dragging kids into the booth and trying to strong-arm them into
signing up for sports camp. He's sweaty, loud, and obnoxious.
And he keeps coming over to our side to see how many sign-
ups we have.

He claims he's going to beat Victor, or else.

Since we were recently in the news and in the newspaper, we're sort of minor celebrities in town. Lysa made the four of us matching T-shirts to promote the camp. She used a bleach pen to draw the chalk outline of a body onto black T-shirts. They look smudgy and amazing.

We sign up fifteen kids in ten minutes. Most of our brochures are gone, along with my voice. And yet the crowd around our booth continues to grow.

What I keep hearing over and over is: *Hey, you're those girls from the news.*

As uncomfortable as this makes me, I try to smile through it. Rachel says my healing needs to begin with my acceptance that this is what life has dealt me. I'm not there yet, but I'm working on being able to say my name out loud without cringing and to claim my identity with a smile. People might still react with waves of pity. But I no longer view myself as a victim. I have to remember that bringing down Principal Roberts was a way to erase that stigma for me. It's hard to suddenly stop looking over your shoulder after a lifetime of doing it. But realistically, there should be no reason for someone to be stalking me anymore. My life shouldn't be any more dangerous than the average high school student's.

I step back for a second just to take it all in and reflect.

Maybe I'm not some freaky weirdo crime geek after all. I hear it over and over: Lots of people are interested in learning more about forensics. The fact that I get to be a part of that is something special.

Spam suddenly grabs my arm, her fingers digging into my flesh.

"Ouch. What?"

She tilts her face up to me, frozen, eyes wild. A look that

could signal an imminent meteor disaster. She continues killing my arm with full fingernails and enough pressure to empty a tube of toothpaste.

"He's *here*." She says this with an appropriate amount of horror.

"The skateboarder?" I ask.

She nods, her eyes wide enough that I can see white all the way around them.

"Tell him we want to talk to him!"

"I can't," she squeaks.

I stifle a laugh. Spam's been stalking this guy for a solid week. Now she's too shy? This must be serious, though. I've only known Spam to fall in love with exactly three things: ice cream, video games, and homemade lemonade.

I start to turn around.

She slaps me. "Don't look."

I quickly look down. "Okay. But is anyone else eyeballing him?"

Spam peeks around me. "I don't think so."

"And you're sure it's him?" I ask.

"Positive," Spam says.

"I don't want someone to recognize him and call him out while he's hanging out at our booth," I say.

"I don't want that either," Spam asks. "What should we do?"

"We need to know who he is and how we can contact him," I say. "Where is he now?"

Spam glances up. "He's talking to Journey."

I sneak a peek over my shoulder. "You're right. He is cute."

"I told you," she says. "Tell me what to do."

"Just casually go over there, don't make a big deal or attract any attention. Ask if you can answer any questions. Or at least find out his name. We deserve to know since we got in trouble over this whole thing."

Spam turns to peek at him and finds that he's looking at her. She freaks and turns back.

"Go. You've got this," I tell her.

She exhales a giant puff of nerves, fluffs her hair, smooths her eyebrows, and straightens her clothes. Game face on, she turns and sidles up next to Journey.

"Would you like to know more about our CSI summer camp?" Spam asks him.

"I would." His smile broadens. "Especially from you, short-cake. You're one of them, aren't you?"

Spam twists the tip of her hair around her finger. "One of who?"

Lysa and I stand back and try to appear nonchalant, like we're not really listening, but we totally are.

"The crime-stopper girls from TV," he says. "My name's Lyman, by the way." He offers her a fist bump.

Spam meets his fist bump and they do the exact same flourish at the end. So weird, how'd she know? I'm surprised at how smooth and calm she seems. I'm barely past my complete stammering, nervous scarecrow stage around Journey.

"Pleasure to meet you, Lyman." Her voice is soft as velvet. "My name's Sp—Samantha."

Lysa and I lock eyes in shock, our eyebrows peaked in the middle like circus tents. Holy crap. Starting in fourth grade she would literally punch you if you called her *Samantha*.

Lyman looks confused. "I thought you're the one they call Spam."

She giggles. "Yeah. That is what my friends call me."

Lyman checks her out. She's wearing a striped top and

striped pants—same color field, different stripes. No one else would ever put these two clothing items together, but Spam pulls it off in the very same way that Lyman pulls off his plaid.

"What do I have to do to get to call you Spam?" he asks.

"You could sign up for the camp," she says, and I swear she's batting her eyelashes.

"Already done." He nods toward Journey, counting out a bunch of small bills.

Journey hands Lyman a receipt. "You'll get the paperwork in the mail for your parents to fill out."

"Thanks, man," Lyman says.

"Then I guess I'll see you at camp," Spam says, being flirty. "Unless . . ."

Lyman looks disappointed. "Unless I can't wait that long?"

She grins and pulls her cell phone out of the pocket of her hoodie. "Snapchat?"

He pulls out his phone and they both open the app. Spam hovers her phone under his. He clicks, then pulls his phone back and grins: "@spamalot?"

She nods.

He keys a few things into the phone. "See you around, @spam-alot." He tips a pretend hat before strolling off into the crowd.

I peer over her shoulder. He sent a Snapchat photo of her talking to me just a few minutes before she turned around and saw him. Her expression goes all dizzy and she fans herself with what's left of our stack of applications.

Lysa and I just shake our heads.

"There was a time when I might have been like this over Journey, too," I whisper to Lysa. "But I at least had the sanity to keep it to myself."

Lysa gives me a look. "Oh, girl, please. You didn't keep anything to yourself. Do you not remember the lectures and almost-interventions we tried to run on you?"

Okay. Maybe I wasn't that covert after all.

"I need a job as a counselor, too," Spam says.

"What about working at your dad's store?" I ask.

She waves away my concern. "The stuff I do for him, I can schedule my own hours."

"Are you sure?" Lysa asks in that tone she uses that sounds like her mother.

"Yes, Mom," Spam says. "Besides, I don't want you getting any ideas about stealing that one away from me."

"You don't have to worry about that," Lysa says. "I can't compete with you for that snappy dresser." There's an element of sarcasm in Lysa's tone. I glance quickly at Spam to see if her feelings are hurt. But she's too much in dreamland to care about what either of us thinks.

"I know," she says. "His style is crazy amazing." She taps my nose to get my attention before drifting out of the booth. "You'll talk to Victor, right?"

I nod. "Yeah. I'll talk to him."

Spam isn't gone thirty seconds before we get another visitor. Detective Sydney shows up and asks to snag Lysa and me for what she calls a face-to-face.

"Where's the other one?" Detective Sydney asks.

"Spam? She left early. Why?" I ask.

"Because I know you three and it's best to nail you down all at once," she says.

Lysa and I exchange worried looks.

Detective Sydney digs in her purse and comes up with the envelope containing Lysa's phone. She hands it to her. "You can have this back now."

Lysa brightens. "Oh. Thank you." She pauses. "Was every-thing . . ."

"Settled?" Detective Sydney asks. "I wouldn't say that. You might still hear from the driver about the mirror on your case. But, for now anyway, we've decided the skateboarder incident is no longer a police matter. You girls just need to continue to mind your own business and you'll be fine."

We thank Detective Sydney for her advice and breathe a sigh of relief. Rachel always says timing is everything. And now Spam's free to pursue a guilt-free relationship with her knight in shining plaid.

Meanwhile, Coach Wilkins is having a meltdown on his side of the camp sign-up booth. Victor has announced that our camp is overfull and is taking names for a waiting list.

Apparently, Coach Wilkins only has twenty sign-ups.

I get him being upset . . . kind of.

But he looks foolish over there balling up his brochures, throwing them on the ground, and stamping on them.

I've got to hand it to Victor. The guy has class. He's willing to wade straight into the middle of Coach Wilkins's meltdown by pretending to rap a song about cool camp. The rap is horri-ble, but Victor is great because his little show takes the pressure off the football players and cheerleaders helplessly watching the coach blow up. Pretty soon, everybody is clapping and stomping along with Victor and Coach Wilkins has worn him-self out.

Miss P would have done something similar, to diffuse the situation. It wouldn't have been a goofy rap, but she would've done something.

► 26 ◄

Being a hostile witness doesn't necessarily indicate guilt, but you have to wonder why someone would be reluctant to discuss what they saw or agree to tell the truth.

—VICTOR FLEMMING

CSI camp registration was a success. Victor allowed us to sign up ten more campers than he planned, plus the waiting list. This means he has the budget to hire Spam as a part-time counselor too. She's beyond thrilled.

All we have left is finals week and Journey's graduation. Then one week of intense setup before camp begins.

Victor and Journey are working on finishing the lab, including the security and safety features. This means when Journey's not studying for finals or reading trial transcripts, he's off running around with Victor.

With all this Journey-free time, Spam, Lysa, and I have started meeting after school at the library. I'm keeping a three-ring binder of the camp activities we've come up with. Lysa is keeping a notebook that tracks the details of Jameson's case as they come to us. Coach Wilkins's public meltdown was added to the list. And Spam's keeping track of Bella sales—we've delivered thirty so far, and have orders for fifty more.

"Victor is expecting us to turn in our list of activities today," I say. "So here's where we stand: Week one, analyzing the crime scene, is done. Week two, hair, fingerprints, and impressions, done. Week three, blood, done."

Lysa cheers after each, but Spam is buried in her phone.

"Week four, ballistics testing. That's mine. It's almost done but I need a few more facts. I knew nothing about guns before I started this."

"You should have asked Coach Wilkins," Lysa says.

I chuckle and Lysa nudges Spam. "You're not even listening."

Spam doesn't look up, she simply waves her hand. "I'll do it tonight."

Lysa and I exchange a *cuckoo* look.

"Spam?" I say.

"What?" She looks up.

"Who are you Snapchatting with?" Lysa asks.

Spam gives us her silly, crooked smile. "No one."

But the way she tosses her hair to the side is a definite clue. "It's Lyman, isn't it?"

She suddenly drips innocence. "Who?"

"Yeah. Right," I say.

"Okay." She drops the façade. "I've been seeing him."

"You mean dating?" Lysa says.

I gasp. "I thought you were going to set up a meeting with us so we could find out what all the secrecy was about."

Spam shrugs. "I didn't think you still needed to do that since Detective Sydney said he was clear. And we're not exactly dating, we're playing games together."

"He comes to your house?" I say.

She gives me the well-worn Spam look of scorn. "Have I taught you nothing about technology? We hang out on Ventrilo while we're playing, which means we can talk privately to each other."

Lysa and I share an eye roll. Only Spam would consider this *seeing* somebody.

"Well," Lysa says politely. "Tell us about him?"

I'm more direct. "What's the big mystery? Did he ever talk to the police? Why did he give you his video and not the police? Did he just move here? Will he be coming to our school?"

"Wow. Slow down, Johnnie Cochran," Spam says. "His mom works nights at the hospital. He didn't tell her about the almost-accident because he says she's super overprotective and would have freaked out."

"I know how that is." I flash them my phone with six text messages. "These are all from Rachel in just the last ten minutes." I pause to text back a reply: E ER THING S GRE T R   H I H   RE   N S H NGING O T WITH S

"Anyway," Spam says. "He said by the time he learned that the driver of the car was claiming *he* was responsible for the accident, he was too scared to tell anyone but us."

"I don't blame him," Lysa says. "I'm still not sure I'm not going to get blamed for having a mirror on the back of my phone case. My father said there doesn't have to be a police investigation for that to happen."

"But is he coming to our school?" I ask.

"No," Spam says. "He homeschools."

I shudder. "Ugh. I'd hate that. The best part of school is friends."

Lysa shrugs. "It can be the best of times and the worst of times, but in theory I agree with you."

"He says he likes it," Spam says. "But he's looking forward to camp. He says summer camps are how homeschoolers learn to socialize. I told him he'd get to meet all of you." Spam starts packing up her stuff. "Anyway, I have to go. I have to get ready for our date tonight."

"Whoa," Lysa says. "It's Friday night. I thought we had plans."

"Calm down, I'm not ditching you," Spam says. "Lyman and I are getting together after. But I have to download some software and upgrade my system before I can go out with you."

"That late?" Lysa says. "And your dad's okay with that?"

Spam shakes her head. "Date. Game. His house. My house. What don't you guys get about this?"

"It must be a lot," Lysa says, switching her attention to me. "What are you and Journey doing tonight?"

"No clue. Between working for Victor and studying for finals I've hardly seen him this week. He is giving me a ride home today, though, so hopefully we'll come up with something." As I say this I spot Journey striding toward us . . . and he's carrying a bouquet of flowers.

▼ ▼ ▼

Journey asked me on a proper date.

It's our first proper date since the prom. And the prom was our first proper date ever.

That makes tonight date two.

He's taking me to dinner at a fancy Italian restaurant. I enlisted Rachel's help with what to wear and she showed up with a new little flowered sundress that looks amazing.

While she's helping me with the curling iron on the back of my hair I notice she's not wearing her engagement ring.

"Rachel, your ring?"

She looks at her hand and shrugs a little. "I gave it back."

"What? Why?"

She shakes her head and I can't believe it. The famous, unmovable Rachel fog of sadness is back. How did I not notice this?

"I love Charles," she says. "I truly do. But things started moving too fast."

"Too fast for you?"

"Yes." But she pauses before she says it and I know.

"No. Rachel. No. You can't make that decision because of me. You can't not do this."

"Erin, Charles and I will still get married . . . someday." She sits down on the bed next to me. "I have loved that man since high school. Which is why we're not in any hurry."

"Oh my god, Rachel. You broke up with him because of me."

"Now, that's not true," she exclaims. "We didn't break up. We're just not charging headlong into a wedding." She swipes some hair off my face. "I have a bright star to launch first."

I tear up and move to give her a hug.

She tears up too, but stops me. "Don't. You'll mess up your makeup. Just go and have the time of your life with that handsome boy. That will make me happy. We can talk more about this later."

Victor calls from downstairs. "Erin. Journey's here."

I race downstairs to be greeted with even more flowers, and Journey, wearing a suit.

"You are the most handsome guy on the planet," I say.

"Okay, got the hint," Victor says. "I'll just go out back and eat worms."

Out in the driveway there's another surprise. A decent car.

"It's no big deal, it's my mom's," he says.

"Trust me. Compared to the beast, this is as grand as Cinderella's coach."

At the restaurant, Journey has made reservations for the

chef's table, which is inside the kitchen. All night long, the chefs come to our table with little tastes of this meatball and a bit of that pasta. Italian sodas in all flavors and garlic bread to die for.

We are having absolutely the best time.

Until I slip off to the bathroom.

As I'm heading back to our grand table, I see two diners that I never expected to see together.

Arletta Stone and Blankface are here, in this restaurant, having dinner together.

I pat my dress. No pockets means no phone. But I have to get a photo of this.

I hurry back to the table and pick up my purse, heading back to the bathroom.

"Is everything okay?" Journey asks.

"Oh yeah," I say. "I just need to—"

One of the chefs dances up before I can finish, singing Italian opera directly to me. My cheeks flame. I wait until he's finished, but then I hurry back to the dining room.

They're done with their meal. Arletta pushes the check to Blankface, who pushes it right back to Arletta. They're too absorbed with haggling over the check to notice me.

I quickly snap the photo and head back to the table.

It's been a great night and I'm still ecstatically happy with Journey. But seeing those two together has popped up a sinister scorpion tail of worry. When I get a chance I'll send this to Spam and Lysa.

"How's Jameson's case? Is it okay to call him Jameson? I love that name and always saying *your father* sounds weird." I'm babbling, a sign of scattered thinking. Fortunately, Journey doesn't seem to notice.

"Of course," Journey says. "Victor's been consumed with the

camp and lab. He says we'll have more time to work on the case in a week or so."

"Have you come up with any other suspects?"

Journey shakes his head. "It's been fourteen years. So, the chance that someone would set my father up, see him go to prison, and then stick around for fourteen years is slim."

I nod. "Yes. I bet that would be pretty rare."

► **27** ◄

Whether you are a victim or only a witness, the stress of the crime
can distort your memory of what happened.
—VICTOR FLEMMING

Finding out that Rachel put her wedding on hold makes me
want to spend more time with her. She needs to know that
even though I was shocked by the news, I'm okay with her having a life. In fact, I want her to have everything she missed
because of me.

I offered to cut my hours back at the camp to part time so
Rachel and I could have some special time. But she won't hear
of it. So it's full steam ahead with Camp CSI summer. Rachel
and I pledge to schedule dinner once a week, just the two of us.

Since camp starts in one week, our assignment for today is
to pack up Miss P's classroom and set it up in the new space.
It's Spam's turn to drive, and Lysa's already in the backseat by
the time I get downstairs.

"I thought you were bringing Lyman so we could meet him."
I climb into the passenger seat.

"He might show up later." Spam makes a wishy-washy wave
with her hand as she backs out of the driveway and heads
toward our local coffee stop. "I'll explain while we're waiting
for our coffee," she says.

"Okay." I pull down the visor to check my hair in the mirror and catch Lysa's worried expression. It's not like Spam to be mysterious or to hold back commentary for a better discussion time.

She parks, and all three of us get out. My curiosity is gnawing at me. "Tell us about him. It sounds like you and Lyman have been hanging out a lot."

"He's really cool. I can't wait for you to meet him." Spam holds the door open. "He'll probably show up at some point. He just wasn't sure if he could get out."

"You make it sound like he lives in lockdown," Lysa says.

"I told you, he's got a wacko hover parent—he has to check in a lot. She wants to know where he's going and who he's going with. Even who he's talking to online. Aggh. He said if we continue to see each other I'll have to meet her."

"What's wrong with that?" Lysa says.

Spam rolls her eyes. "Oh, please. It's annoying. We're practically adults. Who has time for that?" She looks from me to Lysa and back again. Realizing no sympathy is coming, she says, "Seriously?"

I order the drinks for the three of us.

"You make her sound so nosy and intrusive." Lysa laughs.

"Exactly," Spam says.

"In my house that's called parents," Lysa says.

"Mine too. You know Rachel is the hover queen. It's just we've all been friends for so long that no one questions us hanging out together anymore. Didn't you say Lyman just moved here?"

"I don't know how long he's been here," Spam says. "I'm just used to my dad being semi-clueless about what goes on in my life, but maybe that's because he's got the littles he has to keep up with."

"Your dad is amazing," I say. "Trust me, getting Rachel to let me date Journey wasn't easy."

"See, that's what's funny." Spam laughs. "My dad thinks I should be dating. He gets ecstatic when I tell him I'm going to interact with actual people and not just spend the night screaming bad words at game avatars."

We exit the shop with our coffees and discover Lyman leaning against the hood of Spam's car with a skateboard tucked under his arm. His smile radiates happiness.

"You? Screaming bad words at game avatars?" he teases. "I'm trying to picture that."

She literally dances over the walkway and presses her coffee into his hand. "Here. Share. It's an Americano."

She pecks him on the cheek, giving Lysa and me reason for yet another shared look of surprise. Apparently, Spam and Lyman have had some in-person time, too.

"These are my friends." Spam gestures to us. "Friends, this is Lyman."

Lysa and I make silly faces . . . because that's what we do.

Spam just waves us off. "Don't mind them. They're insane. Are you coming with us?"

He gives her a soft look. "I want to . . . but I have some stuff to do today." He hands her back her coffee and looks like he's about to give her a kiss but stops and glances over at us. Instead he goes in for the hug. "I'll come tomorrow." Then he heads off across the parking lot. When he reaches the sidewalk, he drops his skateboard, hops on, and rides off. "See ya," he calls back.

"Not if I see you first." She's joking but stands frozen in place, eyes never wavering, until he's gone from view. With a sigh, she gets back into the car.

I don't want to tease, but for Spam, this is momentous. "You really like him, don't you?"

From the backseat, Lysa worries. "How do we know he's safe? He didn't come forward after the accident. He could be a crazed serial killer, or worse."

Spam scowls. "Oh my god. You always say that. You saw him. He's like a kitten with Bambi eyes and the soul of a puppy. He's smart and deep and sketchy all at the same time."

Lysa nudges my arm from the backseat. "We used to think sketchy meant not good."

"I don't mean sketchy like creepy," Spam says. "I just mean that his facts are sometimes fluid."

"What do you mean by *facts* and *fluid*?" I ask.

"I think they change sometimes. He'll say things, like where he's lived or things he's done, then later I think he says different things. But maybe it's because we're also playing games while we're talking." She backs out of the parking place and prepares to make a right turn onto the street to take us to school.

"So is this a boyfriend thing?" I ask.

"Maybe," she says. "I hope it is. We spend a lot of time together online. And made it through that phase where we've told each other our life stories and still want to hang out. You know how that is."

"Wait," Lysa says. "It's only been two weeks. You can't have spent that much time together."

Spam gives us an exasperated look. "Dude, we hang out online every night and have since before Memorial Day. I just didn't know the guy I was hanging out with was the skateboarder until *after* Memorial Day."

Lysa pinches her lips to the side, a sign she doesn't believe Spam's story. I take a direct approach. "But that's still only been a few weeks," I say.

Spam rolls her head dreamily. "Yeah, but hanging out online

is more intense and personal. There are almost no distractions, it's just him and me. My voice, his voice. You get to know someone much quicker that way. And it's a deeper kind of know. You know?"

Lysa and I clearly don't get this. "No!"

Spam waves us off. She pulls into the empty school parking lot and is presented with her choice of parking spaces since summer classes haven't started yet. Typical Spam, she swings her PT Cruiser straight into the first space.

The one assigned to Principal Blankface.

She shuts off the engine and hops out. But Lysa and I stay put.

"Spam," we both yell at the same time. We refuse to get out of the car.

"What? School's out. She's not even supposed to be here," Spam says.

"That's not the point," Lysa argues. "Besides, I'm sure she'll be here prepping for summer school, which also starts next week."

"What's the big deal? All these other spaces aren't going to fill up. If she shows I'll move," Spam argues.

"Except that the actual reason to have a reserved parking space is so that it's always available and you don't have to track down the scofflaw who parked there and make them move," Lysa says.

"Really? That's what that's for?" Spam asks, adding an extra-wide blink. "I never would have guessed. And, by the way, I've been called a lot of things but never a scofflaw. You're reaching for that one, Lysa."

"If the shoe fits—" Lysa snaps.

I need to get between these two on this or we won't get anything done all day. "C'mon, Spam. Antagonizing the principal will only get us on her bad side. And it could screw things up with the camp. Don't forget, we're on probation."

"You believe that woman has a good side?" Spam flops back into the driver's seat, starts the car, and moves it over one space. She hops out again. "Happy now?"

Personally, I'd rather we stayed farther away from Blankenship's radar by parking where she wouldn't even notice. But I'm not ready to take this up with Spam now.

Before we head up to Miss P's old classroom, we decide to swing through the basement to check out the progress.

The viewing window between the classroom and lab has been installed. And the glass enclosure for the lab is nearly complete. Standing up next to the window between the classroom and the lab, I'm close enough to the work area that I can read the measurements on the beakers. I can see the numbers on the gram scale. "Wow. This is a ringside seat to everything that goes on in there." I'm in awe.

The storage room door opens and the contractor, Clay, sticks his head out.

"Hey, girls." He's holding a paintbrush in one hand and wearing a white disposable fume mask over his face and nose.

"Hi," Lysa says.

He pushes the mask up onto his head. "If you're looking for the boss man, he was here to let me in but I haven't seen him in a couple of hours."

"That's okay," I say. "We know what we're supposed to do. We're going to pack up the other classroom and move that stuff down here."

"Oh. Okay," Clay says. "No problem then. I'll be here most of the day too. I'm just working through my list on the board." He nods toward the glass partition and now I notice Victor's to-do list written in dry-erase marker.

"How long will it take for the paint to dry? Because some of the stuff we're moving is supposed to go in there."

"It won't take long," Clay says. "I'll prop the door open to give it more air and hurry it along."

"Thanks," I say.

Spam checks out the reinforced steel mesh security grid that separates the classroom from the crime lab. She laces her fingers through the metal grate. "Which of us is in the cage, them or us?" she jokes. Catching sight of my scowl, she adds soft monkey sounds. "We'll just say it's them. How's that?"

"Honestly, I don't even care about the lab anymore," I say. "Because the camp is going to freakin' rock." I am looking forward to the camp, but it doesn't hurt to ramp it up a little.

"I hope you kids know how lucky you are." Clay comes out with a bucket of paint and the brush. "If I had had a class like this when I was in high school, I might have made it to college."

We smile and thank him. He's not wrong.

We are lucky . . . and we know it.

► 28 ◄

Forensic evidence reveals more than you think. For example, a
footprint isn't just the re-creation of the bottom of a shoe.
Science teaches us that the length of the foot is roughly
fifteen percent of a person's height, which means
a shoe print can also indicate size.

—VICTOR FLEMMING

Our footsteps echo in the empty hall as we approach room 304,
Miss Peters's science classroom and lab.

We're here to dismantle the last memories of her.

My chest is tight. I didn't anticipate this, but suddenly I'm
expecting everything she ever touched to look like the last time
I saw her. Splashed with blood. Broken. Dead.

Instead, her room looks exactly the same.

And as grateful as I am for that, it's equally unnerving.

There's a large stack of boxes and packing material waiting
for us, along with a note from the Facilities Department to give
them a call when everything is ready to go.

"I've got the computers," Spam says.

"I'll tackle all of the glass beakers, test tubes, and delicate
lab equipment," Lysa offers.

I shrug. "Okay. That puts me on Miss P's desk."

Her grades, class records, and privileged information have
already been transferred to the office, along with anything
valuable or personal. But that doesn't mean that what remains

in and around Laura Peters's desk is devoid of her personality. The drawers are full of handouts featuring her spidery scrawl along the margins. I gather a fistful of half-chewed pencils that she used to stick into a twist of curly blond hair to hold it in place, even though wispy curls always escaped in all directions. I even find a small, shriveled pile of orange peels, wrapped in a napkin and stuffed in her center drawer. I press a few of them to my nose and inhale the concentrated citrus scent. Finding these things warms my insides and makes me happy.

Until I stumble over the liquor globe.

We all remember Miss P's liquor globe. It's about the size of a basketball, but hinged in the middle, allowing the top part to flip open. It's typically used to store liquor, but this was her stash place that she kept stocked with stubby pencils and extra reading glasses. There were also lollipops and fruit, generally apples or oranges, for handing out to hungry students in need of a reward.

This silly globe reminds me of her more than just about any other thing I'm likely to find in this room or anywhere else. I sink to the floor and curve my body around it. Suddenly, it's like I'm two years old all over again. It hurts that she's gone, and even though I'm going on seventeen now, I don't understand any of this.

There aren't enough orange peels in the universe to fill this bottomless pit of empty.

Spam and Lysa quietly join me on the floor, one on either side.

"Look." My voice is raw with emotion.

The three of us place our hands on the globe at the same time.

"What are we going to do with it?" Lysa asks.

"We're keeping it," I announce. "Victor said we could set up a tribute to Miss P in the new classroom. So this will be our tribute."

"I love Victor," Spam says with amazement.

"How will the globe become a tribute?" Lysa wonders.

"Think time capsule," I say. "We'll gather up all the stuff in here that isn't about teaching. Like this stuff." I stand up and start removing photos from her bulletin board. Some are memes, but others are photos of Miss P with people we don't know. Whoever packed up her other personal items managed to overlook these.

I open the liquor globe and carefully slide the photos into one of the compartments. "We can add other stuff, too, from home. Things that remind us of her. Everything will stay inside, but we can take them out and look at them when we're really missing her."

"That's a great idea," Lysa says. "I have things to bring in."

"Me too." Knowing we have a plan for Miss P's tribute brightens up the rest of our task. "What's left?"

"The computers are ready," Spam says. "I updated all the software, cleaned the cache, and labeled and coded all the cords."

"The lab is mostly packed too," Lysa says. "I've done the supply cabinet and most of the beakers and test tubes. Two more boxes should cover it."

"We'll help you," I say. "On our way out to lunch we can stop by facilities and tell them everything's ready to move."

After we finish packing the lab, I put the liquor globe and the treasures I gathered from Miss P's desk into a box and carry them with me. It just feels wrong to leave this stuff behind now that this room has been stripped of everything she put into it.

We head for Battery Burger, our favorite restaurant at the mall, and manage to score a table out on the patio. Miss P's liquor globe gets a prominent seat at the table.

Brianna and her friends stroll by. They stop and gasp. "Is that Miss P's globe?" Brianna says. When we nod, she places her hands on it. "We miss you, Miss P."

This attracts some attention, and at least ten other kids from school trickle over and place their hands on the globe in tribute to Miss P.

The globe is becoming an actual memorial.

▼ ▼ ▼

When we arrive back at school after lunch, Principal Blankface's car is in her parking space and Journey's van is parked a few spaces away.

We enter the classroom to find Journey and Clay talking.

"Hey, Erin." Journey breaks into a smile. "Clay didn't know we were the kids from the news."

"I had no idea I was hanging out with celebrities," he says.

I smile. "It wasn't *that* big of a deal."

"Your old principal might disagree," Clay says. "Now that he's cooling his heels in the slammer."

"Anyway, Victor will be back this afternoon to go over the locks and other safety stuff. Be prepared," Journey says. "He's going to be intense because we can't get the permit to open the camp without those two things."

"No problem, Chief." Clay adds a brisk salute. "I'm here all day, every day until this is done to his specifications." Then he turns to us. "I left a little something for you ladies, too, over on that desk."

Laid out on the desk are three of the paper fume masks. But he's drawn cute animal noses on them.

"The fumes are still pretty heavy in the storage room. So you should wear these if you're going to be in there today." Clay hands one that looks like a cat to Lysa, and another that looks like a sweet puppy to Spam. The last one, with the sharp black nose, he gives to me. "I figured you for a fox because you're the sly, crafty one. Right?"

I laugh and pull the fume mask over my face. "I don't know about that."

"They're cute," Lysa says.

Clay shrugs. "I'm a sucker for animals."

Journey carefully secures the door between the lab and the class with a padlock.

Spam bounds over to him. "Hey. Hold up. We want a look-see in there before you go." She glances back and gives me an exaggerated wink.

"Can't do that, Spam." Journey gives her a firm look.

"No one'll know." She looks around at all of us, including Clay. "Okay. We'll know but we won't say anything. Right, guys? What happens at camp, stays at camp."

"Spam." Journey's voice takes on a warning tone.

"There's not even any evidence in there yet. Is there?" She gives Journey her best one-raised-eyebrow look and then tries to cajole him with an adorable pout. It's not working, and I could've told her it wouldn't. He snaps the padlock closed and, just like a good warden, tugs to make sure it's locked.

He shuffles up to me and slides his arm around my waist while depositing a peck on the top of my head. "Don't be mad," he says.

"I'm not mad." I raise my hands in the air. And I really mean it. I'm cool with it now.

"And don't ask me to let you in." He leans around me,

addressing both Spam and Lysa. "Because I can't and you *all* know why."

Lysa waves. "I got you."

"I got you too," I say.

"They got you." Spam moves away from the door. "But, for the record, I could pick that lock in five seconds. It's pretty wimpy. Just saying."

Journey starts to protest. I press my fingers over his lips. "Don't worry, she won't do that. We won't do anything to get you—or any of us—in trouble with Victor. And we'll never jeopardize your father's case. I promise."

► 29 ◄

The science of ballistics is as detailed and sophisticated as
the study of fingerprints. Maybe even more so.
—ERIN BLAKE

There's a display cabinet behind the teacher's desk and Miss P's
liquor globe will look perfect here. The three of us are quietly
working, but I can tell I'm not the only one struggling with the
empty spot Miss P left behind.

Science was Spam's least favorite class, and yet I'm watching
her unpacking the microscopes and lining them up in the
cabinet with an attention to detail that would have delighted
Miss P.

Meanwhile, Lysa is finding a place for all the stuff that came
from her desk.

When she's finished unpacking the microscopes, Spam
angles her arm around my neck and gives me a rough hug. "I
need to take off," she says. "I have a delivery and setup for my
father. Do you need a ride?"

"Let me check with Victor." I pull out my phone to send a
text. But instead of bars of cellular dominance I have a dis-
appointing red circle with a slash through it. "Wait, no cell
service?"

Spam gasps, horrified. "That can't be right." She whips her

cell phone out of her back pocket and checks the screen. "I have one bar. Nope, gone. Seriously?"

Lysa's already gazing at hers. "Yep. Looks that way."

Clay pops his head out of the storage room and points with his paintbrush. "There's a phone on the wall by the door. You can use that."

I wander over and pick up the receiver on the wall phone. I regard it curiously. It's so big and bulky. "When did they start doing this?"

Clay laughs. "You're kidding, right?"

I give him a blank look.

"You've never noticed there are phones in all of your classrooms?" he asks. "It's a required safety feature."

I dangle my cell phone. "Why would I need to notice something like that?"

Clay shakes his head. "You kids." He closes the door to the storage room and goes back to his painting.

"So call him," Spam says.

It's completely awkward to have to look up Victor's number on one phone and then dial it into another. But at least it's ringing.

After a few seconds, Victor answers. "Yeah?"

"Hey, it's me. Um, Erin." In case he doesn't recognize my voice. "Are you coming back to the school and can you give me a ride home?"

He tells me he's on his way back. I nod and wave to Lysa and Spam. "He's coming. You guys can go."

After I hang up with Victor, Clay comes out of the storage room. "I'm going to wash out these paintbrushes. The storage room is done. I moved a few things so I wouldn't get paint on them. But the only part that might still be wet is the ceiling."

"Okay." Once he leaves, I duck into the storage room to see what needs to be moved back. There are a few boxes of supplies on the floor that belong on the top shelf. I'm tall enough to slide them into place without even using the stepladder.

At first, when I hear voices from the other room I think maybe Spam and Lysa have come back. But it turns out it's Coach Wilkins and his cousin, Arletta Stone. They're peering into the lab through the steel mesh grate. Arletta has her cellphone out and is even taking photos.

"Can I help you?" I step out into the classroom.

"Oh hi, Erin," Coach says. "I was just showing my cousin the new lab."

Something feels off about this. "You should come back when Victor's here," I say. "He'll probably give you a full tour." Or maybe he'll tell them to mind their own business, which is what I'm really thinking.

"We'll do that," Coach says. He tugs on his cousin's arm. "C'mon. We should go."

She drops her phone into her purse and starts to follow him out the door but she pauses in front of me. "It's so exciting that we have one of those labs here in our city now. I'm just crazy about those forensic shows and how they catch people. Aren't you?"

I nod. "Yep. Big fan." I refuse to get too chatty, hoping they'll just leave.

As they're passing through the door, Clay comes back. He notices my wary stance. "What's wrong?" he asks. "Did they do something?"

I shake my head. "No. But I don't think they're supposed to just be lurking around when Victor's not here."

Clay raises his eyebrows. "The guy's been here nearly every day. But he's a teacher, right?"

I shrug. "He's the coach, so yeah. But you ought to let Victor know that he's been hanging around."

"Thanks for the tip," Clay says. "I'll keep an eye on things like that. Anyone else I should look out for?"

I shrug. "The principal, maybe."

"She's been here too. Not as often. She says she's checking on the construction."

I pinch my lips together, not sure what to say.

Clay nods. "Got it. I'll mention both of them to the boss." He turns his attention to hanging some bulletin boards, and I take a seat at the teacher's desk and turn on the computer that Spam set up. I initiate a search for ballistics.

We've turned in our activities for the camp to Victor, but I still have a few facts about ballistics to flesh out.

"This is so amazing," I mutter, while jotting down a few notes.

"What's that?" Clay asks.

"This stuff I'm researching. Like even the slightest remnant of a gunshot can be traced to a specific firearm, where it was sold, and the owner." I look up at Clay. "How do they even do that?"

"Beats me," Clay says with a shrug. "But I guess you're going to find out, huh?"

"I guess so."

Looking up stuff about guns reminds me of Jameson's case. I run back through the facts again. It was his shotgun. They know that. They know where it came from. They even know that it had been handled and loaded by him at some time in the past. What types of evidence could possibly prove that someone else loaded that gun and swapped it with the paintball gun that night?

An eyewitness. Except there wasn't one.

I consider fingerprints and even shoe prints, since those helped me build the case against Principal Roberts.

Have they added anything to the murder board?

I go to the window and peer into the lab. The angle of the murder board makes it a little hard to see from here. But I try anyway.

"They haven't done anything in there in a couple of days," Clay says. "They've been too busy."

"Yeah. They have been crazy busy."

Based on Victor and Journey's workload, I decide it's okay for me to research the evidence in Jameson's trial. Lysa's right. Researching is just reading, and it's all public record.

Except that everything I read leads to more questions.

Police didn't find any unused ammunition on the premises. But they collected a handful of spent brass shells. What happened to the paintball gun and paint balls? Also how did a shotgun with no ammunition kill an innocent kid?

It started with the ammunition so I wonder if there's a way to track the purchase of that stuff. I'm sure I've seen them do this on TV. A cursory check tells me tracking a large order might be possible, but no one is keeping records on a random box of shotgun shells. That's simply not a thing.

About that time, Victor comes flying in the door. He's juggling a shopping bag in one hand and his cell phone against his ear with the other.

"Hello . . . hello?" he says. "Did I lose you?" He drops the bag on one of the desks and heads back toward the door. "If you're still there, I can't hear you so I'm hanging up."

He hangs up the phone and looks at me.

"No cell service," I say.

"Exactly," he says. "And I absolutely love that about this

space. It forces me off the phone with people I didn't want to talk to in the first place."

"Is that about the—you know—" I ask.

"Yes," he confirms. "And I told you, that's for me to worry about and you to forget."

I surrender. Hands up, palms out. Whatever.

"Is the contractor still here?" he asks.

Clay sticks his head out of the storage room. "Yep. Just wrapping up. Journey said you wanted to talk about door locks. If you tell me how many you need I can pick them up at the hardware store."

Victor unpacks the items from the shopping bag. "I've got them right here. We're putting biometric locks on every door." He points to all the different areas. "Exterior doors, both sides. The door between the classroom and the lab. The door to the storage closet. And then this silver one here is for the evidence locker because it works differently."

Clay lays out the boxes. He pencils O ER on the silver box. "Biometric, huh?"

"That's right. Your key is your—" Victor holds up his finger.

"I'm familiar with it." Clay raises his eyebrows. "You don't usually see James Bond technology in the schools, though."

"Biometrics are becoming quite common," Victor says. "Heck, the kids even use it to unlock their cell phones these days. It's the same principle."

"What happens if it doesn't work?" Clay wonders. "Like if there's a power failure or something? Don't you need a fail-safe plan?"

"The locks for the doors have a safety release. If the power goes out, they automatically unlock. The one for the locker works in reverse. If the power goes out it seals it in the closed position. For anything else, a master key will be kept in the safe in the school office. And probably one at the police department, too. But you don't have to worry about that. I just need you to do the installation so we can get rid of the clunky padlock. And then we need to discuss the safety equipment."

Clay examines the parts of the lock that Victor has presented to him.

"I'll get these in tomorrow," he says. "Then we can go over the safety stuff."

"Sounds good." Victor and Clay shake hands.

This gets more exciting by the day. The new classroom and lab are already high tech. But biometric locks are supercool.

"It's good that you're putting in the locks," I say. "Because people have been snooping down here."

"Snooping?" Victor says. "Who?"

"The coach and his cousin were down here today." I give Victor a studied look.

Victor shrugs. "Yeah. Wilkins is all wound up about this. Thinks it's really cool. Wants to be my new best friend or something."

I make eye contact with Clay and nod toward Victor.

Clay clears his throat. "Yeah. The principal has made a few trips down here too. Says she's checking on the construction."

Victor shrugs again. "That's okay. She's just doing her job. Anyone else, though, needs my permission to be in here. Got it?" Victor looks from me to Clay.

We both nod. "Got it," Clay says.

I shoot Victor the thumbs-up.

▶ 30 ◀

Never before in our long, legal history has science played
a role this important in the protection and
enforcement of our laws.

—VICTOR FLEMMING

On the drive home, Victor's abnormally motormouth and can't shut up.

"A shipment is arriving around ten tomorrow. If I'm not there, you can sign for it. It'll be supplies and stuff for both the camp and the classroom. You guys can unpack it and arrange it in the storage room. Oh, and we need to start setting up the evidence locker, too. I've requested the evidence from Jameson's case. That's coming sometime this week."

This sounds promising.

"You need us to help with the evidence locker?"

Victor glances over. "No. Sorry. That's on Journey's to-do list because, you know—"

"Yeah. I know," I say, adding a sigh, which he completely ignores.

"Good." He starts up again. "If Clay gets the locks installed tomorrow, we'll need to create the biometric files. Can you round up all your friends to be there at the same time? Then I can do the basic files all at once. Is that possible?"

"Yes. I think so."

"Sorry if I'm running through this fast," he says. "This thing with the job is giving me a rash."

My head snaps around. "I thought you said it was fine?"

"And it is," he says. "It's fine. They just want a bunch of answers to all of their questions and I have ten other fires burning to get ready for this camp. I don't have time to deal with them right now."

Victor continues to talk and plan all the way into the driveway and even as we climb the stairs together. I already heard from Rachel that she has a meeting after work and won't be home for dinner, so I'm planning to make lasagna and salad for Victor and me.

He dumps his briefcase and stuff on the kitchen table . . . which is still piled with his work folders and papers from last night.

I silently contemplate the mess on the table.

My room was always kind of a disaster, but Rachel and I had an understanding about leaving our stuff lying around the rest of the house. Neither of us do it. But I don't want to say anything. Victor charges up to his room and I start working on the lasagna. Hopefully, by the time I get out the plates for dinner, he'll realize we need a place to eat.

He charges down the stairs, dressed in a pair of sweats, and bounds out the back door. I'm thinking he's going down to shoot some hoops. Instead he returns a few minutes later, lugging a very large box that's at least five feet tall and three feet wide.

"Guess what I bought today?"

"No clue," I say, eyeing the box.

"An actual desk," he says. "So I can get all my junk off the table."

"Good one. Where are you going to put it?"

"I haven't talked to Rachel yet. But I was thinking of setting it up in a corner of the dining room."

I shrug. "We don't use that room anyway."

"That's what I was thinking," he says. "Want to help me?"

"As soon as I get this into the oven."

Helping Victor assemble the desk reminds me of all the things that I've loved about him from the very beginning. He's funny and smart and we can just hang out for hours with each other. We're just easy like that.

I read the instructions and hand him the parts and he does the assembly stuff.

In no time, an actual desk appears before us.

"Impressive," I say.

"Any parts left over?" Victor asks.

"Nope."

"Then we must've done it right," he says. "Now to find the perfect spot."

We first move the desk into the corner, on the shared wall between the kitchen and the dining room. But Victor thinks that's too dark. Then we try it on the exterior wall below the window that looks out over the driveway. Victor even turns around a chair and sits down, trying it out. But in the end, he doesn't like that placement, either.

"I'm used to sitting at a desk that faces out, not facing a wall," he says.

I stand back and survey the area.

"We could take the leaves out of the table, which will make it smaller. Then it will fit against the wall to the kitchen." I stand in the middle, gesturing like one of those guys on an airport runway. "That way your desk would fit in the middle . . ."

"And the credenza could go behind it. Perfect. Grab an end," Victor says.

We move the furniture around, positioning each piece, until the room looks a lot more like an office than a dining room. There's even a space where the credenza used to be that perfectly fits a couple of chairs and a small table, in case Victor has visitors.

He scoops up the large pile of mail that had been stacked on the credenza and dumps it in the middle of his desk. Then he goes to the kitchen table and scoops up all of the papers, bringing them to the desk too. "I will take care of all of this tonight," he says. Then he pauses and gives me one of his high-eyebrow, tilted-head, "wait for it" looks. He burrows his fingers deep into the stack and pulls out a FedEx envelope and frames it between his hands. Actually, it's *the* FedEx envelope.

"This is it. Unopened." He shows me both sides. Then he opens the center drawer and places the FedEx envelope inside. "Let's agree that we will put this in here."

I nod. "Agreed."

We high-five and even do the basketball shoulder slam to seal the deal. When we're done celebrating we turn to see Rachel standing in the doorway.

Her face is blank and her eyebrows are peaked.

I know this look.

I can't say she's mad, exactly. But she's not happy, either.

Victor sees her and lights up. "Hey, sis. Look, I'm cleaning up all of my crap."

"I can see that." She blinks a few times and I can tell she's carefully choosing her words.

"I hope you don't mind if I set things up in here," Victor asks. "Obviously, once school starts I'll be able to move more of this stuff to my classroom. But in the meantime, like Erin says, you hardly use this room."

"Thanksgiving," Rachel says. "We use the dining room on

Thanksgiving." It's subtle, but Rachel crosses her arms over her chest. It's her personal barricade.

Victor shrugs a little self-consciously. "Noted. That's still some months away. But I will make sure the dining room is available by Thanksgiving." He suddenly wilts a little, as if he realizes he might have overstepped bounds. "Listen, if you'd rather, I can move it all upstairs now. There's room and it's not a bother." He gestures broadly. "I was just really enjoying hanging out in the family space."

"No," she says. "It's fine. Really. It just took me by surprise is all." Now she turns her gaze on me. "I was curious to see what you were up to, though. You guys sounded like you were having so much fun. I could hear you all the way outside."

Hmm. So that's the other part of it. Rachel heard Victor and I yukking it up. As much as I love Rachel, that's not something that she and I do.

"I thought you were going to be late tonight?" I ask.

"I was," she says. "But the meeting ended early, so I thought I'd come home and see what you two were up to."

"I made lasagna for dinner," I say.

She pulls me into a hug that is about so much more than dinner. "I was thinking maybe we could go out. Just the two of us. Like old times."

▼ ▼ ▼

Rachel and I leave Victor with a timer set for when the lasagna should come out of the oven and we head off to our favorite neighborhood fish restaurant. I always order the fish and chips and Rachel always orders the grilled salmon.

We chatter casually about work and school, finals, and the camp. The chief and Journey.

"Victor told me you two talked."

I freeze. Is she referring to the Schrödinger cat, FedEx envelope talk or . . . ? What other talk could she be referring to?

"About?" I have to play this one safe. I can't just walk out
on an emotional ledge without knowing what Rachel knows
or where she's coming from.

"He said you told him that I'd let him stay in Mom and Dad's
house and that we'd give you a choice about where you wanted
to live."

"Was I not supposed to say that?"

"No. It's absolutely fine." She pats my hand on the table.
"Erin, he raved about you for the longest time. He loves you so
much. You know that things haven't always been civil between
me and Victor. But this family connection is something my
brother has needed for years." Rachel smiles. "You've become
a healing force in our family."

"No. Rachel. You're the one who held us together this whole
time."

"I love this family," Rachel says.

"I love this family too," I whisper.

I'm a little nervous and edgy through the rest of dinner, but
by the time we're done and Rachel's paying the check, it appears she's unaware of the probabilities of our family makeup.

▸ 31 ◂

I catch a ride to work with Journey and while he's over on the lab side, watching Clay install the locks, I stroll around the space that will be our new classroom.

I take Miss P's liquor globe from the counter and bring it to one of the desks. Today, Lysa and Spam and I are going to say a few words in her honor and put things inside the globe as a tribute to her. Mentally, I'm also putting the last image I have of her in here too.

It's time for that horrific vision to be retired.

I hear soft footsteps as Lysa and Spam slip through the door. Lysa has a tiny purse over her shoulder and a glossy black leather document pouch under her arm. The tip of the silky teal scarf that trails out of the pouch makes me smile. I remember the day that Miss P took that scarf from around her neck and wrapped it under Lysa's collar because it was the perfect match to what she was wearing.

A few steps behind is Spam. She's wearing a T-shirt and a pair of jeans and carrying a cardboard tray of coffee. That's it. No purse or backpack.

I scowl at Spam. "Dude, you didn't bring anything?"

"Don't trip." Spam pats her back pocket.

We take up places around the globe and I tip open the top. Lysa pulls the scarf out of her bag and presses it to her nose.

"I kind of hoped it would still smell like her," she says. "But it doesn't." She passes the scarf to Spam, who sniffs it and passes it to me.

I bunch the scarf into the shape of a nest and bury my nose in it. I can't smell her either. But to be honest, the only smell I associate with Miss P is oranges. "You were generous with everything, Miss P." I stuff the scarf into the globe.

Lysa retrieves the rest of the offerings from the document folder. There's a photo of her posing with us. "You were beautiful . . . inside and out." She drops the photo into one of the slots in the globe. "I also wrote out one of her sayings in calligraphy." She displays it to us, then reads it aloud. "Just because you don't see something doesn't mean it's not there."

"That's perfect," Spam says. "Just because we don't see her doesn't mean she's not here."

I open my shoebox. "I made copies of her class notes. The ones I saved, anyway." I hold them up. "Look, her handwriting is all over them."

"Nobody in the whole world writes like that," Spam says.

"I also brought all the photos from her bulletin board and put them in there . . . and I know it's a little weird, but I saved these orange peels. They're from an orange that she gave me right before . . ." My voice trails off. "Anyway." I shove the photos into a compartment and let the orange peels trickle into the globe.

"We'll call the orange peels potpourri," Lysa says.

Finally, Lysa and I turn to Spam.

"What?" she says.

I gesture to the globe. "You were supposed to bring something too."

"Right." Spam retrieves a flash drive from her pocket. She drops it into the globe. It hits the bottom with a thunk.

I frown. "We don't even know what's on it."

"It's everything," Spam says.

"What do you mean everything?"

"I scraped everything we had that has anything to do with Miss P. I got the data from both of your cloud files, which included all the notes . . . assignments . . . science projects . . . photos of her old classroom . . . the contents of her computer and her phone records. There's even some random internet searches I did when we were trying to figure out who killed her. Anyway, everything that had anything to do with Miss P is on there."

"Wait, what?" Lysa says. "How did you get *our* cloud files?"

"Have you met me?" Spam tilts her head, adopting a look of moral innocense.

"You're saying that everything I brought and everything Lysa brought is all contained on this jump drive."

"Well, not everything," Spam says. "Obviously, the photos from the bulletin board aren't on here. Or the teal scarf. But it's likely that everything else is there."

Lysa and I shake our heads. Spam's nothing if not amazing.

"Okay. One last time." I close the globe and press my fingers to it. Lysa and Spam add theirs. "To Miss P," I say.

"Miss P," repeat Spam and Lysa.

I carry the globe to its place on the shelf behind Victor's desk. I set it just so, and give it a good polish so that the burnished, Old World finish shines.

When I turn around, Lyman is peeking in the doorway.

"Hey, Erin," he says. "There's a guy up here looking for you. Says he has a shipment."

Spam dances toward the door, arms wide. "You made it."

▾ ▾ ▾

When Victor said he ordered some stuff, he wasn't kidding. I sign for five giant boxes.

Fortunately, Journey's still here and Lyman just arrived, so we have extra help muscling the boxes down the stairs and into the supply room.

Once everything has been moved, Journey heads back over to his side to work on the evidence locker, which shares a wall with our storage room. Journey demonstrates this by pressing his face to the floor and making ghostly sounds into a vent between the rooms.

I notice another small vent in the wall between the storage room and the classroom.

"Why are there are so many vents in here?" I wonder.

"This probably used to be a locker room," Lyman says.

"How would you guess that?" I ask. "You don't even go to actual school."

Lyman points at the drain cover in the middle of the floor.

I nod. "Not bad, Sherlock."

While we were goofing around, Lyman unpacked all five boxes and sorted the supplies. "How do you want this stuff arranged?" he asks. "Alphabetically? In order by size? Or maybe they should be arranged by things used together? You tell me."

I draw a blank, and apparently so does everyone else.

"Miss P had one small cupboard. So things were organized by where they fit," I say.

"We can do better than that," Lyman says. "There's plenty of room in here. You just need to tell me how you want it."

While we're deciding how to set up the storage area, Clay pokes his head in the door. "Hey, kids. Just so you know, I'm installing the lock on this door right now, so two things: Be careful coming out, and after I'm done, don't close the door. It has to be programmed."

Most of us just kind of grunt and nod in response to Clay. But Lysa responds with words. "Thank you, sir. We will be careful," she says.

"Have you ever noticed that Lysa has amazing manners?" Spam says.

This is Spam's version of Lysa's mom-mode and even though I know it threatens to get them into a fight, I can't help but agree. "She's our official ambassador."

Lysa puts her hands on her hips. "Yeah. Cut the crap. Let's get this done. It's almost time for lunch."

Lyman holds up a couple of the items we brought down yesterday from Miss P's supply cabinet. "What about this stuff: flour, wax, Play-Doh? Those aren't science class materials, right?"

Spam pats him on the head. "Ahh, the joys of homeschooling. You missed all the fun, like dripping iodine solution onto little piles of baking flour to test for carbohydrates."

"Because if it's carbs, it turns what color?" I say.

"Black," she answers, and then sticks out her tongue at me. "I paid attention . . . most of the time."

"Play-Doh?" Lyman asks.

"For molding your own test tube holders," Lysa says.

"Don't get me started on the wax," I say. "It's great for capturing impressions of something. Like did you know there's a spray wax that they use for saving tire treads or shoe impressions in snow?"

"That's kind of cool," Lyman says.

"Yeah, and if you could get someone to touch it, you could probably steal their fingerprint with wax too."

The room goes quiet and I suddenly realize everyone's staring at me. "Okay. I know that sounded bad and I'm not saying I would do that. I'm just saying wax is amazing, moldable stuff."

"Don't even joke about that," Lysa says. "We got in enough trouble over the skateboarder video."

"You did?" Lyman's head snaps up.

Spam kneels next to him. "We did . . . a little bit. And it was kind of dicey for a day. But we got through it and it's completely over. No worries." She gives him a hug and wanders out of the storage room.

"That reminds me." I grab my bag, dragging out my makeup kit. Inside is the hinged lifter with Lyman's fingerprint. I hand it over to Lyman. "This belongs to you."

Lyman inspects the square in his palm and gives me a quizzical look.

"Yeah. That's your fingerprint," I say.

His look changes to skeptical and maybe even a little angry.

"It was on the car that almost hit you. We lifted it because . . ." I look to Lysa.

"We did it because we could and we thought we might need it to help you," she explains.

Lyman holds the card between his fingertips. "But where did you get the card?"

I relax. He's not angry, just curious . . . like all of us.

"Oh, Victor gave it to me." I step up on the stepladder and find a box. I hold it up. "He just ordered a whole box of them in all different sizes. They're really cool and easy to work with. I'm sure we'll be playing with them during camp."

Lyman opens his wallet and carefully sticks the fingerprint inside. He wanders out of the storage room after Spam.

While they're gone, Lysa and I make an executive decision on an organizational approach that combines putting the heavier things on the bottom and grouping things together by how they'll be used. Example, flour and salt stay together because they are both used for investigative experiments.

When Lyman and Spam come back in, Spam has a label maker. Lysa hands the things to me and I hand them off to Lyman. Before too long he has everything on the shelves and lined up completely straight.

Lysa admires Lyman's skill. "That's amazing. How'd you do that?"

Lyman blushes a little. "I worked at this little grocery store last summer. The guy used to check my shelves with a ruler, so I learned how to eyeball it and make it straight."

Spam is using the label maker. "Which store was that?" she wonders.

Lyman blushes again. "It wasn't around here," he says. "It was near where we used to live."

"I can't keep track of everywhere you've lived," Spam says, giving us a look. She mouths the word "sketchy" to us.

I give her a shrug. Judging from my own life, I figure everyone has a secret or two.

Lysa applies the last of the shelf labels. "Okay, done," she says, breathing a sigh of relief. "Now lunch."

Victor sweeps in and calls for all of us to join him in the classroom.

"Or maybe not," I say.

► 32 ◄

Biometric tech is a whole umbrella of new tricks and procedures
which include palm prints, irises, facial recognition, voice
patterns, and even mannerisms. If there's something
unique about you, biometrics can track it.
—VICTOR FLEMMING

As we file into the classroom, Journey moves some chairs into
position at one of the tables. Victor lays out some electronic-
type gadgets. Then he begins pacing and rubbing his hands
together in that excited way he gets when he's getting ready to
show something off.

Journey takes a seat in one of the chairs. I head over to take
a seat in the chair next to him and he quietly shakes his head.

Whoops. Okay.

I move back to stand near Spam, Lyman, and Lysa.

Victor keys in on Lyman. "Who's this?"

"Oh, this is my boyfriend," Spam says. "He came to help us
out today. But don't worry, you don't have to pay him or anything."

Lysa and I exchange smirks. Spam admitting to a boyfriend.
What's next?

Lyman offers his hand. "My name's Lyman, sir. Nice to meet
you."

Victor shakes his hand. "Nice to meet you, Lyman. Thanks
for helping out."

"Lyman's an amazing organizer. Wait until you see the storage room," I say.

"Great." Victor continues pacing. "Okay. So, we're just *five* days away from launching the first CSI camp in this city."

We all cheer.

Immediately, the classroom door opens and Principal Blankenship enters the room. My stomach drops because I'm sure she's here to chastise us for making too much noise . . . or breathing too much air . . . or being in her space.

I check my Bella bracelet and there's no light. I glance at Spam. She places her hands in front of her, imitating how Blankenship walks around with her notebook. She's not carrying the notebook, which means she doesn't have the tattletale bookmark.

Victor acknowledges her with a nod, but she hangs toward the back of the room.

Maybe I'm worrying for nothing. I remind myself this isn't school, it's a job. But my stomach tends to squeeze itself into the size of a coin purse whenever she's around.

"The lab and evidence room are done. Most of the basic equipment is in. We moved the AFIS fingerprint scanner over here because PD is upgrading to mobile units anyway." Victor points to Clay, who is hanging off to the side. "Where are we with the safety equipment?"

"Everything's ordered, just waiting on delivery," he says.

"We can open without the ventilation system because I can hold off doing any tests in the lab until we have that," Victor says. "But we have to have the alarms and fire extinguishers in or we won't pass the permit stage. You were also supposed to get a price for the automated fire suppression system? We don't have to have it, but it would be nice."

Clay nods. "Yes, sorry. I'll install the alarms tomorrow. The extinguishers are on their way and I'll call again about the automated system."

"Good. Journey and I are driving to Salem tonight to pick up some donated supplies," Victor says. "We can circle back on this in the morning."

I give Journey a grouchy look. He failed to mention a trip with Victor. His response is a helpless gesture. I know it's not his fault and I also understand that Victor's got the time pressure of opening day to worry about. It's just every day there's something new keeping Journey and me apart.

Miss Blankenship checks her watch and raises a slender finger. "Do you need me here for this?"

"Yes, just a few minutes more," Victor says. "I was just giving an update. We now have locks on all the doors."

We all glance around at the various doors. They are each standing open and all of them have gleaming new doorknobs with small keypads and screens above the knobs.

"These are the biometric locks. They'll be keyed to your fingerprints. This will provide us the security we need for the lab, as only certain fingerprints will open certain doors. We'll also be implementing a fingerprint attendance system for the kids in the camp."

Lyman looks surprised. "How will that work?"

"Easy," Victor says. "A biometric system takes a fingerprint and converts it to a code that can be used to open a door or add a name to an attendance file. The actual fingerprint isn't stored or viewed. It's just the unique identifier, like your name."

"Interesting," Lysa says.

"Camp attendance will be a test, but if it works the way I know it's going to, the whole school will go in this direction in the fall." Victor nods at Blankenship. "Right?"

Blankenship offers a slight nod in response. "I'm detail

oriented and your biometric system offers a lot of detail. So it's possible I could be persuaded."

I'm kind of amazed. Victor's charm has made her almost tolerable.

"I can explain all of this in even more detail," Victor says. "But then your heads would explode." He pauses for laughter, but doesn't get any.

My stomach grumbles and Blankenship checks her watch again.

The rest of the room stays silent.

"I get it," he says. "Let's set up those files."

Victor takes a seat at the table, next to Journey, and begins arranging the electronic equipment. "I want you to use the thumb on your dominant hand. You don't need to press down hard, just fit your thumb against the screen and hold it there until the system beeps." He opens a stamp pad and drags a small slip of paper in front of him. "To get a good scan you'll place your thumb straight down. Don't press, just touch." He demonstrates using the stamp pad, producing a nice, light, oval thumbprint. He holds it up for us to see. "This is perfect. It's not smeared, stretched, or distorted."

He repeats the process several times, rolling his thumb one way or the other, each time producing a misshapen version of his print.

"If you roll or tip your thumb in any direction it will make your scan difficult to read. You can practice a few times with the stamp pad if you want."

Miss Blankenship makes a bored cluck and switches from one foot to the other. Her impatience is not lost on Victor.

He sweeps the slips of paper to the side and positions the scanner. "Everybody got the drill? Let's do this. I'm the administrator, so I'm already in the system." He spins out a piece of paper with a colored chart. "You can see here how the doors are arranged, numbered and color coded. Green is for campers, no door access. Yellow is limited access. This will be for the classroom and storage room. Various teachers and administrative personnel will have access. For the summer, this will include our camp counselors. Finally, red equals restricted access. For the moment, the only restricted access on campus will be the two entrance doors to the lab as well as the door to the evidence locker. And the only ones who have access are me and Journey."

Victor looks up at me. "Erin. You ready?"

I step up and press my thumb onto the screen of Victor's device. After a few seconds, there's a flash of light and a beep. "Okay. You're all set. Who's next?"

Spam goes next, then Lysa, Journey, Miss Blankenship, and even Clay.

"We're giving Clay yellow access for now, which is the same as the camp counselors, but we can delete him when his work is finished here," Victor says. "That's what's so great about this system. You don't have to worry about collecting keys or rekeying locks."

"What about me?" Lyman asks.

"Lyman is signed up for the camp," I say.

"Oh. Good idea," Victor says. "This will be a great way to test every level of the system. Campers should not be able to open any doors at all, but will be counted on the attendance scan each morning. Step up here. Let's try this."

Lyman steps up to the table and plants his thumb on the scanner.

"Okay. Now we can test the doors and make sure they work . . . or don't work, as the case may be."

Victor closes the door between the class and lab. There is an electronic buzz as it locks. Then he applies his thumb to the keypad and a second light buzz signals it's unlocked.

Victor closes the door and Journey steps up and tries. He's able to unlock the door too.

Victor waves me over. "Okay, Erin. Let's see how you do." He closes the door to the lab with a satisfying clang.

I step up and press my thumb to the screen. The system responds with a negative, electronic bleat. My friends laugh. I shrug.

Who cares, anyway?

Okay. Maybe I do care a little. But for the most part I've let it go. I flash them all nasty smiles but stay quiet.

"I have a question," Miss Blankenship speaks up. "Does the system keep a record of who goes in and out of each door?"

"It does," Victor says. "Which is one of the great things about utilizing a system like this over traditional keys. Once it's dispersed throughout the campus, we will have a record of everyone who comes and goes, in every room."

I glance over at Spam and watch as the space between her eyebrows narrows.

I know what she's thinking. Biometric scanners are cool and everything, but we're not exactly in favor of the adults always knowing where we are all the time. Like Lysa and the teen tracker her parents installed on her car. It sends a text to her parents if she goes outside of her boundaries. And they can always look back and see every place she's been.

"But will it keep a record of denied attempts to enter a door?" Blankenship asks. "Or access with the key?"

Victor looks intrigued. "Hmm. Good question. I don't know the answer to that. I can check into that further, if you like?"

"Would you, please?" she asks.

Her questions are kind of sketchy, but the truly suspicious behavior is how nice she's being to Victor.

Victor turns to Clay. "We've tested all the doors, so I think you're done for the day. Journey and I need to get on the road. You're all dismissed," Victor says.

Miss Blankenship whirls and heads for the door.

Spam races up to her before she can completely escape. "Oh, Miss Blankenship. I have something for you." She pauses, a slight scowl on her face.

Spam hands her one of the Bella pins. It's a volcano wearing a graduation cap. Blankface examines it closely.

"It's a special school pride pin that I made for graduation." Spam shrugs. "It's for the booster club."

Blankface examines it stoically. Then she shrugs and clips it to her sweater.

Bam!

► **33** ◄

When something stands out as different, it can be tracked.
—PRINCIPAL BLANKENSHIP

I wait while Victor and Journey close and lock up first the lab and then the classroom. The three of us walk to the parking lot together. I give Journey a tight hug before sending him off with Victor again. They're driving to Salem to pick up some supplies that are out-of-date for a commercial lab, but perfect for either the camp or the classroom. Victor estimates it's about $5,000 worth of stuff. So it's worth the drive. But they won't be back until late. And Lyman has plans with his mother tonight.

So that means it's a girl's night.

Lysa's driving. We're planning to grab dinner, then deliver some Bella orders, and after that we're going to a movie.

I text Rachel to let her know and she texts back telling me to have a good time.

After dinner and ten successful Bella deliveries, we return to the car, but Lysa immediately starts looking around for something. She looks in the console, the backseat, in between the seats. She's becoming frantic as she even checks the trunk.

"What are you looking for?" I ask.

"What did I do with the leather pouch that I brought Miss P's shrine stuff in?"

I shake my head. "No clue. I remember seeing it, though."

"I have to find it," she says. "It's my mom's."

"We must have left it at school. We'll look for it tomorrow," I say.

"You don't understand," Lysa gasps. "It's Givenchy."

"I promise a night in the storage room won't turn it into *Tar-jay*," Spam says.

I giggle. Whenever Lysa goes on about some designer, Spam brings up her favorite store, Target. Only she pronounces it as if it were a French word.

"It's just that I borrowed it without asking, which is okay as long as I don't leave it somewhere. I have to go back and get it," Lysa says, sounding a little frantic.

"Now?" both Spam and I ask at the same time.

"Yes. Now," Lysa says. "You guys know my mom. 'I forgot' is not an excuse."

"But how—"

"With these," Lysa interrupts, holding up her thumb.

"I don't know." It seems weird and maybe even a little wrong for us to go into the school buildings at night. "I'm afraid Victor will think we're taking advantage. Don't forget, we're still on probation."

"We're not students now or even family members," she says. "Effective today, we're employees. Victor said so himself."

Good point. And I do know how her mom loves to dole out situations to help Lysa remember the rules. She actually calls them "situations" instead of "punishments," which is what they really are.

"Okay. But we're just going to go in, get the pouch, and

leave," I say. "No messing around. I can't do anything to disappoint Victor."

"Of course," Lysa says. "What else would we do?"

Spam nudges me. "This is where you say, while we're there we should sneak into his lab and touch all of his stuff." She cackles.

"You guys. I'm seriously over it with the lab. I don't even care about it anymore."

"Uh huh." Spam wiggles her eyebrows.

Her teasing is getting on my nerves.

▾ ▾ ▾

When we arrive at the school, the parking lot is completely empty. Any car would stand out, but Lysa's bright red Mustang is practically a beacon.

The campus is dark and deserted too, but we know there's a security guard who stops by every so often on rounds. It's a little creepy to be here when it's so quiet, so we hurry around to the back of A-building and down the cement steps.

Even though it's going on eight o'clock and still somewhat light outside, the hallway is dark. Pitch-black. Typical basement.

The three of us simultaneously pull out our cell phones and turn on the flashlights, sending out three beams to slice through the darkness. From there, we find our way to the classroom door. My thumb unlocks it.

Spam shines the light up under her chin. "Can I just say how much I love this biometric stuff?" She moves into the classroom ahead of me, feeling along for the wall switch.

"Don't," I say. "The light will show through the windows." I point to the high windows. The dim light that filters in isn't strong, but with our phone lights it's enough for us to maneuver around the furniture.

"I thought we agreed that it was technically okay for us to be here," Lysa says.

"Technically, it probably is. I just don't want to have to explain to the security guard that we're here for your mom's stupid document pouch," I say.

"Givenchy isn't stupid," Lysa says.

I tiptoe toward the storage room. "It's probably in here." I stop to shift things out of my right hand and turn off the flashlight and Spam and Lysa run into me.

"Shhh. Ow, that was my toe," Spam whispers.

"Quiet," Lysa orders.

"Stop it, you guys. I'm trying to do this. And why are we whispering?" I unlock the storage room door and just as I'm about to walk through, Lysa tugs hard on my sleeve.

"Erin," she hisses.

"What?" I keep moving forward into the storage room, but she pulls me back.

"Seriously, look," she says.

Now I'm annoyed. "What?" I say a little louder.

"Shhh." She shines her phone light across the classroom. First, on Miss P's shrine. The top is hinged open and some of the contents are scattered across the counter. And then, more importantly, on the door to the crime lab, which is standing open a few inches.

"Is somebody here?" My stomach roils.

"The parking lot was deserted," Lysa says.

"Call Journey," Spam says. "Maybe they left it like this . . . or came back."

"I walked out with them. They locked everything up. And he just texted me ten minutes ago saying they're almost to Salem."

Spam is putting things back into Miss P's shrine. "The flash drive's gone," she announces.

"Maybe it's on the floor," Lysa says.

Spam prowls around, shining her phone light into the corners. "Nope. Gone."

"Who would do something like this?" Lysa says.

"Clay told me that Coach Wilkins has been hanging around down here every day."

"Why?" Lysa asks.

"Exactly," I say.

"Did they mess up anything in here?" Spam walks into the lab.

I don't even follow her, that's how paranoid I am about getting caught in Victor's lab. Instead, I stand at the door and hiss at her. "Come out of there."

"Wait." Spam glides by the AFIS computer and swipes her finger on the keyboard.

"Don't touch anything," I say.

The screen lights up. She jumps a little and then she peers at the screen. "Uh oh."

Lysa slips into the lab, next to Spam. "What's uh oh?"

"You guys. Get out of there." I refuse to set even one foot into the lab. Victor and I have a deal and I can't . . . I just can't.

"Oh wow." Spam's moan tells me this is serious.

"Come out, now."

"She's coming." Spam flies out of the lab with Lysa in tow. She grabs my arm as they run past. "Hide."

"Who's coming?"

"Blankface." Spam moves quickly to the storage room. I close the lab door and follow them. We barely get the storage room door closed before I realize my Bella bracelet is lighting up red and vibrating.

- **34** -

Information is power.

—VICTOR FLEMMING

We hide in the storage room and dim our phones just as the *tap, tap, tap* of high heels enters the room. Blankface flips the switch, bathing the classroom in light. Some of the light seeps in through the vent along the floor. If I press my cheek to the cement I can just barely see the globe on the top of the display case. Spam put it back together and left it closed.

Blankface walks straight up to the globe and opens it. I select the camera app and angle my phone into the vent, then hit *record video*. Now all three of us can watch her movements on the screen.

Blankface spends a few minutes rifling through the stuff in the globe, then takes something from it and slides it into her jacket pocket. She carefully closes the globe and adjusts its appearance so it looks normal, as if it hasn't been tampered with.

She proceeds straight to the door of Victor's lab, pulls out a key, and lets herself in.

Even in the dark, the three of us exchange silent gasps.

We can't monitor Blankface's activities in the lab from the

vent. She doesn't stay in there long. It only seems like forever, as we're lying crouched on the cold cement floor.

When she finally exits, her phone is in her hand. She carefully shuts the lab door and even polishes the metal with the hem of her jacket. Then she pauses to complete something on her phone before slipping it into her pocket and *click*, *click*, *click*ing across the classroom as if nothing out of the ordinary just happened. She leaves, turning off the light on her way out.

I pick up my phone and stop the video recording. "Holy crap, what just happened?"

"Blankface owned Victor's lab," Spam says as she sits up.

"But why?" I ask.

"Maybe she was looking for us," Lysa says. "My car is in the parking lot."

"No. She was totally mindful and directed. Look at this." I replay the video. "She walks in, goes straight for the globe. Then right into Victor's lab. When she comes out she's doing something on her phone."

"Sending a photo?" Spam says.

"Of what, though?" I spot Lysa's document pouch on the bottom shelf. "Hey, here's your Chanel pouch-thingy. Crisis over."

"It's Givenchy," she says. "But the crisis isn't nearly over."

Lysa turns her phone to show me. It's a photo of the AFIS computer screen in the lab.

Someone recently ran a fingerprint and this was the result.

There's a giant banner across the top—MISSING PERSON—and a name I've never heard before. "Todd Kenneth Jenkins. Who's that?" There's also a date that goes back years and two photos. One of a baby and one of a teenager.

Lysa shakes the phone in my face. "Look at the picture."

I look—and then do a double take because this can't be right.

It's Lyman.

Spam grabs the phone and stretches the image to make it bigger. "It says it's an age-progressed photo, but dang, it's him. Unless . . . do you think he has a twin brother?"

Her lip trembles as she hands the phone to me so I can study it too. I read the smaller print. "It says he disappeared from his home when he was nineteen months old." The information sinks in. "Lyman was kidnapped?"

Spam points at me. "His fingerprint? What did you do with it?"

"I gave it back to him . . . today."

"Maybe he dropped it or left it lying around and Victor or Journey decided to run it to see what came up," Lysa says.

I shake my head. "No. I watched him. He carefully tucked it away in his wallet."

Spam sits back hard against the wall. "This is really scary."

"We have no choice," Lysa says. "We have to tell Victor."

"We can't." Both Spam and I say it at the same time.

"Victor and I are doing great right now. We've . . . we've . . . ." I suddenly realize that I haven't even told my best friends how Victor could be my real father, and this isn't the time to launch into that. "Anyway, we're on probation. He'll never believe we just found his lab like this. He'll think we broke in. Everything will be ruined. He *trusts* us. And . . . probation."

"What about poor Lyman?" Lysa says.

"Exactly. We'll be putting him right back into a sketchy situation with the police," Spam says solemnly.

Lysa gives Spam a freaked-out look. "Are you insane? He's been kidnapped. He's already living a nightmare." She looks frantically between the two of us. "He deserves to know."

"Wait. We don't have to be the ones who tell, because somebody else will do it," I say. "The person who ran that fingerprint is probably telling him right now. We can just act shocked right along with everyone else."

"Or not," Spam says softly, with a certainty that I wasn't expecting. "I'm pretty sure Lyman ran his own print."

"What? He's the last person I would suspect," I say.

"I have no clue what was up with Blankface." Spam exhales. "But I think Lyman figured out how to get into Victor's lab."

"Impossible. Victor tested each one of us on every door. Lyman's fingerprint failed to open a single door. There's no way he could have gotten in."

Spam drags her fingers down her face, distorting her features as she goes. "Except he might have made a Play-Doh finger."

There's a long pause.

"What are you saying? Where would he get an idea like that? And how could that possibly work?"

Spam points at me. "You started it by bragging about using wax to steal someone's fingerprints. But it's possible I might have told him how to do it."

"Wait. What?"

Spam issues a heavy sigh. "*MythBusters* did an episode a few years ago on biometric fingerprint locks, and they were able to open one by making a Play-Doh finger and putting a photocopy of the correct fingerprint on the end of it."

I glance at Lysa. Her eyes are huge. She puts her fists to the sides of her head and mimes a brain-explosion.

"Seriously?" I agree with Lysa. "You figured out how to fake your way into Victor's lab?"

She's the picture of guilt. "Blame *MythBusters*, not me."

"And you didn't tell me?" I'm both glad and mad at this fact.

"You said you were over getting into the lab," she says.

"And I am. I just can't believe you didn't tell me."

"You didn't tell either of us, but you told Lyman?" Lysa is as incredulous as I am.

Spam rolls her head from side to side. "It's not like I told him, exactly. We were just talking about the locks and I mentioned *MythBusters* and he said he saw that episode." Her eyes dart between us. "That was it, I swear."

"Okay, but where would Lyman get a photocopy of Victor's fingerprint?" As soon as the words are out of my mouth, I gasp, remembering Victor demonstrating the method he wanted us to use by stamping his own thumbprint onto various slips of paper. "Oh crap. All he had to do was pick up the paper with Victor's print on it." I glance at Spam. "Did you—"

"No." She shakes her head vehemently. "And he didn't say a word to me. But it makes sense."

I'm horrified at how this looks. "This is totally something I might have done."

"We completely, totally suck," Lysa moans. "We know something we're not supposed to know and we can't report it because we have a history of breaking the rules. Plus . . . probation."

"No one will believe we didn't break into the lab," I say.

Spam and Lysa look at each other helplessly and agree. "No one."

35

The actual contents of a crime lab must remain
mysterious to the public at large.

—VICTOR FLEMMING

"So who left the lab door open?" Lysa asks.

"Blankenship?" Spam says.

"She used the key," I say. "And she wasn't surprised to see the globe back together."

"She never seems surprised by anything," Lysa says.

"It is suspicious that she went straight into Victor's lab, though," I say. "Victor was perfectly clear, everyone is supposed to stay out of there."

"Maybe she's like you, Erin," Spam says. "Rules don't necessarily apply."

I glare at Spam. Yes, I'm tense and irritated because when this blows up, I'll be the one getting blamed. "Me? What about your flaky—oh, no, wait—*sketchy* boyfriend?"

Spam backs up and points her finger at me. When she does, a ball of paper falls out of her hand.

"You can't blame me for this. And you shouldn't blame him, either," Spam says. "You of all people know how it feels not to know things about your life that you should know." Her intensity loses steam and winds down. "You know?" Her voice cringes with apology.

I *do* know. And that's the hardest thing about this situation. I don't blame Lyman. Not one little bit. I bend down and pick up the wad of paper that Spam dropped.

"What's this?" I ask.

Spam waves it off. "I don't know. It was with the stuff on the counter from the globe. I kept it out because I didn't remember it being in there with our stuff."

"That's because it wasn't." I smooth it out. It's actually a cocktail napkin with scalloped edges and purplish stains on one side. On the other side a message is scrawled in thick black ink: A COWARD DIES A THOUSAND DEATHS . . . but YOU ONLY ONCE!

"What the—"

I hold the napkin up for Lysa and Spam to read.

"That's from Shakespeare," Lysa says.

Spam smirks. "She's delusional. That's a Tupac lyric."

"It's totally Shakespeare," Lysa argues.

"Tupac!"

"You guys are missing the point. This is clearly a threat. We need to figure out why it's here and who it's for."

"We need to go back to Spam's and work this out," Lysa says.

I tuck the napkin into my bag and we slip out of the storage room, across the classroom, and up the stairs. After carefully peeking around corners and confirming that the school is deserted, we make a mad, panicked run to Lysa's car, jump inside, and slam the doors, without running into anyone.

All I want to do is race to the safety of my attic and collapse onto the sofa. But the threat penned on this napkin has me shaking. It's as if catching my mother's killer made no difference at all. The terror is as fresh as it ever was.

Something bad is about to happen. I can feel it.

▼ ▼ ▼

While I roll the whiteboard out of the storage closet, Lysa retrieves the laptops and tablets from the chargers and Spam brings us down an array of fruit and chips for snacks.

"You have to promise not to say anything about Lyman to anyone until I have a chance to talk to him," Spam says.

"Trust me. I'd prefer not to say anything about Lyman to anyone ever," Lysa says. "But you have to promise to stay away from him until we figure this out. He could be dangerous."

I mime zipping my mouth closed and locking it with a key. I don't even want to think about how Victor would react to knowing people were in his lab.

The first thing I google are the words on the napkin. "Okay, you're both right. The threat is derivative of a Tupac lyric . . ."

"I told you. It's the opening of 'If I Die 2nite,'" Spam says. "Which, I'll admit, is creepy."

Lysa opens her mouth to protest but I hold up a finger, silencing her.

"Which *is* derivative of a quote from Shakespeare," I say.

Lysa makes a face at Spam.

"The question is, who is it for?" I say. "Victor? Journey? Me?"

"Miss P?" guesses Lysa.

"She's already—" Spam whispers.

"Right. We have a lot to figure out," I say. "Let's get to work."

A hush and the blue glow from all the devices settles over the room. Spam spins her chair to face the television. She logs on to her game to try to hook up with Lyman.

Lysa and I start by searching the name on the wanted poster: Todd Jenkins.

It's too common. There's an actor, a doctor, and a photographer named Todd Jenkins, to start, and none of them is Lyman.

"Not finding anything," Lysa says.

"Me either," I agree.

"Go back and plug in the date from the poster. Look for news stories about the kidnapping," Spam calls over her shoulder.

Lysa and I split up the task. I search for news articles about child kidnappings around that time and she searches his name around Columbus, Ohio, where the missing person notice says he was born.

I receive a text from Journey that he and Victor made it to Salem and managed to get all the stuff into Victor's car. He says they'll be on their way home soon.

I reply. Then I text: SO IS THERE N THING O RO ISING IN THE

He writes back: WH T O O E N

Not really thinking this through, I continue: O NOW N THING OO I EE I EN E OR

WH he writes back.

Of course he wants to know *why,* I'm asking bizarre questions. ST NT SI ING O T THE OO ST O RE E RNING O T

THE ONTENTS O RI E SHO RE IN STERI O S TO THE I T RGE he writes. TH T S WH T I TOR S S N W TW HOW W S THE O IE

"You guys, we never decided what movie we saw," I say.

"We didn't see a movie, remember?" Spam says.

"Yes, but everyone *thinks* we saw a movie, so we need to get our stories straight."

Lysa shakes her head. "I suggest we stick with the truth."

"Oh, I see. So we should just tell everyone you borrowed a designer leather thing from your mom without permission and left it in the storage room, and when we went back to get it we watched the creepy principal violate Victor's rules and enter his lab. Only to then figure out our friend also broke into the secret, uber-secure lab to run his own fingerprint, proving he was an abducted child. But we didn't want to tell anyone because we'd get in trouble."

Spam and Lysa adopt similar "yeah that's not good" expressions.

"Exactly," I say. "Lying about a movie is so much easier."

Suddenly Lysa gasps. "I found something."

Spam and I move to look over her shoulder.

Lysa covers her mouth with her hand, reading ahead of us. Then I get to the spot and cover my mouth with my hand too.

It's an article from fourteen years ago about a couple who were found dead in their home from a drug overdose. And the same night, their toddler son went missing.

Spam looks between me and Lysa, tears welling up in her eyes. "His parents are dead? How awful." She thumps down into a chair. "He probably just found all of this out a few hours ago. And he's alone."

"With a kidnapper," I add.

Spam gives me a grim look.

Lysa searches off that article, finding more details. "Wait a minute. Wait a minute. Okay. So, yes, Lyman's parents were known to have drug problems."

I lean over Lysa's shoulder to read the article along with her. "They had both been in rehab several times. But not in months after their son was born."

Spam shakes her head. "Poor Lyman."

"Have you met his mom?" I ask.

"You mean the kidnapper?" Spam asks.

"Yes. The one you called the hover mom?"

"Not yet," Spam reports. "Why?"

"Because, according to this article, there's a good chance that she's his real aunt." Lysa swivels the laptop so Spam can see the article. "She disappeared the same night."

"Wow," Spam says. "I can't imagine what he must be feeling right now."

I *know* what Lyman's feeling.

"He's feeling like his whole world just blew apart," I say.

◄ **36** ◄

Missing children is a complex issue. They are classified as
either missing, abducted, runaway, or thrownaway.
—NISMART-2, U.S. DEPARTMENT OF JUSTICE

We're lucky that Mr. Ramos isn't very nosy because we can just
blast in here and invade Spam's basement, any time of the day
or night, and he never checks on us or asks a single question.

"Look, this is huge," Lysa says. "As big as catching Miss P's
murderer. And when they hear our story everything will
make sense because Lyman was the skateboarder and this is
probably why he didn't come forward. We'll tell them the
truth. They might be a little mad at first. But we'll make them
understand."

"We have to make sure it is the truth before we tell anyone
anything," I say.

Spam brings the whiteboard out of the closet and starts a
new list. "The age-progressed photo looks *exactly* like him. He
told me they move all the time and that his mom works nights
at hospitals."

"He's homeschooled," I say. "Probably to keep his records out
of the system."

Lysa taps her pen on the table. "What else?"

"He found us," I say.

"Oh my gosh." Spam perks up. "That's right. He knew everything about us from the newspaper and TV. He even knew about Erin's mom and Journey's dad." She smacks her forehead. "I'm so stupid. I'm so used to talking about you guys that I didn't even think it was weird that he asked so many questions."

"All I know is when questions about my life kept bubbling up they made me determined," I say. "Finally, I got to the point where I was going to get answers one way or the other."

"I think we can conclude that Lyman suspected there was something not right about the facts of his life," Lysa says.

I nod. "Trust me. It's possible to know things like that without knowing them exactly."

"So, Lyman became friends with us, *and* figured out how to get into the crime lab. But how did he know about the AFIS computer and how to run a fingerprint?" Lysa asks.

Spam sinks into her chair, flops her head onto the table, and covers her face with her arm.

"Let me guess," Lysa says. "You told him step-by-step how Erin did it?"

Spam sits up. "In all fairness, that newspaper article gave up most of details. I maybe only said a few things."

"Running a print is incredibly easy," I say.

"The main thing is you have to let me talk to him before we tell anybody," Spam says. "I owe him that."

"Okay, then let's go to his house," I suggest.

"We can't," Spam says. "He says his mom has a phobia about unexpected visitors."

Lysa and I make eye contact. She nods. "Right. Adding *wary of visitors* to the list."

Spam scrawls the words onto the board. "I know it's starting to sound like Lyman just used us to find his truth. But I really do know him and I'll get through to him, I promise. I just need you guys to be patient."

I inhale deeply and breathe out slowly, hoping this simple act will unlock the layers of stress that are threatening to suffocate me.

"You say you know him, Spam. But you really don't. His life is a complete mess," Lysa says. "And you didn't know about any of it."

"In all fairness, I suspected something. Not this, though. I didn't expect this," Spam says. "And, if it's all true, then none of it is his fault. So lay off a little."

"Spam's right. Lyman's the victim here," I say.

"You guys should spend the night," Spam says. "Then we can keep working on this."

"I'm sure Rachel would be okay with it," I say.

Lysa nods. "I can probably do it, but I'll have to go home first and pack a proper bag. You know my mom."

"I'll go with you. Spam can stay here and troll for Lyman," I say.

"I can go too," Spam says.

"No, you can't."

Spam looks confused.

"Spam, you know how you get around interrogations—"

Lysa interrupts. "If my dad even looks at you funny you'll urp up everything you know about Lyman. You know you can't hold it in."

Spam slumps in her chair. "You're not wrong."

"Alright, we're going," I say.

Spam holds up the leather pouch. "Don't forget this."

▾   ▾   ▾

The ride to Lysa's house is quick. I'm worried about the Lyman thing, but I'm also worried about something bigger.

"What about Blankface? What was she doing in Miss P's memorial globe and then in Victor's lab?"

Lysa shrugs. "Being nosy. That seems to be her superpower."

"Is that all, though? She was taking a pretty big risk."

"She obviously thinks she's more important than Victor," Lysa says.

"But is she trying to *hurt* Victor?" I ask.

"Why would she want to do that?"

"I forgot to tell you, but when I was out to dinner with Journey the other night, Blankface was in the same restaurant having dinner with Arletta Stone."

"No way," Lysa says. "What could those two possibly have in common?"

"I don't know. But they've both been hanging around Victor's lab. Yesterday the coach brought Arletta down there and she was taking pictures on her phone."

"Why?" Lysa asks.

"Good question. I'm worried about Victor. I don't think he's paying attention to stuff. Haven't you noticed how distracted he is?" I ask.

"I've noticed he's busy," Lysa says.

"Yeah. But he's also scattered. There was a problem when he was at the FBI and it's still a problem. He might not be paying close attention to what the coach or Blankface are up to. And apparently, everyone in town knows he's reexamining Jameson's case. That could be dangerous."

"Wow. Okay," Lysa says. "My dad calls that multiple bogies, like attacks coming from all sides."

"That's exactly what Victor's dealing with. Which is why I

really can't disappoint him with this lab thing. I can't be another bogie."

"I understand. Don't worry, we'll figure this out." Lysa pulls into her driveway and her movements become very deliberate as she psyches herself up to deal with her parents. "But first we have to make it in and out past my parents, the Incredible Hulk and Wonder Woman.

I smile. Lysa's parents pretty much are a dynamic duo.

▼   ▼   ▼

Watching Lysa handle her parents is pure poetry.

As we step in the front door she calls out, while slipping the leather pouch into the coat closet.

Her mom pops through the doorway to the family room. "Hey, girls," she says. "How was the movie? What did you see?"

I freeze, because we never agreed on a movie.

But Lysa easily spins a line as smooth as café au lait. "Oh, the lines were really long," she says. "So we just decided to go back to Spam's and watch a video. We watched the first *Mad Max*."

"Old school." Her mom lights up. "That's one of my all-time favorite movies."

"I know," Lysa says. "And I can see why. Anyway, we want to watch the next one, so can I spend the night at Spam's?"

"Her father's home, right?" Mrs. Martin asks.

"Oh yes," Lysa says. "Along with all of her little brothers."

"Okay. Fine with me," she says. She pats my elbow. "Good to see you again, Erin."

"Good to see you, too, Mrs. Martin."

Mrs. Martin walks out, but then walks back in. "When you leave here you're going straight back to Spam's house, correct?"

"Yep," Lysa says. "I just need to get my stuff."

We go into her bedroom and she packs a few things—pajamas, toothbrush, nail polish.

I give her a look. "Nail polish?"

She shrugs.

"Bye," she calls out as we slip out of the house.

As soon as we're settled in the car and she's backing out of the driveway, I send Spam a text saying: WE RE ON O R W

She writes back: NO   N S HERE N HE S RE ING O T

"Oh no." I read Spam's text to Lysa.

Lysa presses the gas pedal. "Is she in danger? Tell her to do whatever she needs to do to stay safe. Call 911. Lock herself in a bathroom. We'll be there in ten minutes."

Spam writes more and I read it aloud. "It's not that kind of freaking out. She just wants us to stall. She wants more time to talk to him alone."

Lysa glances at me. "Do you believe that?"

I shrug. "If she wasn't safe she'd say something." I truly think she just wants to make it okay with him.

Lysa gives me a stricken look. "We can't stall. You heard my mother. There's GPS on this car. They will know if we don't go directly to Spam's house."

"Okay. Okay. Go to my house and you can text her when we get there that I had to pick up some things as well."

There's no one home at my house so I let myself in and Lysa and I head up to my bedroom. She sends a text to her mother about where we are, while I throw a few things in my bag to take to Spam's.

I send Spam a text. NOW

She replies: NO

Lysa is edgy and aggravated. "Where's your laptop?"

I point to the attic.

She leads the way into my closet and up the ladder like she's done it a hundred times, which is funny since she only recently came to know that this space even exists.

I hand her my laptop, then flop down on the sofa. I stare up at the open beams while listening to her fingers click away at the keys.

"Wow," she says. "Geez. Thi . . . This is . . . Gosh. What the—"

I roll over on my side and prop my head up on my hand. "What?"

She flashes me a sad look. "I'm reading a study that says between 1997 and 1999 over two hundred thousand children were abducted. . . . by family members!"

"Wow. Are you serious?"

She gives me a hard look. "I am *more* serious than my dad."

I roll back on the sofa. "I don't think I've ever seen you *that* serious. Two hundred thousand?" I try to let that number sink in.

"By *well-meaning* family members." She uses air quotes around well-meaning.

"I don't even know how to process that," I say.

"I don't either." She closes the laptop. "But we need to get back over there before Lyman leaves. He needs to understand this isn't his fault."

The reality of Lyman's situation hits me. I grew up immersed in survivor's guilt, wondering why I was left alive and if a family member was to blame for my mother's murder. Lyman is actually living with a family member who did the unspeakable. Lysa's right. He's going to need some serious support after getting news like this.

I roll off the sofa and land on my feet. "Let's go."

► 37 ◄

Well-meaning family members might think they are right to
illegally remove a child from their home, but really
they are only making the situation worse.

—VICTOR FLEMMING

When we get to Spam's house, she's sitting outside on the back
steps, sobbing. This is a sight neither of us have seen before.

Lysa curls in next to her and throws her arm around her
shoulders.

"Spam, where is he?" I ask.

She waves her hand and croaks, "Gone."

Lysa hugs her. "Did you tell him . . . about his parents and
his aunt?"

"He knew," she sobs. "He knows everything."

"Okay." Lysa nods. "That's good."

Spam gives her a stark look.

"I don't mean it's good that this happened," Lysa stammers.
"I just mean that if he knows, it's because he *did* run his own
print. And that's good because it means we have control of the
information."

"What do you mean by control?" I lean against the railing,
watching Lysa coax Spam out of her hysteria.

"If it's just the four of us who know, then we don't have to
worry about someone swooping in out of nowhere and busting

it open before we're ready." Lysa nervously gnaws at a hang-nail. "Maybe, for once, we can actually help someone get out of trouble the *right* way."

Spam vehemently shakes her head. "No! Huh uh. Lyman ordered us to stay out of it." She starts to quiver again, but pauses to take a long, calming breath. "He was super-crazy furious. Said I invaded his privacy."

"He's the one who left it open on the computer," I say.

"Right? But he thinks I hacked in to get it." She shrugs. "I probably could have, but I didn't. The part that hurts is I really like him." She looks back and forth between us. "But he was just using me to get what he wanted."

"What does he want, Spam?" Lysa asks. "Because no one *tries* to blow up their life. Not like this."

"He wants to be normal." Spam sighs. "His aunt found out he made actual friends here and she was going to make them move again." She gestures, hands in the air. "He's a smart guy. He knows that's not normal. He suspected she was hiding something for a long time. At first, he thought he would get to know us and ask us what he should do. He thought maybe we could find out if there really was something going on. But that could have been risky too. He said he saw the opportunity to do it on his own and he took it." Spam's tears start up again. "Giving him back his fingerprint gave him the idea. He apologized, but said he took a few of the lifters from the box in the storage room, too."

I take her arm and help her up. "Let's go down to the base-ment and see what we can figure out."

Down in the basement, we take up uneasy spots in front of the laptops that Lysa doled out to us earlier. We need to come up with something to help Lyman, but I'm at a complete loss.

I glance at Spam. She can't seem to stop sniveling.

Lysa is intently creating order out of her area. She lines up the laptop with the edge of the table, adjusts the angle of the tablet, and straightens her notebook and pens. "What did he say? Did he mention a plan or say when they were leaving?"

"No," Spam says. "I mean, he's mad at us for finding it, but he's also mad at his aunt. Furious with her, actually."

"What does he say about her?" I ask. "Is she nice, mean, psycho?"

"Is he in any danger?" Lysa asks.

"He *loves* her. All along he's told me that she's awesome and smart. He says she works really hard, but that she's nice and caring." Spam shrugs. "He loves her even though she's also a little psycho with the moving and the paranoia."

Lysa taps her pen on the notebook. "That's not paranoia. She has a reason to be scared. She kidnapped her sister's kid. And it doesn't matter that her sister is dead. When they catch up to her she's going straight to jail."

Spam and I both kind of recoil from her bold prediction. When Lysa channels her father, she's intimidating.

"But his parents were on drugs," Spam says. "Doesn't that count for something?"

"No." Lysa is firm. "You can't just break the law because you think it's the right thing. She could have called the police on them and had him taken away from them."

"Maybe she tried," I argue.

"She obviously didn't try hard enough." Lysa slams her hand on the table, bouncing the pens in all directions. Then she concentrates on rearranging them again. "Sorry. I'm trying to come up with a solution. But I know what my father would say if a client came to him like this."

"What?" Spam asks. "Lyman needs sound advice."

"My father would tell them to turn themselves in. Take the

punishment and then get on with life as a law-abiding citizen. Seriously, how awful and stressful must it be to move every year and never be able to stop looking over your shoulder?"

"Okay, but Lyman didn't do anything wrong, and he's the one who stands to suffer the most," Spam says. "He told me he refuses to go into foster care; he doesn't care what anyone says."

"I didn't think of that," I say. "If Lyman's aunt goes to jail, what happens to him?"

Lysa shrugs. "His parents are dead, so yeah, it's not a pretty picture."

"Spam, try to get him to come back. There's got to be something we can do," I say.

"Apparently, I have a grandmother. You could help me find her." The disembodied voice in the dark room startles us as Lyman steps down into Spam's basement.

His hands are in his pockets and he walks sheepishly toward us. He nods back at the stairs. "Your dad was taking out the trash when I came up the driveway, so he let me in. He's a pretty cool guy."

Spam's frozen in her place at the table. It's as if she doesn't believe her eyes that Lyman has returned. "Are you still mad at me?" Her voice is a tiny squeak.

"I was never mad at you. Not really." Lyman strides over to her and wraps his arms around Spam's head, pressing it to his chest. He gives her a tiny noogie. "I'm pretty much an idiot."

She pulls away and looks up at him, her eyes welling up again. "Did you just give me a noogie?"

He scoots himself into her chair with her. She melts against him. "I couldn't help it. You're too cute." He looks up at Lysa and me watching them, wide-eyed. "Remember me? I thought my name was Lyman—now I'm not so sure."

"We get it," I say. "No worries. We'll keep your secret."

Lyman gets up and paces around the table, rubbing his hands together nervously. "Spam, I'm really sorry for what I said tonight. I was dealing with a lot and was kinda freaking out."

"Understandable," Lysa says. "We can try to keep it a secret. Or at least help you figure out what you should do."

"I found out my baby picture has been printed on milk cartons," Lyman says. "And I'm having a hard time wrapping my head around that."

I let his words sink in. I've spent most of my life at war with my unfortunate past. But your picture on a milk carton? That's intense.

"I don't want you guys to think bad about my mom, either," he says, still pacing.

"Uh, not to be tacky," Spam says, "but which mom?"

"My *mom* is the woman who raised me. I don't know what all caused her to do this. But she must've felt like she was out of options." Lyman circles the table. He's talking to us, but his eyes are on the ceiling. "I wish you could get to know her." He stops and leans against the table. "From what I've pieced together, she gave up everything so I didn't grow up in a home with drugs or wind up in foster care or some other horrible option. If we get caught, her life will be destroyed and it will be my fault. The best thing I can do is to separate from her so she can go on and live and breathe."

Lyman's description of his mom reminds me of Rachel. She diligently kept her promise. She did everything she could to give me a great life. Now it's her turn to have her own life with the chief. I understand exactly what Lyman wants and why he wants it.

He makes his way back over to Spam. "Spam, you are smart

and amazing. If you can help me find my grandmother, I'll go there. Hopefully, she'll take me in. Once I'm gone, my mom can disappear. She's really good at it. And then I won't have to go to foster care."

Spam slaps the table. "We've got this."

"We can totally help you," I agree.

Lysa rolls her head from side to side, stretching out the tension in her neck. "We can. And I am with all of you, at least in spirit. But we all need to be aware that by not reporting this we're technically aiding and abetting."

There's a long, silent moment while we study each other's faces.

"We're kids," I exclaim. "What are they going to do to us?"

Spam giggles. "And we're back in business.

► 38 ◄

Trying to identify one specific person on the internet is like trying to find a toothpick in a tornado.

—SPAM RAMOS

Spam erases the skateboarder side of the whiteboard.

Lyman stops her. "Wait. You said I was cute?"

She smirks. "Get over yourself." But then she blows him a kiss. She points to Lysa. "You're on legal. Start with his parents. Dig up everything. They died taking drugs and we know it wasn't their first time." She glances at Lyman. "Sorry. Not judgy."

Lyman shrugs. "It's okay."

"On it," Lysa says.

Spam writes on the whiteboard: Lysa = legal. "Oh, this isn't a priority, but we should know what aiding and abetting could mean to us."

Next Spam points her marker at me. "You're on proof. You know this stuff better than any of us. We can't *think* we found Lyman's grandmother and have him go to some strange woman's house and give her a heart attack. We have to *know* it's her. Go wherever you feel like you have to go."

I nod, crack my knuckles, and hit the laptop.

Spam writes on the board: Erin = proof.

My phone suddenly rings, startling everyone. I look at the caller. "It's Journey." I answer it tentatively. "Hi, babe."

"Hey. Did I wake you? It's only ten o'clock," he asks.

"No, no. You didn't wake me. What's up?"

"Victor and I are back here at the lab—" He pauses as Victor talks to him. I can't hear exactly what they're saying, but I'm struck with terror. Did we not put something back in the right place?

I mute the phone. "They're at the lab." I flash my wild, fear-filled expression around the table.

Everyone pauses and no one dares to breathe.

"Victor was just wondering—" He pauses again and my heart is nearly pounding out of my chest. "Oh. Never mind. He found it."

"He found it," I repeat. "Good." Everyone around the table relaxes again.

"How about if I come over?" he says.

"Uh. Oh, well . . ." I fake a yawn. "I'm really tired. I was just getting ready to go to bed."

"But aren't you at Spam's?" he asks.

I'm completely freaking out. "Yes. Yes, I am"—another fake yawn—"but we're all really tired and getting ready to go to bed." I gyrate my hand for them to make noise.

Spam fake yawns, loudly.

"Hi, Journey," Lysa says.

I nod. "He says hi back to all of you. How'd you know I was here?"

"Oh. Rachel told Victor so he wouldn't worry about you."

"Ahh. That makes sense."

"You sound weird," he says. "What are you doing?"

"I'm fine."

"But you don't want me to come over?" He sounds a little hurt.

"No. It's late. Another time. Talk to you later. Bye." I hang up the phone and breathe a sigh of relief for getting through the call without blurting out something incriminating.

"Journey would be a problem?" Lyman asks.

"No," I say hesitantly. "Not really."

"It's for his own protection," Lysa says. "Journey's Victor's intern. The less he knows about this, the better it is for him."

Spam stands at the whiteboard and points a marker at Lyman. "Start at the beginning. Tell us everything you know about yourself and your mom. Example, what's your birthday?"

"August 30th," Lyman says.

Spam points at Lysa. "Check the missing persons flyer on your phone. Is the birthdate the same or different?"

Lysa scrolls back through her phone. "Same," she says.

Spam grins at Lyman. "Congratulations, dude. You have a real birthday." She scrawls his real name in a top corner of the whiteboard and underneath it she writes: DOB 8/30. "What else?"

"My mom goes by Laine Becker, but that's not her real name," Lyman says.

Spam hovers the marker over the whiteboard.

"Her real name is Lydia Booker . . . and she's a doctor."

"Whoa. How did you find that out?" I ask.

"It's on the wanted poster." Lyman shrugs. "I ran her print before mine."

"Wait, she works as a doctor but she's wanted by the FBI?" Lysa is incredulous. "That doesn't sound right."

"No," Lyman says. "Lydia Booker is a doctor. Laine Becker is a nurse's aide."

"How did she explain moving all the time?" Lysa asks. "Does

she make it fun, like it's an adventure, or does she just say you have to go?"

"She apologized for it," Lyman says. "She knew it was hard on me. It was hard on her, too. We'd leave everything behind and only take what we could get in the car. Every new place we'd start all over. She said we had to move because she had a lot of student loans that she couldn't hope to pay off and we were moving to escape bill collectors."

Lysa and I make eye contact.

"Kernel of truth," I say.

"Exactly," agrees Lysa.

Lyman looks confused. "Obviously we were moving because of me."

"Yes," Lysa says. "But most of the time when people lie there's a kernel of truth to their story. Knowing that your mom is a doctor, I think the student loan story is also true and might help us find your grandmother."

"How do you know you have a grandmother?" I ask.

"There's a contact in my mom's phone to call in case of an emergency. Her name is Millie and I asked my mom about her once," Lyman says. "She paused for a really long time and then she said Millie was my grandmother."

"Do you know Millie's last name?" I ask.

Lyman shakes his head. "Just Millie."

"But did you try calling the number?" Spam asks.

Lyman sighs. "Disconnected."

The three of us groan.

"What if she's—" Lysa slaps her hand over her mouth to keep from stating the obvious.

Spam waves her hand. "A disconnect doesn't mean anything. Lots of people have changed their numbers in the last ten years because they gave up their landlines."

Spam points to me. "Type in a search for Millie Jenkins and select images."

Within seconds I'm able to turn my laptop around for all to see. There are a bunch of images, but they are mostly of young women. Too young to be Lyman's grandmother. There's also one that's way too old.

Spam pats her chair for Lyman to come sit next to her. He smiles softly as he joins her. I admire the deep and soulful way they look at each other. It's clear they have a special connection. "Jenkins was your father's last name," she says. "Millie is probably on your mother's side. Let's try Millie Booker."

I type in "Millie Booker" and press enter. My phone lights up. It's a Snapchat from Journey with a blurry picture of his hair on a white pillowcase. The caption says H IR ISSES O .

"Aww." I make a cute, pouty face. "Journey." I wave my phone.

"We don't have time for him right now," Spam says.

"I know, I know." As I scroll through the images of Millie Booker, I wonder how Journey's going to take the news when he finds out we helped Lyman. Will there be a problem between us because I kept something this big from him? I'm pretty sure I wouldn't be happy if the situation were reversed. And depending on how this works out, I'm going to have to tell him. "Nothing that looks promising on Millie Booker."

Lysa slides a piece of paper across the table to Spam. "Here's everything from the article."

Spam reads it off and transfers the names to the whiteboard. "Okay. Your parents' names are Katherine and Andrew Jenkins. Anything about siblings or grandparents?"

Lysa shakes her head.

"What about ages?" Spam asks.

"Katherine, twenty-six, Andrew, twenty-eight, and the baby was nineteen months."

Spam looks at Lyman. "What do you think, is your mom the older or younger sister?"

"My mom is older," Lyman says. "I think by maybe three years. She said she and her sister stopped talking a long time ago."

"Did she say why?" I ask.

Lyman shakes his head.

"Without the right last name we'll never find Lyman's grandma," I say.

"That's not necessarily true." Spam taps the marker on the board. "Lyman, can you get that phone number? The one you said was disconnected?"

"It's on my mom's phone. I'd have to go home to get it." Lyman checks the time. "Actually, I need to go home anyway. She'll be getting up to go to work soon and she will freak if I'm not there."

"Okay. Go home and get the number," Spam says. "Text it to me when you have it."

"Will do." Lyman gets up and heads for the stairs. He stops, turns back, and goes to Spam, wrapping her in a warm hug. He kisses the top of her head. "This was a crazy night and I don't know what I'd do without you." He looks at Lysa and me. "I don't know what I'd do without all of you."

He bows and pretends to tip an imaginary hat and then he leaves.

Spam stands completely still, watching him until he's gone. She sighs, then turns back to the whiteboard.

Lysa and I are just staring at her.

"Are we doing the right thing?" she asks.

I shake my head. "I don't know. I can't even get my head around what the right thing is in this situation."

"We're not doing the right thing," Lysa says. "But we are doing what we always do, which is the thing that feels the most right."

▶ 39 ◀

While movies and TV glamorize my profession by showing
us out in the field . . . crime scene analysts
basically work in laboratories.
—VICTOR FLEMMING

Spam hunches over her computer, wildly pecking keys. A couple of tears slide down her cheek and she brushes them aside with her sleeve.

"Spam, are you okay?" Lysa asks.

"Yes. Maybe. I don't know." She sits back, letting out a heavy sigh. "I'm pretty sure this is the right thing. I'm just worried I won't see him again."

"I know it sucks," I say. "But there isn't a better solution, is there?"

Spam shakes her head. Her lip quivers.

"How can you find his grandma's last name from a disconnected phone number?" Lysa asks.

"The Criss-Cross Directories." Spam stands up at the whiteboard and draws a giant triangle. "It's an online tool that you can use to find people. There are three basic identifiers: name, address, and phone number." She writes these words at each point on the triangle. "If you know two of the three, finding the third one is easy. But there's a chance it can still work even if you only know one."

Lysa gives her a sketchy look. "Are these directories legal?"

Spam chuckles. "What? You know me, right?"

"Which is why I'm asking," Lysa says. "We could be in enough trouble as it is. I don't want to compound it and make it worse."

Spam nods. "No worries. It's legal. It's a tool that private investigators use. My dad has an account."

"Why would your dad have an account like that?" I ask.

Spam tilts her head. "I don't know if he's still actively doing it. But he subscribed to it because he was trying to find my mom."

Of course. Spam's mom walked out on the family when Spam was in fourth grade and they've not seen or heard from her since. "He never found her?"

"Nope," Spam says. "It's like she left the planet."

Lysa and I exchange looks. "Sorry."

"Ah, it's not that bad," she says. "Thanks to her, I've got these cool trust issues that keep me from getting close to people . . . except for you guys . . . and now Lyman."

Spam's phone pings with a text message coming through. She reads it. "Aggh. He says he can't get to his mom's phone." She types a message back to him. "I'm telling him to check the computer. She probably has her contacts backed up there."

After a few minutes, another message comes in with the phone number. "He got it. Now, let's see if this is going to work." Spam accesses the directory. "Okay. I'm typing in Millie and the number. Fingers crossed."

We're all waiting.

"Okay. No address." She closes her eyes and crosses her fingers, chanting, "Please, please, please. Just a name. That's all we need."

There's a ping. She opens her eyes and looks. "Johnson.

Lyman's grandmother's name is Millicent Johnson." Elated, Spam jumps up and writes this on the board under the facts we know.

Lysa and I don't share her euphoria. "Spam, that's a pretty common name. There could be a million Millicent Johnsons," I say.

"Seven hundred and forty-one thousand hits," Lysa says. "In just one search."

Spam points to the list on the board. "Yes. But how many Millicent Johnsons are there who lost a daughter to drugs and a grandson to a kidnapper, and has a daughter who is a doctor?"

She has a point.

"First, we'll skim through the top photos to narrow our search. Then we'll start searching for specifics. Trust me. This works."

"If it works, then how come your dad didn't find your mom?" Lysa asks.

"Clearly, she didn't want to be found," Spam says. "There's a good chance that Millie would really like to get to know her grandson."

"Let's hope." This is a lot like what I was feeling not knowing who my father was. The main thing I wanted was to know that he was at least happy to find out that I exist. Maybe now is a good time to tell them about Victor. "By the way, I think I found out who my father is."

"Wait. What?" Lysa is so shocked she leaps out of her chair and it clatters backward.

"Holy crap," Spam says. "When did that happen and why didn't you tell us?"

"It was only a couple of days ago, but everything's been so crazy we haven't had a chance to talk about just stuff. Anyway, there's a chance that it's Victor."

"Wait. What?" Spam tilts her head, trying to figure this out.

"It's a long story . . . but he and my mom . . ." I shrug. They can figure out the rest.

Spam and Lysa surround me, hugging and squealing.

We're making so much noise that Mr. Ramos appears at the bottom of the stairs, bedraggled, in his bathrobe with hair sticking up. "Holy cow," he says. "What's going on down here? I thought you were being murdered, and after I let that boy into the house."

"Sorry, Dad," Spam says, trying to look contrite. "We'll be quiet, I promise."

He wags his finger. "You better. Any littles who wake up because of your noise, I'm sending them down here for you to deal with."

"Fair enough," Spam says.

After Mr. Ramos leaves, I tell them about my conversation with Victor. To me, the best part of the story is how happy he was to possibly have a daughter.

"Hopefully, that's how Lyman's grandmother will feel too," Spam says.

We narrow the search for Lyman's grandma down to three Millie Johnsons—two who live on the other side of the country, and one who lives about five hours away in Washington State. The last one is the most logical because it's near where the articles about Lyman's parents were written.

Spam prints out all three profiles. "We'll show these to Lyman tomorrow. He might be able to eliminate one or two just on the facts."

It's approaching midnight and it has been a pretty long day. Spam goes to the closet and drags out the sleeping bags and pillows. Lysa goes into the bathroom to change into her pajamas and brush her teeth.

I sink down into a pile of pillows, but I bring the laptop with me. Instead of being tired after today's drama, I'm ramped up. "Are you guys really ready to go to sleep?"

"I am," Spam says with a yawn.

"Me too," Lysa agrees.

"I'm going to surf the net for a little while," I say. "Okay?"

Spam crawls into her sleeping bag. She waves. "Have fun. Don't do anything I wouldn't do."

Lysa gives her a disgusted look. "You know that either one of us would naturally stop way before you would, right?"

Spam smiles as she snuggles down into her sleeping bag. "Yeah. But I like saying it anyway."

I dive into computer search mode. We found some solid answers for Lyman. I should be able to find the same for Journey.

► 40 ◄

It's never a slam dunk, but a defendant can request a new trial
if evidence surfaces that might change the
outcome of the original verdict.
—VICTOR FLEMMING

"Erin. Erin." Someone is shaking me.

I'm majorly annoyed as this rude interruption yanks me out
of the fog of a fantastic dream where I'm in a courtroom, on
the witness stand, about to deliver the perfect hammer of
evidence that will win the case.

In reality I'm in a sleeping bag, on the floor of Spam's basement. The laptop stands open on my chest and I'm surrounded
by wadded up paper and scribbled on Post-it notes. Spam and
Lysa are hovering over me.

"Did you stay up all night surfing the net?" Lysa asks, accusation dripping from her words.

I yawn and stretch. "I don't think it was all night."

"Lightweight," Spam says with a giggle.

But I suddenly remember what I was doing and what I found.
I sit straight up. Spam catches the laptop as it tumbles off my
chest. "Oh man."

"What?" Lysa asks.

"I have to see Journey. I think I found something that might
help his father's case."

"What," Lysa asks.

I hold up my hand. "Wait." First, I check my phone to see if the links I sent to myself came through. I can't risk losing what I found last night. Fist pump. They're there.

Next I send Journey a text asking about his plans for the day.

He texts back that he's already at the lab with Victor and will be there for most of the day. I ask if I can come over. I have some information for him.

He texts back that Victor says we should all come, there's plenty of work to be done and only a few days before camp opens. Journey reports Victor is offering pizza as a bribe.

OR RE ST I text back.

WHENE ER he writes.

RT I reply.

And the three of us hit the ground running to get ready.

"We're picking up Lyman on the way," Spam says.

As we're heading out the door, I send a text to Rachel letting her know our plans for the day. She writes back that Victor had already mentioned he needed all available hands to get everything ready for the camp.

In less time than it normally takes for me to pick out an outfit, we have Lyman and we're at our favorite coffee place. Lysa and I handle the drink orders while Spam and Lyman huddle in the corner over the Millie profiles we found.

I keep glancing over at them, trying to read their body language. But there appears to be no emotion involved, just the two of them hunched over the documents and their phones.

When the coffees are ready, they join us and we transition back to the car.

I can't believe I'm the most curious of the three of us, but I can't stand waiting. I have to know. "Well?"

"We found her," Spam says.

"Are you absolutely sure?" Lysa asks.

"Yes." Lyman laughs. "In the background of one of the Millie photos you can see a portion of a photo on a shelf . . . and it's my mom. I'm positive I've seen it before."

"Which one was she?" Lysa asks.

"The one in Washington State," Lyman says. "She's not that far."

"So what are you going to do?" I ask.

Lysa and I are in the back, Lyman is in the front passenger seat. All eyes are on him. Spam's literally holding her breath and waiting for him to speak before she starts the car.

"I have three days to get everything ready and spend some time with my mom. Then I'll leave and go to my grandmother's. I just hope she's been wishing for family." His voice wavers, but he pauses to clear his throat. Spam places her hand over his. "I'll plan to leave Friday. My mom works a long shift on Fridays and is usually so tired when she gets home she doesn't even check on me until Saturday afternoon. I'll leave a note telling her what I've done and why. That will give her the weekend to disappear."

"Would you like us to meet with her after you're gone and tell her how we helped you? So that she'll know you're really okay?" Lysa asks.

"No." Lyman is adamant. "She needs to think that I'm the only one who knows the truth. Otherwise, she'll really freak out."

"I get it," I say.

"Do you want us to take you home now?" Spam asks.

"If it's okay, I'd like to hang with you guys the rest of this week. I'm really sorry I'm going to miss the actual camp. It sounds like fun."

▼ ▼ ▼

The classroom is abuzz with activity. Coach Wilkins has a bunch of papers spread out on the long counter behind the teacher's desk. It looks like he's collating packets for all the campers, including Victor's.

"Hi, Coach," I say.

"Hi, Erin," he replies.

Victor is just heading out. He stops and grabs my head with both of his hands and makes a demonstration of planting a big smooch on my forehead.

"You kids are lifesavers. See those boxes over in the corner? That's what we picked up last night." He wiggles his fingers in the direction of the supply room. "Make it disappear. Then you can start putting together kit boxes—think crime scene kit. One for each camper and maybe a couple of extras. I left a list on the desk. I'll be back in a couple of hours." Victor sweeps out the door, blowing kisses to Lysa and Spam on his way. He even gives Lyman's shoulder a squeeze. "Good to see you again," he says.

As I watch him go, I can tell he's distracted. This isn't Victor's normal MO. I just hope he really is dealing with all of this like he promised.

Journey and Clay are on the lab side assembling a long white conference table. Together they stand it on its legs. Then Clay begins unpacking leather office-style chairs. He waves.

I wave back a cup of coffee that I brought for Journey, who bounds over to the door.

"Where's mine?" Clay calls out.

"Sorry, I didn't know you were here or I would have brought you one."

Lyman grabs a couple of boxes and leads the way into the storage room. Lysa and Spam follow him.

Journey checks his watch. "I ordered the pizza." He leans against one of the desks. "So, what was going on last night? You sounded really weird and you basically hung up on me."

I glance at the storage room. Everyone else is in there. I hate lying to Journey. But what choice do I have?

"Nothing," I say. "You know how it is with Lysa and Spam. Sometimes they get on each other's nerves and I'm in the middle. It's all okay now, though."

"Really?" he asks. "Because Lysa said hi, but Spam's avoiding me. And Lyman's here again? When did that become a thing?" Journey edges toward the storage room. To keep him away from the door, I move in the opposite direction. I don't want him overhearing any risky conversations they might have.

"He and Spam are in *that* space." I make fluttery romantic eyes, but Journey only looks more confused. "Victor doesn't seem to mind." I grab Journey's shirt and lead him toward the center of the room. "Anyway, I have something to show you."

He glances into the lab. Clay's now lying on the floor, tightening the screws on wheels on the chairs. "I should be in there helping Clay," he says.

Clay waves. "No worries. I've got this."

I tap some keys on my phone. "So, last night I stayed up surfing the net because I'm still working on the ballistics stuff for the camp."

"I thought you were tired," Journey says.

I'm a terrible liar. "I was when you called, but then I couldn't sleep. Anyway, I came across something you need to see."

"What's that?" Journey asks.

"Remember how your father claimed he didn't have any shells for the shotgun?"

"Yeah," Journey says.

"Well, I hope you won't get mad, but I looked up the transcripts from his trial. There's not much listed in as evidence."

"I know," Journey says.

"But they found a bunch of shell casings that had been fired from his gun."

Journey looks sad. "Yeah. That's one of the things that kinda stuck with me. Either my father is straight-up lying or someone else was shooting his gun."

"Exactly. So, look at this." I open my phone to an online article. "I'll send it to you, but basically forensics investigators have discovered something new. The heat produced by firing a bullet can actually *etch* the fingerprint of the person who loaded that bullet onto the brass casing of the shell, preserving it forever."

"Wow." Journey takes my phone and scans the article. "That's like—whoa!"

"It might be a long shot, but if you believe your father is telling the truth, show this to Victor. There's a machine called CERA which extracts prints from the cylindrical shape of a bullet casing and process it so it can be run through AFIS."

"Victor probably knows about this, right?" he says.

"Probably, but he's been so scattered lately, a reminder couldn't hurt," I say.

Journey shakes his head. "No kidding. Getting this camp up and running has been insane."

I wrap my arms around his waist. "Anyway, I hope you're not mad."

Journey kisses me on the forehead. "I'm not mad at all. This could be an excellent find. And you can read up on stuff all you want. Just don't . . .

"I know . . . cause any problems."

Coach Wilkins finishes his packets and wanders over to join us. "Wow. Fingerprints etched into the brass. That forensic stuff is wild, isn't it? I remember this one story where they found a frozen Viking in a glacier and not only managed to get his DNA, but they figured out he had been murdered. A Viking! Can you imagine that?"

Clay comes out of the lab. "My favorite one is the guy who killed a whole family and then ordered a pizza, but got caught because he didn't eat the crust."

The coach brightens. "I know. Totally stupid."

I exchange side-eye with Journey. This is stuff we like to talk about too. It's just a little weird to see adults as enthusiastic about it as we are.

"Yeah, your uncle is really bringing it to our little city. Criminals better beware." The coach checks his watch. "I'm going to take off. Tell Vic I left the registration packets for his campers on the counter over there. I know he's busy and I figured as long as I was doing mine I could do his, too."

"That was nice. I'll tell him. Bye." I wait until the coach leaves and the door completely closes before I turn to Journey and Clay. "It's not just my imagination. There's something weird about that guy, right?"

"What do you mean?" Clay asks.

"Well, at the camp sign-ups he was like brutally competitive with Victor, and now he's acting like Victor's best friend."

"He just thinks your uncle is cool, that's all. And, frankly, I think he's pretty cool as well." Clay goes over to the steel mesh door and gestures to Journey. "I'm ready to work on the desk and I could use your help."

"I'll be right there." Journey turns back to me. "I really do appreciate everything you've done, but I have to get back to work."

"Me too." I nod toward the storage room.

Journey glances back at Clay, who holds up his thumb. "Oh, that's right. Duh. You can't get in there without me."

Journey goes to open the door for Clay, and I slip into the storage room.

Lysa and Spam are handing items to Lyman for him to stack on the shelves. Lyman's shelves are a thing of beauty. Everything is precisely lined up and arranged in a way that will be easy to find and use.

"Lyman," I say, "how are we ever going to keep these shelves straight without you?"

"Maybe Victor should hire Lyman as a counselor for next year," Journey says.

I had no idea he walked into the storage room behind me.

Lysa, Spam, and I all share the same freaked-out, harried expressions.

Even Lyman seems a little bit frozen in time.

No one dares to speak.

"What'd I say?" Journey asks.

I shake it off. "Nothing. We're just really impressed with Lyman's mad organizational skills. Right?"

Lysa and Spam are all over each other agreeing with my statement.

Journey frowns. "That's pretty much what I was saying too. Anyway, pizza's here."

We all rush for the door to try to leave this awkward situation as far behind as possible.

► 41 ◄

Aiding and abetting means knowing about a crime and
not reporting it. The penalty can be equal to
the penalty for the crime itself.
—LYSA MARTIN

I'm caught in the middle.

Spam wants a goodbye dinner for Lyman. Which is great.
And she wants to pay for it with some of the money we've
raised by selling the Bella. Which is also great.

My problem is that Journey will—understandably—want to
come to the dinner with me. And I'm worried about him finding out about Lyman's situation—specifically about Lyman's
mom. We all agree she deserves a chance to get away. But if
Journey finds out about her, I know he'll feel obligated to tell
Victor. He'll even say it's to help her.

"Don't worry," Lysa says. "We'll just be extra careful not to
leak any critical information."

"Right. We'll just act normal," Spam says.

Lysa and I just look at her.

"Okay. Maybe 'normal' wasn't the right word," she says. "But
we can do this."

I hope she's right.

▼　▼　▼

Lysa, Spam, and Lyman are already seated at a table when we arrive.

Because their backs are to us, I try to make some noise as we approach. I even walk in a wide circle so they'll be sure to see us coming.

Lysa spots us first and nudges Spam. They abruptly stop talking as soon as we arrive. And it's completely awkward.

"Hey," Journey says to the group. Has he noticed their odd behavior?

The waiter comes to the table. Now that Journey and I have joined the group, he recognizes us as the crime-stopper kids he read about in the newspaper. He hurries off and returns with the owner. The owner insists on taking a photo of us to post on their blog.

"It'll be good for business," the owner says. "The whole city is so proud of you kids. Our restaurant is part of a national chain. This will look very good for us."

Journey is psyched about the photo. He gets out of his chair and pulls me with him so we can pose behind Lysa, Lyman, and Spam.

"Wait until you hear about the forensic camp for kids that we're starting next week," he says. "That will really be newsworthy."

"Oh. That sounds very exciting," the restaurant owner says.

While Journey is carrying on with the owner, the rest of us are kind of freaking out. The last thing Lyman needs now is publicity.

The owner readies his cell phone and tells us to squeeze together.

Lyman abruptly jumps up. "Excuse me." He tries to slip past me.

"No. Wait," the owner says. "One second for the photo."

"Oh, I'm not with them," he says.

The owner and Journey frown at his comment.

"I mean, I am with them, right now. Tonight," Lyman stammers. "I just wasn't one of the crime stoppers." He tries for a humble smile before slipping away from the group.

Journey grabs Lyman's jacket.

"Stay," he says. "You might not have been part of the team then . . . but you are now. I can tell just by the way the girls act toward you."

Lyman is caught. He has no choice but to pose for the photo.

The owner shows us the photo on his phone. It's a great shot of all of us. Lyman looks particularly good, as he was standing directly under a floodlight fixture.

"Great," Lyman says with a smile that's really more of a grimace.

Not wanting to stand out any further, we quietly order our food.

Only a space alien who had never seen a group of human kids have dinner before would think that our actions and conversation were anything close to normal.

Spam and Lyman sit woodenly next to each other and barely touch their food, even if they are holding hands under the table.

Lysa tries to get a conversation going, but her attempts sound a lot more like interrogations.

I'm hoping for a juicy topic to come along and distract us, but I can't think of anything.

"Oh, I talked to Victor," Journey finally says after a very long lull in the conversation. We all lean forward, anxious for something to soak up the awkward. But we're so suddenly and unbelievably attentive to Journey that, for a moment, we throw him off his game.

He pauses, staring at his plate.

"Yes?" Lysa asks.

Journey shakes his head. "Sorry. I forgot what I was saying."

"You said you talked to Victor . . ." I try prompting him.

Lysa and I make desperate eye contact across the table. This dinner might have been the worst idea ever.

"Oh. Now I remember," Journey says. "Before we left the lab tonight I told Victor about that article you found and I reminded him there were brass shells collected from the property. He agrees that's exactly the kind of thing we're looking for. Something they didn't know to test for back then, that we can test for now. He thinks it could be an important break for my dad."

"Really?" I ask.

"Yeah," Journey says. "He's even tracked down one of the machines and is working on seeing if we can borrow it."

"That's great." I scan the table. "Doesn't that sound great?"

"Yeah, great," Lysa says.

"Sounds great," Lyman says.

"Really great," Spam says.

Journey looks around the table. "Seriously, what's going on with you guys?"

We all shake our heads and deny that there's anything going on. Spam stares at her plate.

"I'm totally not buying this," Journey says. "And I'm starting to get mad, so whatever is going on, I need you to tell me. Just so you know, if it's something with Victor or the lab, I'm not going to promise to keep my mouth shut, either, because they're transferring the evidence from my father's case into our evidence room tomorrow. So, if you guys are pulling anything shady, I need you to tell me now and I need you to knock it off. I can't afford to let anything derail my father's case. Not when we're this close." Journey's breath is coming in hot gasps now. He wads up his napkin and drops it in his plate.

We are stunned into silence. None of us dares to look directly at him or even at each other. Awkwardness hangs over us like a thick layer of fog.

When no one speaks, Journey shakes his head and looks directly at me. "Please. Please don't do something to screw up the evidence from my father's case. The reading and giving me information is fine. It's good even. But you promised you wouldn't do anything more."

I take his hands in mine and look deeply into his eyes. "Don't worry. I haven't and I won't. We haven't done anything to affect the lab and we're not doing anything that could compromise Jameson's case. Right?" I scan the faces at the table.

Everyone nods, but no one dares to speak.

Our refusal sounds pretty lackluster, and even if we do mean it, Journey's not buying it.

► **42** ◄

We are in full-on camp countdown mode.

Today is the last regular work day before camp starts on
Monday. I ride in with Victor, and Journey's already waiting
in the lab when we arrive. I can tell from the wary way he looks
at me that he's not completely comfortable with how we left
last night.

Clay shows up a few minutes later, lugging a heavy toolbox
in each hand. Both Lysa and Lyman are coming with Spam and
they should be here soon.

Victor scrawls rambling to-do lists all over the glass window
and we waste no time getting to work.

By midmorning, everything is progressing perfectly.

Thanks to Lyman's incredible organizational skills and attention to detail, the four of us finish assembling thirty-two
camper crime scene kits, which include a mini fingerprint kit,
flashlight, disposable camera, and instruction cards outlining
each activity. They're stacked on the display counter behind
the instructor's desk.

Victor has approved our schedule and activities, so I'm

typing up the hour-by-hour official schedule on Victor's computer.

Spam is creating slide presentations. Every morning we can run a new set of slides as a way to introduce the activities and get the campers excited.

Lysa is putting together the master list of the campers' names, ages, contact information, and allergies. She's also working on name badges and a seating chart.

We are perfectly on schedule. And we're going to look amazing from day one.

Unfortunately, the crime lab and Clay's to-do list aren't in quite as good order. But Victor said they didn't have to be.

"As long as there isn't a sudden crime spree in Iron Rain we're okay," Victor says. "As long as there isn't a sudden crime spree we have a little more leeway with the lab. The important thing is that the classroom is ready for the inspector tomorrow morning."

Clay is feverishly installing the fire alarms and the brackets for fire extinguishers. "All the alarms and extinguishers will be in by this afternoon," he says.

Meanwhile, it turns out that Lyman is pretty creative. With lots of weird suggestions from each of us, he's arranging the crime scene tableau.

The first day of camp is going to feature the weirdest Halloween display ever.

Lyman started with a life-size plastic skeleton from Miss P's old classroom. He's dressing it in some old clothes and sunglasses Spam brought from home. He sprawls the skeleton dramatically across a chair near the front of the room.

Journey makes prints of his shoe and tapes them to the floor.

I leave an obvious fingerprint on the lens of the skeleton's sunglasses.

Lysa has made up a batch of Miss P's fake blood. She puddles some on the floor and splatters some on the side of the desk. She's also added a few additional props: a bottle labeled OISON and a jar labeled R GS.

Clay is so impressed by our scene that he donates an old hammer. He says we should make it look like the murder weapon. Spam manages to wedge the clawed end of the hammer in the skeleton's eye socket and moves the sunglasses up on his forehead.

By the time we're done, the scene is authentic and scary enough that Miss Blankenship actually lets out a tiny shriek when she stops by unexpectedly and *click, clicks* right into it.

On the heels of Miss Blankenship, two police officers show up in the classroom on official business, looking for Victor. Lysa summons Victor by tapping on the glass.

I recognize the older one. It's Officer Baldwin. He was the first one I talked to after finding Miss P's body. And he told me then that I was going to be okay.

"Hey, Officer Baldwin," I say. "Do you remember me?"

He brightens into a big smile. "Well, there's our girl," he says. He looks around, making a sweeping gesture around the classroom and lab. "Looks like you've got some fancy stuff going on here."

"It's going to be interesting," I say.

Officer Baldwin sets the file box on one of the desks. It's labeled COLTER, RODNEY.

"Is this what you've been waiting for?" he asks.

"Not me," I say. "But yes. My uncle has been waiting for it."

Victor thanks the officers, signs a receipt, and takes the box. Journey uses his thumb to unlock the steel door of the evidence room.

We watch as Victor opens one of the lockers and puts the

box on a shelf. I move to the steel mesh wall between the lab and classroom so I have a better view of what they're doing.

Victor lifts the lid on the box. On top are a few sheets of paper—it looks like a list. He runs his finger down the list of items and stops.

He shows the list to Journey, pointing to a particular line.

Victor reaches into the box and runs his hand around. When he pulls his hand up, he's holding a plastic bag with some spent shells in the bottom.

Journey makes eye contact and gives me a strong nod.

Victor leaves the bag of shells in the box, and slides the box into a locker. He and Journey step out of the evidence room. Journey tests the door to be sure it's closed and securely locked.

► 43 ◄

Most of the children who have been abducted by a family member are returned alive. But they frequently suffer harmful and damaging memories.

—MISSING CHILD WEBSITE

Lysa and I force Spam to come out with us.

Tonight's the night. Lyman's leaving. We agreed that none of us will know how or when. That way, if we're questioned afterward, we can honestly say we didn't know.

Plausible deniability, Lysa calls it.

They've already said their goodbyes, so there's no reason for Spam to mope alone, at home, when she could do her moping out with us. After plenty of prodding, the three of us are in line for tickets to the latest chick flick and my mouth is watering from the smell of freshly popped popcorn.

"I hope you guys don't mind, but I gave him four hundred dollars from the Bella money," Spam says. "That should be enough to get him there safely."

"He'll be fine, Spam," I promise.

"He will," she agrees. "It's me I'm worried about."

"You'll be fine too," Lysa says.

Just as Lysa moves to the front of the line, I get a text from Journey. H E THE ER   ON O R W   S S EET S
T THE   T N W T H S R N THE TEST.

O   O   EE   I text back.

ESSSSSS   he replies.

"Forget the movie," I say, waving my phone. "They're on their way back. Victor's running the test tonight and we can watch."

"In that case, drop me off at home," Spam says as we head back to the car.

"No. You want to be there when Victor proves that Journey's dad didn't kill that poor kid, right? This is historic." I nudge Lysa. "Tell us, Counselor. Has Iron Rain ever exonerated an inmate before?"

Lysa gives an irritated huff. "You only call me counselor when you're using me to support your case."

"That's not true. This time I'm calling you counselor because I think you'll know the answer."

"Call me Lysa and I'll still know. But, to answer your question, I don't think Iron Rain has ever exonerated someone who has been incarcerated for fourteen years. That's a really long time."

"See, Spam? You don't want to miss that."

But her face is completely devoid of emotion, which is not a trait that would normally ever be applied to Spam. Her voice is unusually flat too.

"I just . . ." She trails off as if she doesn't have enough energy to continue talking.

"We get it," Lysa says, buckling her seatbelt and starting the car.

"I feel so bad for him. He shouldn't have to tear up his whole life to protect his mom."

"You mean aunt," Lysa says.

Spam nods. "Aunt-mom. You heard how he feels about her. I know it seems like I haven't known him that long, so how could I be so connected? But I *knew* him. I told him things about me that I've never told the two of you."

Lysa and I glance at each other.

"I'm going to be honest here," Lysa says. "It worries me that you got so attached so quickly."

"Me too," I say. "You were always the one who had no tolerance for boys. And now look at you."

She gestures to her sad face. "Well, take a new look, this is unattached. I'll probably never see him again. Our goodbye was practically a handshake."

"There's a chance you'll see him again. When he turns eighteen he can come back," I say. "Plus, you know how to find each other in that game. Right?"

"That's why I wanted to stay home; I was thinking maybe he'd show up for one last raid before he goes."

There's a ping as another text from Journey comes in to my phone. "Oh, Journey says Victor just spilled something on his shirt and wants me to bring him a fresh one. Let's go to my house, pick up a shirt for Victor. Then we can stop and get something to eat. By then it will be time to grab some coffee and meet them at the school. Once the test is over, we'll drive you home. You'll be home by nine-thirty or ten at the latest. That's plenty of time to try to find Lyman on the game if he's still around."

Spam rolls her head against the back of the seat. "Fine," she says.

▾ ▾ ▾

When we arrive at my house, Lysa and Spam wait in the kitchen while I run upstairs and grab a clean shirt out of Victor's closet.

I fly back down the stairs with a white shirt for Victor tucked under my arm. Lysa and Spam are curiously eyeing the dining room, now set up like Victor's office.

"When did you do this?" Lysa wonders.

"It looks so different," Spam says.

"Victor needed a place to work. Once school starts and he can officially move onto the campus this might change. But for now, this is his office."

"Does Rachel even still live here?" Lysa asks.

"Oh yeah. She does," I say. "She stays at the chief's a lot. But we still see each other every day."

"Is Rachel and the chief weird for you?" Spam asks.

I shrug. "Not really."

I catch Lysa and Spam exchanging a look and I remember my intention to stop hiding my feelings. I lean against the door into the dining room.

"Yeah, it is kinda weird. There's been a shift in our relationship. But it might be a good thing. It used to be I couldn't breathe without Rachel in my business. Now it's like she and Victor tag team, and his style is more hands-off."

"Is she happy like this?" Lysa asks.

"I think so," I say. Then remember my mission for honesty. "Actually, she's a completely different person now, you should see her. She's way happier. Turns out I was holding her back."

"I'm sure that's not true," Lysa argues. "You and Rachel are family."

"We are. But Victor told me she didn't set out to be a 911 operator, she wanted to be a police officer. But she thought that wasn't a wise occupation for a single parent."

"She stayed and stuck it out with you though," Spam says. "And that counts."

"Kids aren't supposed to think that their parents would have been better off without them," Lysa says, pinching her lips together in a frown.

"I get that. But she deserves to have her own life too. Right?" I straighten the papers on Victor's desk. "Things with Victor are better than ever—which is why he can't find out about . . . you know."

"Does Rachel know that Victor might be your father?" Lysa says.

I pause. "I'm pretty sure if Victor had told her, she would have said something to me. So I'm guessing the answer is no."

This is a reminder that at our next dinner I need to broach the subject with Rachel.

A Snapchat arrives from Journey.

It's a video of the turnoff sign to Cape Disappointment. One of our favorite landmarks. This means they're about thirty minutes away.

"We better get going."

▼ ▼ ▼

We park next to Victor's car in the school parking lot and I'm the first one out.

I head straight for the stairs, but by the time I reach the door I realize I've got a problem.

"Hey . . . somebody get the door." I'm juggling Journey's special coffee, Victor's clean shirt, my messenger bag, *and* my cell phone?

I glance behind me. Dang! Lysa and Spam aren't even to the stairs yet. Okay. It's possible that I'm a little overexcited and, also, that I mostly ran here from the parking lot.

I try shifting everything to my left arm to see if I can free my right thumb to activate the lock. When that doesn't work,

I lightly kick the door in the hopes that Journey will hear me and come let me in.

They obviously can't hear me, so I have no choice but to wait until Lysa and Spam get here. I can't help it—I'm going to totally geek out watching Victor and Journey pull off this test.

This could be it. The moment of getting an innocent man released from prison. How amazing would that be? Journey could be reunited with his dad. I'm proud of the fact that I'm the one who found the article on the CERA machine and the idea of checking for fingerprints etched into the shell casings. Even Victor said it was a good call. And he admitted he had been too busy to focus on the case.

Those shells probably made Jameson look like a liar fourteen years ago. And now they might set him free.

I hear Lysa and Spam coming down the stairs behind me.

"Finally. Can someone get the door?"

Lysa waves the fact that she has her cell phone, purse, and iPad in one hand and a fully loaded cardboard coffee carrier in the other. "Obviously, I can't," she says.

We both look to Spam.

Spam is oblivious. She has her cell phone in one hand and her Bella tracking phone in the other and she's moving around, waving her arms to try to get a stronger signal.

"Spam, what are you doing?" I ask.

"I get that the basement gets crap reception, but there's not even any connectivity on these stairs." She continues waving her arms. "What if Lyman needs me?"

"Open the door," I say. "There's Wi-Fi in the classroom."

"That's right." Spam slips both phones into one hand and presses her right thumb onto the pad, unlocking the door. She opens it and we pour into the classroom.

The light is off in the classroom but on in the lab and

shining through the large window. I catch a glimpse of Victor and Journey from the back. They're sitting next to each other at the lab conference table. I'm so glad Journey is getting this opportunity to work with Victor. They are so much alike.

We dump our stuff on the nearest lab table and I turn to flip on the light.

Suddenly, Clay appears blocking my way.

"Clay! You scared me! What are you doing."

Then I see the handgun, pointed right at my face.

"Oh my god!" Spam shrieks.

► 44 ◄

Just because you don't see something
doesn't mean it's not there.

—MISS P

I'm too stunned to move or react. Nothing here makes any sense.

Clay waves the gun from side to side. "Step back. Slow and easy. Hands up."

I glance at Victor and Journey. Why aren't they doing anything? Why aren't they taking care of this? Why aren't they even moving at all?

"Clay?" I say.

"Shut up," he barks. "Just do it."

I back awkwardly into Spam and Lysa. This is completely surreal. We look like characters in a bad TV show.

"What is this?" Spam whispers.

"Clay? I don't understand," I say.

"Cell phones? Let's have them," he demands.

The three of us don't move, but shift our gaze to the cell phones lying on the nearby desk. Clay follows our gaze.

He smashes the phones a couple of times with the butt of the gun and shards of glass spit in all directions. "Drop them in the sink," he orders.

Lysa scrambles forward, scooping up the cell phones and dumping them in the nearest sink.

"Turn on the water," Clay orders.

Lysa turns on the water, then she steps back behind me and clutches Spam.

The lab door is propped open with a chair. Upon closer inspection, I realize that Victor and Journey are strapped into chairs with duct tape. Their heads are tilted forward. I can't see their eyes; they aren't moving.

Are they dead?

I'm consumed by a surge of rage, fueled by despair.

I grab two of the nearest coffees, flick off the lids with my thumbs, and fling the entire contents straight at Clay's face.

"Run!" I scream to Lysa and Spam. I whirl, heading for the door to the lab. "The glass is bulletproof!" If we can get inside and close the door we might be safe.

Clay curses loudly and deflects most of the liquid with his arm. It's been a while since we bought the coffee so it wasn't scalding hot enough to do any real damage, but it makes him accidentally fire off a shot anyway.

Lysa and Spam clutch each other and duck at the sound of the bullet ricocheting around the room. They won't make it into the lab and I won't go without them. I edge back to them, but I can't take my eyes off Victor and Journey, so I don't see it coming when Clay slams the left side of my head with his fist, which is wrapped around his gun. My head jerks to the right and the whole world turns a watery gray. My knees weaken. I grab the edge of a desk as a large area of pain blooms slowly over my left ear.

I press my hand against my wound. A large knot swells and throbs.

I shrink back from Clay. But he's right there, holding the gun pointed directly at my forehead.

"Oops." I want it to sound mouthy and unafraid. But it comes out like more of an apologetic croak.

"Try that again and I will put a bullet in your brain."

Spam and Lysa clutch at my arms. I'm unsteady and dizzy.

"Why are you doing this?" I ask, my voice thick and drowsy.

"Shut up," he says. "All of you, into the lab."

He motions for us to walk ahead of him. My fingers wander into something warm trickling down the side of my face. "But we're not allowed in the la—"

"Walk," he roars.

"Erin, don't antagonize him. He's literally homicidal," Lysa whispers.

Gee, Lys, ya think? The whole left side of my head is literally screaming at me exactly how homicidal he is.

I keep quiet and flow along with them into the lab. I'm dying to get a look at Victor and Journey. As we pass through the door I scan them for signs of trauma. I don't see any, so maybe—hopefully—they're still alive.

They're each taped to a chair. Their feet are taped to the pedestals. There's tape around their torsos. And their arms are taped to the armrests. On their faces are disposable fume masks like the one Clay wore when he was painting.

"You," he orders, waving the gun at me. "Smarty pants. Tape your friends into these chairs. Now. Move."

He pulls out two more chairs from the conference table.

"Sit," he orders them.

"You don't need to hurt us," Lysa says. "Just take what you need and go." Her voice is firm, calm, and well modulated, just like her mother's.

"Really?" Clay stifles a laugh. "You're telling *me* what I need." He drives his foot into the soft spot behind my knee, nearly taking me down. "TAPE. Good and tight. Start with their mouths, I'm sick of listening to all of you. Tape their hands to the arms of the chair. Tape their ankles together. And then tape around their shoulders. Trust me, there won't be a last-minute salvation where you wind up on TV talking about how you saved the day. Not this time."

My head throbs and I'm trembling so hard I can barely stand. Also, he just said he was going to kill us.

This isn't a dream but it might as well be. What in the world is going on?

Lysa knows how to keep her emotions in check, so I start with her. I'm afraid to even look at Spam, because we'll both lose it.

It's weird how I manage to do it, but I separate my brain and my hands into two different worlds.

My hands work fast. Taking care of business. Completely unemotional. I could tape down a row of kittens and it wouldn't faze my hands.

My brain is another story.

It's murky, sketchy, woozy, and on fire, all at the same time. I'm trying to plan three steps ahead. But there's this fog that I can't seem to crawl out from under. And I'm worried to death about Journey and Victor.

Why is Clay doing this? What could he possibly want? Lysa says psychopaths love to talk about themselves and display how much smarter they are than everyone else.

"I don't know what you want, but you must be pretty smart, Clay. I'm guessing Victor underestimated you." I glance at Victor, feeling a little sick to my stomach. Then I shift my gaze to Lysa. Her eyes tell me this is a good direction.

"Shut. Up," he says.

Lysa nods for me to keep going.

"I'm just impressed. I've been dying to get into this lab and look at you. Bam, you're in!"

"I cut the power," he brags. "No power, no door locks."

"But you're still hanging around, tying people up. Which means you didn't get what you needed. Am I right?"

"Less yakking, more taping," he orders.

"I'm trying," I complain. "But it's really sticky and not easy to pull off the roll."

"Just do it," Clay growls.

I finish securing Lysa and move to Spam. I gently put the tape over her mouth and she keeps dropping her eyes down. Up and then down. Up and then down.

Based on Spam's look I get the message that there's something on me. I slide my hand down, along the waistband, over my hip. There it is. Spam slipped her Bella phone into my back pocket.

I tug my shirt down over it and turn my hip away from Clay.

I don't know what's going to happen once I finish taping Spam. I can't bear to look in her eyes. Her terror only makes mine worse. The blow to my head is giving me double vision.

"Step back." Clay waves the gun in the direction he wants me to move. As much as it kills me to do so, I step back, away from Lysa and Spam. Their eyes are huge and round with terror.

Keeping the gun trained on me, Clay uses his other hand to turn a couple of disposable fume masks face side up on the table. He covers his own nose and mouth with his elbow before spritzing the inside of both masks with something.

He keeps his gaze on me and the gun at the ready as he slips one mask over Lysa's nose and mouth. Then he repeats the process on Spam. They struggle a little, but they're only breathing through their noses, and within a few seconds their eyes flutter shut and their heads tip forward.

"You don't have to do that," I yelp, stepping forward. "They'll be good. I promise."

"It's just a little bit of ether," he says. "I can't stand looking at their eyes."

"Ether?" I scream. "That's dangerous. Please, take it off."

"Shut up," Clay says. "They'll be fine. I have another job for you."

I follow his request and step back, but I'm not feeling very conversational. I give him my most angry, steely gaze.

"Now you're going to help me with my next problem," he orders.

What problem? Nothing's making any sense. What can I possibly help him with?

"Is there something wrong with the construction, Clay? Is there a problem with the inspection?" I ask. I'm grasping at straws but it's all I've got.

"Shut up. I need to think." Clay tucks the gun into his waistband and pulls his keys out of his pocket.

I zero in on his key ring.

It's a carved wooden ring, with a dolphin motif in the center—a twin to the one Journey's father gave him. The next thing I notice is the rather large Swiss Army knife.

Clay opens the blade and holds it up in such a way that the light glints off it.

"Here's a question for you, smarty-pants," he says. "Do I need to hack off the whole thumb or can I get by with just the skin? And which thumb should I should use—your uncle's or your boyfriend's?"

► 45 ◄

Forensic evidence can change the outcome
of a criminal investigation.
—VICTOR FLEMMING

"Don't be an idiot." It's all I can think/blurt out.

The chairs are on wheels. I grab the back of Victor's chair and try to wheel it away from Clay, but Victor's feet keep it from rolling smoothly. I turn the chair and push it. This puts me between Victor and Clay. I glance at Journey and my heart sinks. How am I going to save them all? Light glints off the blade of the knife.

"You don't need to cut anything," I add.

"It's the fastest way," he says.

"Really? I didn't think you'd be that stupid." I try to keep my voice level as I push Victor's chair toward the evidence locker door. "Cutting off a thumb with that knife will take longer than you think, and it'll get really messy. You'll wind up with incriminating evidence all over you."

Clay grins. "I'll give you this, you're a smart one."

I press my hand against Victor's neck. His skin is warm, which means he's still alive. I jostle the chair and scan his face, praying, *Wake up. Wake up.* There's a slight moan and I'm encouraged.

"I thought you said cutting the power disengaged the locks? Why didn't you just do that?"

"Doesn't work on the evidence room," Clay says.

That's right. The evidence locker had a different lock.

Victor groans softly and slightly flexes his hand. "Shhh," I whisper.

"Give me a minute and I'll get the door open for you." I roll Victor's chair right up next to the door. But there's a problem.

The way Victor's hand is taped down to the arm of the chair leaves his thumb about six inches away from the fingerprint pad on the door lock. I try to stretch the tape, but it's too tight.

"Clay, I need you to cut this tape a little so I can reach his thumb up to the door. Then you can get what you came for."

"You better not be working me," he says.

"I'm not." I rub the spot above my left eyebrow that continues to throb. It feels like my brain is about to blow out of my head. "Look." I step aside and hold Victor's thumb up toward the keypad. "I just need a few more inches."

Clay approaches me and slices through a strip or two of tape, allowing me to stretch Victor's thumb far enough to connect with the keypad. The lock clicks and the deadbolt slides back.

I push Victor to the side and behind me. "There. I don't know what you need to do but just do it and get it over with. "

Clay grabs my arm and pushes me ahead of him into the evidence room. I haven't been inside since this room was outfitted with the lockers. All three walls are lined with heavy steel lockers in a variety of sizes. The units fit right in under the high windows that run along the back wall.

To my knowledge the only evidence that has been delivered is from Jameson's case. Clay did seem interested in the case. It can't be that he's going though all of this because he just wants to see it? Clay swings the locker open. We were both here when the evidence was delivered, so he knew right where to find it. I try to edge my way to the door.

He grabs my arm and yanks me back. "Get back here."

My shoulder slams into the lockers and pain shoots through me.

"Find those shells," he orders, pointing at the box with his gun.

"What?"

"You know. The shells," he says. "The ones with my finger-prints etched into them."

Ohhh. Stunned doesn't begin to describe it. Whacked? Ambushed? Gobsmacked? Yes. All of that and more. I gasp. "You killed Rodney?"

"Stop stalling," Clay orders, poking me with the end of the gun.

I dig around in the box. There wasn't that much evidence in Journey's father's trial. The plastic bag of brass shells has slipped to the bottom. My fingers close around them. As I bring them out of the box, Clay snatches them from my hand. With the gun, he prods me into the corner of the locker room.

"Stay in that corner." He backs out of the door and starts to close it. Then he pauses, looking at Victor. He places his foot on the bottom of Victor's chair and shoves him into the evidence locker room with me.

He steps out and closes the door with a very final-sounding *clang.*

I rip the dust mask off Victor's face.

"Put that back," Clay orders, pressing the barrel of the gun against the holes in the mesh. "And stay away from him."

I carefully put the mask back on Victor's face, but I pinch one edge so it sticks up. I throw my hands up and move to the other side of the evidence locker, away from Victor.

Clay rummages in his toolbox and comes out with a handful of white plastic zip ties. Starting at the top of the evidence locker door, he slips a tie in place and cinches it tight, lashing the door to the doorframe. Working quickly, he adds seven more ties down the length of the door. The door won't open until all of the zip ties have been removed.

My heart sinks.

I know from the last time I had those plastic things around my wrists and ankles that there's no way to get them off without heavy-duty scissors or long, drawn-out sawing with a very sharp knife.

When he's finished, Clay pats the door. "There," he says. "That ought to hold the two of you."

Next, he turns his attention to my friends. He pushes Journey, Spam, and Lysa up to the table. To the casual observer, it looks like they're just hanging out, ready to have a meeting or a discussion, except for the creepy masks covering their noses and mouths.

Next, he goes into the lab area and twists the handle opening the gas valve. He takes out a bottle with a label large enough for me to read: ETONE. He splashes it liberally around the entire lab.

"Clay," I say, trying to reason with him. "You don't want to do that. Just go. It's not too late. You can still get away."

He pauses for a second, which makes me think he's considering leaving us alive. But then he just goes back to setting up the room.

"Talk to me, Clay. Tell me why you're doing this."

He shakes his head and continues about his business.

It's terrifying how visible he is through the glass walls of the lab, and he doesn't seem to care at all. He opens a cupboard and pulls out some plastic bottles of chemicals.

He dons plastic gloves and protective goggles. Then he pours about an inch of some liquid from a glass bottle into a beaker. Next, he rifles through a box of aluminum foil, crumbling layers until he has a ball of foil large enough to plug the top of the beaker. After that, he wraps several layers of foil over the plug and secures them with a rubber band.

Finally, he turns the beaker upside down and clips it to a beaker stand like that.

Underneath it, he positions a petri dish filled to the brim with another liquid.

He steps back, looking pleased.

With the stage set, Clay returns his tools to the toolbox. For my benefit, he makes a display of dropping the bag of shells in there too, along with his gun. He grabs his toolboxes and slips out the door, making sure it closes and locks behind him.

"Clay, wait." I try to reason with him. "Please. Don't do this."

He takes a long, mean look at me. "Nobody cared about this case for years, until now." He opens the door to the classroom to leave. "So this is on you."

"Clay. Tell me what you did in there. What's going to happen?" I beg.

"Ever hear of a chemical fuse?" He checks his watch. "You have about twenty minutes to say your prayers before this lights up. Amazing what you can learn on the internet, right?"

Oh my god. Potassium chlorate combined with sulfuric acid is a chemical fuse. And it *will* start a fire. That with the leaking gas and splashed acetone will destroy this whole room. And it will probably look like an accident, too.

"Clay. Wait."

He turns the light out as he exits the lab.

It's pitch dark and I have twenty minutes.

I pull Spam's Bella phone out of my pocket. The screen is locked. Crap.

I try to remember her favorite passwords. I key in her birthday. Nothing.

I try it backward. I try her father's birthday. No dice.

How do I not know Spam's mother's birthday?

Maybe Lyman. I'm trying to remember his birthday.

I just try typing the letters for "Lyman"—5, 9, 6, 2, 6. The phone blinks on and it's open. Yes! I try to make a call, but there isn't enough of a signal for it to go through. I try dialing 911 anyway and an error code appears on the screen.

Crap.

I glance at Victor. He'll know what to do. I rip the mask off his face and toss it aside. I gently smack his cheeks.

"Victor. Victor, wake up."

He groans.

I go to the mesh doors and shake them hard. They don't lock from the inside, but with eight zip ties holding them closed, getting out will be impossible unless I can find something sharp. I open every locker.

All empty.

The contents of Jameson's evidence box are mostly paper. If only I could paper cut my way out of this. I remember how my stomach lurched when I saw the giant knife tumble out of my mother's evidence box. What I wouldn't give to have that here now.

I go back to the phone. It's open and connected to Wi-Fi. Spam's selection of favorite apps pops up. Right on top is that game—the one she and Lyman play. Lyman could get us out of this. Even if he only called the police for us. I open the app and the game automatically signs me in.

I don't know the name of Lyman's character, so I just post as Spam. SOS NEE HE   What does she call it when things happen not in the game?

In real life. That's it.

I type again: SOS IN   NEE HE   IR   N I   O   RE THERE

I pause and watch the cursor blink off and on for a few seconds, but those seconds feel like hours.

What am I going to do?

My gaze stops on the windows over the lockers. I step onto the arm of Victor's chair and my foot slips off and kicks him in the ribs. He groans. But I manage to pull myself up on top of the lockers. I have to stay on my belly because there's only an eighteen-inch gap between the top of the lockers and the ceiling.

I knew the windows wouldn't open, but maybe I can kick out the glass and crawl out to get some help. I slam my foot against the glass. Nothing happens.

I try it again. Still nothing.

I give it a flurry of kicks, alternating feet.

"It's bulletproof," Victor says. His voice is thick and slow.

I look over the top of the lockers. Relief floods my body.

"Victor!"

I jump down from the lockers and start clawing at the tape. Once I have one of his arms free, he helps me work on the rest of the tape.

"Oh my god. Are you okay?"

"What happened?" he asks.

I let it all pour out—about Clay and him hitting me and taking the spent bullets.

Victor's eyebrows raise. "Whoa. I did not see that coming."

"Me neither," I agree. "He seemed so nice."

Victor moves around, loosening his muscles. He tries the door and runs his finger along the number of zip ties holding it closed. He nods at the lab. "What's that set up over there?"

"Sulfuric acid and potassium chlorate." I give him a grim look.

Victor tears off the last of the duct tape. He grabs the mesh and tries shaking it violently. "I'm smelling gas. We need to get everybody out of here." Victor shakes the door, but it's so tightly secured that it doesn't even rattle. He tries to wedge his thumb through the mesh to reach the locking mechanism. But the mesh is too small.

"What can we do?" The metallic taste of fear forms at the back of my throat.

"I don't know," Victor says. He pats his pockets. "No cell phones, huh?"

I wave Spam's Bella phone. "No signal."

"We need to get a message out," Victor says.

Spam's phone suddenly begins to vibrate. I look at the screen and a red light is flashing. Throbbing. Flashing. Throbbing. My head is hurting so bad and my vision is so blurry I can barely read it. I cover my left eye with my hand.

Oh my god. It's the Bella app!

Principal Blankenship is nearby.

Victor paces worriedly.

"Help me back up to the window," I say to him.

"I already told you, you can't break it," he says.

"Just do it," I shout.

He helps me up and I turn on the flashlight on Spam's phone. Then I flash the light across the campus. What's SOS—three long and then three short? I don't remember. And it really doesn't matter. I just need to get her attention. I flash three long and then three short. I wave the phone around in a circle. I flash from side to side.

Victor stands below, watching me. "What do you hope to accomplish with that?"

"Blankenship's here. I'm hoping she'll see the light." I keep working the flashlight beam. Right. Left. Up. Down. Long. Short. Back and forth.

"But—" Victor is just about to tell me how this will never work when all of a sudden, an upside-down face appears in the window. Blankenship's face. The face of the one person who has actual keys to this room.

She's puzzled. And angry. When she recognizes me she's *very* angry.

"Key," I shout at her.

It's clear she doesn't understand, so I mime using a key to unlock a door.

Victor stands on the chair and peers over the lockers.

She's even more shocked, but when she sees his face she turns and runs.

I jump down off the lockers. "How much time do we have?"

Victor studies the beaker. "Best guess? Less than five minutes."

"She can make it," I say.

"The key won't help." Victor tries to pry the zip ties.

"What can we do?" I say.

"Call Chuck. This is going to get messy," Victor says.

I wave the phone. "No cell service."

Suddenly, the door to the classroom bursts open and Lyman races in. He pauses and turns back to flip on the light.

"Lyman!" I bang on the door to the evidence locker. "Hurry! Get us out!"

Victor glances at me. "He can't do anything."

"Yes, he can!" I scream. "Lyman, hurry!"

Lyman races to the door of the lab. He's holding a Play-Doh finger.

Victor squints in amazement. "What the—"

Lyman presses the finger against the lock.

It doesn't work. Lyman is shocked.

"It just worked," he says, pointing to the classroom door.

"Try again," I say.

He reshapes the finger and tries again. It still doesn't work. He looks panicky.

"Keep trying," I say. "Don't give up."

Blankenship races in. She stops and sizes up Journey, Spam, and Lysa duct-taped to the chairs. Then she shoves Lyman out of the way and uses her key to unlock the door.

Blankenship heads toward us, but Victor points to the group at the table. "Get them out of here," he says. "That room is about to blow."

She and Lyman move into action. She kicks off her high heels as she rolls Journey out of the lab and across the classroom. Lyman is pushing Spam and pulling Lysa behind him.

"Take off their masks," I shout.

Lyman and Blankenship pause long enough to rip the masks off their faces. They toss them aside and push them out of the classroom.

Victor throws himself against the door of the evidence locker, then again. "Help me," he grunts.

We time it and slam the door at the same time.

After about ten tries, two of the zip ties snap.

"Two down. Six to go," Victor says. "One, two, three . . . go."

I'm giving it every ounce of strength I have and there is zero budge to the door.

Blankenship runs back in. She has scissors in one hand and a small Swiss Army knife in the other.

Victor watches the beaker. A thin stream of white smoke trails up from one corner of the wad of aluminum foil.

Blankenship tries to wedge the scissors in between the zip tie and the doorframe, but it's too tight and the scissors break apart.

"Taryn, you need to go. It's going to explode," Victor says. "We'll take cover in the lockers."

I glance at the lockers. While they might protect us from an initial blast, if there's a fire, it will be like hiding in an oven.

I'm shaking and so terrified I can't even think.

Lyman suddenly races back in the door. He grabs Clay's hammer from the crime scene display and charges at the door of the evidence locker with the hammer over his head. Using the claw part, he whams it against two more zip ties, splitting them.

Blankenship manages to wedge the knife blade in between one of the ties. She pulls down quickly and it snaps off.

Lyman takes out two more with the hammer.

"Hurry," Victor says, urging them on. He and I keep our eyes on the beaker. The thin stream of smoke is getting thicker.

There's one zip tie left, positioned high up on the door.

"Stand back," Victor orders.

Blankenship and Lyman move back and he and I ram the door as hard as we can, busting off the last zip tie.

At that same moment, there's a fizzle sound and a bright flash of light.

Victor grabs my arm and barrels out of the evidence locker.

Blankenship grabs Lyman and we charge toward the door on the other side of the lab.

A fireball follows right on our heels.

We start up the stairs and a huge blast pushes at our backs and blows us to the top.

We tumble out into the cool night air just as another boom and giant fireball explodes below us.

► 46 ◄

Going strictly by the rules, a criminal trial is not
a quest for the truth, but an indictment
of what is believed to be true.
—VICTOR FLEMMING

The air feels cool.

The sheets feel cool.

Everything feels cool.

Only, the left side of my face is on fire.

I try to sit up, but my arm is tangled in the sheets.

"Hey, hey. Easy. Careful."

My eyes flutter open. Rachel is sitting by my bed. "You're okay. I'm right here."

I yank myself out of the fog and struggle to sit up. "Where is everybody?"

"Victor's fine. He's in another room. They're checking him out now for solvent exposure."

"What about—"

"Everyone's fine. Journey, Spam, Lysa . . . even the new boy," she says.

I'm too dizzy to sit up. I flop back in the bed and search for the controls to raise it up. Rachel finds the controller and does it for me.

"I need to see them. Take me."

"Relax. You'll see them soon," Rachel says. "They were exposed to solvents, which requires medical supervision, but you, m'dear, have a concussion."

I rub the side of my face. It's numb and throbby. "Is it serious?"

"It can be," she says. "You need to stay down." She straightens the covers and smooths my hair. "Charles says if you kids hadn't pulled off that escape, the sabotage could have gone undetected. All the things that man set in place might have looked like an accident after the fact, especially with Victor gone." She swallows back a sob, pausing briefly. "I could have lost you both at once."

The door opens just a crack and Lyman peeks in. "Hey, forensic girl."

"Lyman." I give Rachel a pleading look. "Let him come in. Please?"

She goes to the door and ushers Lyman inside. "Just a minute. She needs to rest."

"Thank you," Lyman says.

"I'll check on Victor," Rachel says. "He's right next door."

"Thanks, Rachel," I say.

Lyman sits down in the chair next to my bed. "Spam sent me to check on you."

"Is she—"

"She and Lysa and Journey are all okay. Whatever that stuff was that he used to knock them out has ravaged their noses and throats. But the doctors say in time they'll heal just fine."

"I owe you my life. We wouldn't have made it out without you."

"I owe you mine, too," Lyman says.

"What happened? Are you still going to . . . you know?"

"My grandmother's?" He shakes his head. "I don't have to

now. When Spam sent the SOS—or actually, I guess it was you—I had already written a note to my mom and packed my things. All I needed to do was get to the train station. I logged into the game to leave one last message for Spam and found your message. I dropped everything and went straight to the school."

"Oh no."

"It's okay," he says. "My mom came home early, found the note, and tracked me by my cell phone. She got here just as everything was blowing up. And . . ." He pauses. "She turned herself in. No more running."

"Oh, Lyman. What's going to happen now?"

"I'm not exactly sure, but we sat down with the police chief. My mom explained everything . . . she *had* petitioned for custody of me but it was declined because she was single and worked long hours as a doctor. Also, her student loan payments *were* really high."

"Why would any of that stuff matter?" I ask.

"My parents swore they would stop using drugs, and the social worker wanted to believe them. Anyway, the night she took me, she had just stopped by their house on her way home from work and found my parents completely passed out. She decided to take me home with her to keep me safe. It was supposed to be just for the night. But the next morning she learned they died from overdoses. She was afraid that she would lose her medical license. So she decided to run."

"Why?"

"She's a doctor. She should have recognized the signs of an overdose. If she had called paramedics, there was a shot they could have given them and they might have survived. She said she probably should have called for help, but that wasn't the first time she'd found my parents in that condition."

"How awful. How do you feel about that?" I know this isn't an easy question.

"I'm relieved to have it out in the open and grateful to her for what she did," he says. "But I'm also sad. She gave up her whole life as a doctor to protect me, and now . . ." He shrugs. "She's probably going to jail."

"What did the chief say?"

"He said she probably will have to do some jail time, but he will try to help her."

"What about your grandma? Do you still want to meet her?"

"I've already talked to her on the phone. She's coming here. She'll stay in our house, with me, while my mom gets things squared away. So the good news is you're not getting rid of me. I hope that's a good thing."

"Seriously? It's awesome. Spam must be thrilled."

The door flings open and Victor bangs against both sides of it trying to wheel himself in, in a wheelchair. "Can you believe they're insisting I use this thing?"

Journey appears behind Victor and holds the door open so Victor can roll himself in. The chief is right behind Journey.

"Oh, be quiet," the chief says, slipping in front of Journey. "At least you're alive, thanks to our girl here. How's the head, sweetie?"

Lyman waves and moves out the door.

I rub my temple. "It's been better. But hey, squeaked one through again." I give him a soft smile and he returns it.

"We sure did," Victor says. "You must be a cat with nine lives."

Journey squeezes past Victor and the chief to get to the head of the bed. He lightly kisses the throbby, bruised side of my face.

"Is it bad?" I ask.

Journey nods and presses his hand over my wound.

His warmth radiates through me. I scoot over to make room for him and he sits on the edge of the bed.

"Are you both okay?" I ask.

Journey takes my hand and squeezes it. "I'm fine."

"I'm fine, too." Victor shakes his head. "But I'm plenty angry about the lab blowing up. And, also for missing the cues about Clay."

"You weren't the only one who missed that; I actually went to him for advice on how to tell you things," I say.

"Yeah, well next time just tell me, okay," Victor says.

"Did he really kill that kid?" I ask. "It seems so unbelievable."

"It's quite a story." The chief pulls up a chair. "Back then, the contractor was just getting started and he had this gimmick to drum up business. Clay would send Rodney in at night to vandalize certain properties. Then Clay would show up the next day and offer a reasonable bid to repair the damage. Most of the time they'd get the jobs without any competition."

"So how long did this go on?" Victor asks.

"About a year," the chief says. "Long enough for Clay to build up a reputation as a reliable contractor people could trust. Journey's family was going to be their next target. But Clay said Rodney went soft watching Journey's parents care for their young son. He liked the way he felt around them and wanted to be part of a family again."

"Wow." I look at Journey. "The power of family."

Victor squeezes my foot.

"I was an officer when this was going on, not directly responsible for this case or anything, but I remember it," the chief says. "Jameson claimed someone was harassing his family and no one believed them. According to Clay, the 'harassment' was coming from Rodney. The young man left Clay and secretly took up living in the ruins of the cannery and, ultimately, in the attic of the Michaels's home. He knew that Clay wanted him to come back, but he moved around like a ghost and managed to avoid him. Apparently, he developed a real fondness for you, Journey. He told Clay you were the little brother he never had."

"Somebody was living in our attic? That's super creepy," Journey says.

"Clay was afraid that Rodney would eventually rat him out?" Victor asks.

"Exactly. Rodney threatened to do just that if Clay didn't leave him alone," the chief says. "Clay knew Rodney was living at the cannery. He had been hanging around, spying on the family, and trying to get to Rodney. He must've gone through Jameson's truck when he wasn't home and found the shotgun. He watched Jameson set the trap and he knew exactly who that trap was set for. That night after everyone went to bed, he loaded the shotgun and swapped it with the paintball gun. Rodney was asleep in the attic when the trap was set. He knew nothing about it."

Spam slips in the door and gives me a little wave.

"Wow. Clay seemed like a nice guy. Who knew he was that coldhearted?" I say.

"He reeked of it," Spam says. "He was too nice."

"Here's the amazing part," the chief continues. "Once the deed was done and Rodney was silenced, there wasn't anything that would have connected Clay to Rodney . . . until your idea to test the shells, Erin."

"See that?" Victor says, beaming. "You saved the day again. You really are my star pupil."

"He took the shells with him," I say. "They're in his toolbox."

"Don't worry, we'll find them." the chief says. "It would help if we had something else to tie him to Rodney. But the shells might be enough."

"Check Clay's key ring," I say. "He's got a carved wooden ring like the one Rodney gave to Journey when he was a baby.

"We'll definitely look into that."

I look up at Journey. "So when are they letting your dad out of jail?"

"The legal stuff is complicated," Victor says. "But we'll get to work on it."

The door opens again and a nurse peeks in. She is shocked by the number of people in my room.

"What is wrong with you people?" she says. "This young lady has a concussion and needs her rest. All of you *out*. Out. Out."

"No," I plead. "Don't make them leave."

"Oh yes," she says firmly. "They're leaving. Now. Shoo."

Everyone files out of the room.

Victor is the last to go. He gently presses his hand to my forehead.

"I'm intensely proud of you," he says.

► 47 ◄

Family means no one gets left behind or forgotten.
—STITCH, OF *LILO AND STITCH*

After two days in the hospital and a day in bed at home, I'm almost back to normal. Well, as normal as I've ever been.

Victor told me to get dressed up, he has a surprise.

I come downstairs wearing slacks and a nice top, but he throws his hands in the air. "That is not *dressed* up. May I see an actual dress, please?"

I can't imagine what he has planned that would require a dress. I go back upstairs and change. When I return, he grins and rubs his hands together. "That's more like it." He heads toward the door but pauses, giving me a strange look. "We're still family, right?"

"Of course. Why?" He's acting weird, but then a near-death event tends to do that to you. I'm probably acting weird myself.

It takes all the way until we're in the car and Victor is driving before I ask. "Where are we going?"

"You'll see," he says.

"That's what you told me when I asked about the camp. . . . And where Rachel was. Where is she, by the way?"

"You'll see," he says.

"Noooo," I clench my fists in frustration.

"Just relax. You'll have the answers to everything soon. I promise," he says.

"Why are you being so mysterious?" I ask.

"Because you're being so nosy. Can you just go with the flow and—"

"Let me guess . . . I'll see."

"Now you're getting it," he says.

After a short drive, we wind up at the courthouse. Victor parks and leads the way into the building. He's practically skipping while I'm lagging behind, trying to figure out what we're doing here.

"Come on, slowpoke," he says. He clearly knows his way around. He leads us through a few doors and down a long hallway. He peeks into an office. "Judge Carter is expecting us." The woman points to the left.

Victor goes to the next door and opens it. A sign tells me we're entering Judge Carter's chambers. "Wait in here," he says. Then he quickly ducks out.

It's a large wood-paneled office. So large that at first I don't notice Rachel and the chief sitting in chairs in front of a desk. Rachel's carrying a small bouquet of flowers.

Aw. I think I get it. "Is this a surprise wedding?"

Rachel and the chief exchange looks. They shrug and shake their heads.

"Then what? Somebody tell me what's going on."

Victor bursts back in with the judge and a packet of papers. He takes the flowers from Rachel and offers them to me. "Erin," he says. "If you will you do me the honor of allowing me to adopt you and make you my official and forever daughter, Judge Carter here is willing to handle the legal, business end of that arrangement."

What? I'm stunned. Shocked. Shaken . . .

Fortunately, there's a chair nearby and I flop into it.

Victor looks concerned. "Whoa. Are you okay? Is it your head? Was that a no?"

"No."

His face looks crushed.

"No. It's not a no, it's just a—" I look at Rachel. "What happens to us?"

Her eyes get watery, but she has the most beautiful smile I have ever seen. "Nothing and everything happens to us. You are still my beautiful daughter and the sun and the moon and the stars and if I didn't understand it before, I know now that you are more than likely the very best parts of the two most important people in my life—your mother . . . and my brother. And I'm more than happy to share the amazing young woman that you are with him."

I nod. "Okay, then. Yes. I've always wanted a dad. I'll be your daughter."

In a crazy whirl of events that I will barely be able to remember five minutes from now, Judge Carter asks both Victor and me why we are seeking this adoption. And then he tells us something we already know, which is that once we take this step we will become a family and neither one can back out or ever tear us apart. And then says it's so.

My heart is bursting out of my chest. I feel like I need some air. I get out of the chair and head for the door.

"Where are you going?" Rachel asks.

I point to the door.

She laughs. "Give me back my flowers. Now we're having the surprise wedding."

"What?" I hand her back her flowers and flop down in the chair again. My knees are shaking so hard.

Rachel kneels in front of my chair. "My mission every day since *that* day has been to keep you safe and perfect. But despite my most ardent efforts, twice now I've almost lost you and my brother completely. This second time was a stark reminder that all we really have is today. And we each need to live it to the fullest. I hope you're okay with that."

I nod and flash the biggest smile ever because that's much easier than trying to talk with all this emotion clogging my throat.

Rachel and the chief wrote their own vows, and the only dry eye in the room belongs to the judge, who declares them husband and wife.

Victor nudges me. "How about that. You went from zero to two dads in a single day."

"What are we going to do with the FedEx envelope?" I ask.

"What do you want to do with it?" he asks.

"I think we should burn it," I say.

"Okay," he says. "Bonfire at dusk. Bring marshmallows."

▼ ▼ ▼

We're just getting into Victor's car when his cell phone rings. He pauses to answer it.

"What? Yeah. No." He listens for a couple of seconds and then turns sharply to look at me. "Wait. Hold on. I'm putting you on speaker and then I want you to repeat that."

Victor holds out his phone so we can both hear the guy on the phone. "I said, I sent you a note about the paternity test you requested."

"Yeah?" Victor answers. His gaze is tightly pinned to me.

"The samples became contaminated once they got here," the guy says. "We couldn't do the test. Can you send them again?"

My mouth drops open. I motion between the two of us and he nods.

"Thanks anyway, John," Victor says. "I don't need those results anymore anyway."

Victor clicks off his phone.

"So we still don't—" I ask.

"That's right," Victor says. "And it doesn't matter." He laughs as he starts up the car.

I'm laughing too. But then I stop. "What about the job thing?"

"Listen, I know I told you not to worry about that even though I know you can't control how you feel. I don't want to be that dad, Erin. I want to be the guy who makes mistakes, but tells you the truth. I've answered all their questions honestly, and I'm pretty sure it's going to work out okay."

"I'm pretty sure it is too." It turns out that Victor's not like all the other adults in my life, simply telling me what to do and how to feel and keeping what's real away from me.

"I'm waiting for you to ask about the camp again," he says.

"Okay," I say. "Tell me about the camp?"

"You'll see," he says, grinning.

I shake my head, buckle my seatbelt, and sit back against the seat.

▼ ▼ ▼

I'm a little edgy when I realize that Victor is driving us to the school. I'm not fond of places where I almost died.

The Administration building is cordoned off with crime scene tape. The beautiful white pillars and marble are scarred with blackened fingers from the smoke. Victor says it could be months before the building can be used again.

He leads us over to the gym.

Inside, sharing space with Coach Wilkins and sports camp, is Camp CSI, humming along under the supervision of Miss Blankenship—though I hardly recognize her with her jet-black hair down and flowing around her shoulders in soft curls. Lysa and Spam and Journey and Lyman are spread out, working with dozens of kids divided into different age groups.

I'm stunned. "Everything was destroyed. How were you able to pull it back together so fast?"

"Taryn called in some favors," he says.

"Taryn?"

"Turns out our principal, Miss Blankenship, had some surprises of her own. Did you know she went to school with your Miss P? It's the reason she applied to come to this school."

Miss Blankenship wanders over with the clipboard against her chest.

"I'd like you to meet my daughter," Victor says to her.

"I know Erin." She swivels her head toward him in that familiar odd way. "But you mean niece, not daughter. Right?"

"No. I mean daughter." Victor holds up our adoption certificate. "Fresh off the press."

"Wow." Her eyes light up. "What a day, huh?"

"You knew Miss P?" I ask.

She offers a sad smile. "We were roommates all through college. She was my best friend."

Miss Blankenship pulls a photo from underneath the papers on her clipboard. I remember it from Miss P's bulletin board. I took it down and put it in the liquor globe. What I didn't realize at the time is that it is a photo of Miss Blankenship and Miss P in their caps and gowns.

"Wow. You look so different. But I don't understand. Why were you such a . . ." I pause, searching for a diplomatic way to phrase my question.

"Stick in the mud?" she offers with a guilty smile.

"Yeah. Okay. I'll go with that."

She draws in a long breath. "Laura was a people person. People, especially kids, were her thing. She used to joke that she was Glenda . . . and I was the other one." She pinches her lips into a thin smile. The first real one I've seen on her.

"She was definitely Glenda." I remember the cheery glow that always seems to surround Miss P. It's my favorite way to think of her.

"After all of this I've learned my lesson and I've made a pledge to try to be more like her," Blankenship says. "Because that's what she would want for me and for you and for the school, too."

"This school meant a lot to her," I say. I suddenly key in on one piece of the puzzle that I never figured out. "Did you leave a quote on a napkin in Miss P's tribute globe?"

"You saw that, did you?" Miss Blankenship looks surprised. "It was one of our favorites."

"So was it Tupac or Shakespeare?"

"Yes." The twinkle in her eye suggests continued prying won't get a better answer.

"I suppose I can allow one mystery to go unsolved."

Miss Blankenship fingers a strand of hair that cascades over her shoulder almost as if it's something foreign. "I hope you and your friends will give me another chance."

"On one condition," I say.

"What's that?" she asks.

"You might have to let us call you Miss B."

She smiles. "I think I prefer that to Blankface."

The heat of embarrassment creeps onto my cheeks. "I-I don't know—"

"It's okay," she says. "I asked for it."

"Hey, excuse me. Can I interrupt just for a minute?"

I turn around, surprised to see Arletta Stone trying to get Victor's attention.

Victor greets her warmly. "Arletta, right?"

"Yes." She pauses, tapping a sealed envelope against her palm. "I don't know how to say this, but I can't thank you enough for reopening the Michaels's case. It means a lot to me that he's been cleared."

Victor slips his arm around my shoulders. "Erin gets the credit for this one."

"Well, you probably know that I testified at his trial . . . said some things I probably shouldn't have. I've felt bad about those things for years."

"I'm sorry. What are you saying?" Victor frowns.

"I didn't lie exactly, I just repeated the urban legends we were told as kids. But my stories didn't help his case. The worst part is I said those things because I wanted his building and I was hoping to force him out. Anyway, now when he gets out I want to help him get back on his feet." She hands Victor the envelope. "This is a letter of commitment from an investment group who is willing to underwrite the historic hotel he wants. I'm hoping for a small museum . . . in one corner. But I'll leave that up to him."

Victor takes the envelope. "You want me to pass this along to Jameson?"

"If you would, please," she says. "There's also a letter of apology. Do you think that will be okay?"

"One thing I've learned," Victor says, "is that it's never too late to do the right thing."